DEADLINE ISTANBUL

DEADLINE ISTANBUL

THE ELIZABETH DARCY SERIES

PEGGY HANSON

Peggy Hanson

WILDSIDE PRESS

Published by Wildside Press LLC.
www.wildsidebooks.com

FOREWORD

Deadline Istanbul is a blend of reality and of dream-like memories, of fact and fiction, of people I may have met with those purely made-up. My love affair with Turkey goes far, far back, to Peace Corps days in the 1960's and has been renewed with more years of living there and innumerable visits to virtually every corner of that wondrous land.

In all those years of living in and visiting Turkey, I never came across the dead bodies and mysterious crimes my protagonist Elizabeth Darcy can't seem to avoid. Even as a correspondent for Voice of America, I didn't encounter much murder—first-hand, at least.

In this book, I've taken liberties with Turkey and its people, as well as with expatriates who live or work there. I hope I have managed to present them both with the richness they deserve. There are good people, bad people, kind and cruel people. In short, exotic surroundings do not change human nature.

1

Dear friends, listen to me now,
Love's like the shining sun,
A heart without love
Is nothing more than a stone.

What rises up in a stony heart?
No matter how softly it begins,
The tongue's soft words
Soon turn to war when poison spews.

Yunus Emre, 13th Century Turkish poet

1996

Lights flickered along the dark sides of the Bosphorus. Happy lights, he thought. He pictured romantic dinners in restaurants with lights down low. Parties of well-dressed guests from all nations nibbling on *meze* and drinking *rakı*. Making sophisticated jokes about politics. Gossiping. Good stuff for backgrounders, if not news. Grist for the reporter's mill.

Peter Franklin was dressed for one of those parties—that one up there. From here he could see the gleaming crystal glasses, held by coiffed women and well-tailored men who had stepped out on the veranda for some Bosphorus night air.

If his mysterious contact arrived, he'd go, as planned. Parties always offered interesting contacts and possible networking. But opportunities to meet major players, like the one he awaited now, were far more rare and could not be ignored. The party would have to wait.

If his contact came. He was almost sure he knew who that would be.

Water lapped at the bottom of the boat and a ferry leaving Beşiktaş landing gave off a mournful toot.

The first bridge, strung like a necklace across the water, framed the distant domes and minarets of Süleymaniye, the greatest creation of the sixteenth-century architect Sinan. On a nearer point lay Topkapı Palace, eerie and quiet. Its lighted walls hid the secrets of centuries, of long-dead Sultans and their *harem*s of women from all over the Empire.

Peter loved Istanbul. He loved its mosques, its alleys, its history. He loved its women and its cosmopolitan food. He soaked up its magic.

This story had become Peter's baby. He'd taken months to weave the threads together. He would have his confirmation soon.

His small boat rocked on the wake of the Russian cargo ship passing in the night. The boatman kept the light off, as requested.

The other caique came slowly, silently, beside his boat, floating on the current.

Peter never had a chance.

The last sound he heard was the plaintive call to prayer from the historic mosque along the wharf.

Peter missed the party.

2

I like to walk in cities; to ask the
way; to find what I want to find
by getting lost in the back streets,
across the wastelands where the
gardens are, and the shops and the
bazaar stalls; to flow with a throng
of people at lunch hour, then find
an empty street and go slowly.

Mary Lee Settle, *Turkish Reflections*

Afternoon sunlight glinted pale-gold across the Bosphorus. Sea gulls followed the ferry in raucous competition, trying to catch a piece of sesame-covered *simit* thrown by a passenger. The smell of fresh-salt water permeated the air. I pulled my raincoat around me.

Damn, damn, damn.

Everyone in the *Trib* newsroom had been shocked. Popular, gregarious Peter. Aggressive reporter. Much-respected at the *Trib*. I took it personally. He was my friend, colleague, and partner on some prize-winning investigative stories. We both loved digging out the truth.

Now here I was, alone in Istanbul. To do Peter's job. Not an assignment I'd ever thought to have, or wanted to have.

The Embassy dispatch said Turkish police had completed an investigation and thought Peter had died of an accidental overdose of an illegal drug.

Easy for the police to say, but I didn't buy it. Peter was a professional. I had to clear his name of this posthumous insult.

My editor Mac had read my mind. "Not your job to investigate this. Don't do it! I don't need two correspondents dead."

Mac knew perfectly well I'd follow my own advice, not his. I assured him I'd be careful. He punched my arm playfully, a worried frown on his face. We understood each other.

Plaintive Turkish wails of love gone wrong swirled around the few of us riding outside along the ferry's railing. The sad tunes fitted my mood. Where had the music come from?

Two people down from me along the railing, a man with dark, olive-shaped eyes, wearing a black leather jacket, seemed to be the source. The radio must be in his pocket. His thick mustache matched his dark hair. He smoked a cigarette and looked away from me. Macho in the extreme. A Turk's Turk, right from an old Camel ad.

The wooden ferry made a clean swath through the dark water. Bubbles of white wake stretched out and widened behind us, untraceable footprints on our liquid path.

3

*"I have seen the terrible punish-
ments meted out in hell to tie-wearing
atheists and arrogant colonialist
positivists who make fun of the common people and their faith..."*

Orhan Pamuk, *Snow*

Erol Metin walked from the Silver Wolves' meeting to the bus stop in Üsküdar. From there he would catch a ferry to the European side of the Bosphorus.

Nizam, the leader of the Silver Wolves, had been right in his monologue tonight to the brothers Turkey was headed the wrong direction. One could never say so publicly, but Atatürk himself had started that, in the eyes of the Silver Wolves. After all his heroism in defining and protecting the nation at the end of World War I, Atatürk—or at least his successors—had veered off course.

Yes, there never would have been a Turkey without Atatürk. One had to admit that. Even Nizam admitted that. But why did the Father of the Turks have to wipe out Islam to save Turkey? Why did he have to embrace the West? Pushing the Greeks into the sea made sense to Erol and his group. Banning the fez and veil did not.

Erol's purpose in life was to right that wrong, among others. Turkey was not the West; it belonged to the East. It was a magnificent leader in the East. The home of the Caliph. A bulwark for Islam.

Whatever means it took to help Turkey regain its rightful place, he would do it.

Erol was young and idealistic. He did not separate goals from methods.

⚴

Already I was being handed from
arkadash to arkadash, that word for
friendship, one of the most important
words in the Turkish language.

Mary Lee Settle, *Turkish Reflections*

The ferry passed Rumeli Hisar, that great fortress built by Mehmet the Conqueror in 1452. Its stone walls formed an asymetric pattern on the hill. Grass inside the walls was turning yellow for the winter.

When I thought of Peter, my insides felt both asymmetric and yellow. I hoped this ferry ride would clear my jet-lagged brain on where to start. .

Peter's body must have stayed near the water's surface or it never would have been found under that veranda in Ortaköy. And it must have entered the Bosphorus near the restaurant. From the north, the Black Sea side.

The currents of the Bosphorus run deep. On top they flow north to south, from the Black Sea to the Sea of Marmara. Far below the surface, the water goes the other way—a self-cleansing cycle. Except things kept going into it.

Like Peter's body. A shudder started at the back of my neck and ran down my spine.

I hardly looked at Macho-Man-with-the-music as I made my way into one of the ferry's comfortable sitting rooms. But I had to pass him, and I could swear he leaned out to make sure I'd bump him as I tried to slip past.

Whether he was trying to attract or repel me, it was un-Turkish to invade my space like that. Accosting foreigners is looked down on, too. "*Ayıp,*" they say. Shameful.

As I passed him, I looked straight at the man. His eyes were singularly opaque. I couldn't read them. He was looking at me but not interested in me. As a person, I was erased.

Feeling as though I'd brushed against evil, I sat beside a fresh-faced young woman wearing the traditional Islamic head scarf, the *jilbab*. She was one of the few women on the boat wearing one, but seemed as self-possessed as the others.

Since this was Turkey rather than the Arabian Peninsula, the pink *jilbab* was color-coordinated with the girl's long-sleeved *khamis* worn over modest slacks. Not an inch of skin appeared between bottom hem and shoes, but her attractive femininity showed through. I felt a sisterly kinship and we gave each other warm smiles. The chill I'd experienced from the Camel man began to thaw.

I savored a tulip-shaped glass of sweet mahogany-colored Turkish tea bought from a man carrying a swinging tray shouting, "*chai, chai!*" My new-found friend in the *jilbab* had one, too. I viewed her as an ally against the big rude guy outside. Turkish women have devastating put-downs for men who get out of line. They turn them into little boys with a flick of the apron string.

Just before we docked, I thought perhaps she'd be called on to defend me. I saw a leather jacket in the opposite row. The dramatic profile. The man in the leather jacket was no longer looking away from me.

He had me in the crosshairs of his eyes.

Past the exiting crowd, the charming scene of Galata Tower from the ferry disappeared in a cloud of dark smoke belched out by our engines. Through that black haze, Istanbul no longer felt like the safe haven I'd always viewed it.

Somewhere behind me, haunting music followed. Too afraid to turn around, I got the message. My tracker wanted me to know he was there.

5

A nail will come out but
its hole remains.

Turkish proverb

Bayram Çengel sat at Peter Franklin's desk in the *Washington Tribune* office on the hill stretching up from the Golden Horn, that dagger-shaped inlet of water that once separated the Ottoman government from the foreign envoys on Pera Hill. His knees went weak when he thought of Peter's sudden death. Peter was big. Not big like Atatürk, of course, no one could be that big, but someone respected by all. A role model for any aspiring journalist. Peter Franklin, the Washington Correspondent. The man who knew everything. How could he have died?

Bayram felt lucky to have gotten this job at the tender age of twenty-two. He'd done a course in journalism at a private university on the Asian side. But it was only a two year course. Everything he knew about news, real news, had come from Peter.

The Turkish newspaper Bayram had worked for was often well-written but it, like others of its kind, expressed a certain political view. Objectivity did not come into it, though investigation did, at times. Peter had combined the two. Pure luck that Peter chose Bayram from other applicants. Or was it? Peter may have seen how eager the young man was to pull himself out of the poverty he'd grown up in. Peter understood.

It was almost sacriligious to be sitting in Peter's chair. Certainly, it was sad.

Earlier today he'd met the new person at the airport. Elizabeth Darcy. He'd seen her byline on *Trib* articles.

She had a nice smile, at least.

As a traditional Turk, Bayram doubted that a woman could take the place of a man, especially a man like Peter Franklin.

Perhaps he would give her a chance. Really, he had no choice. He'd stocked the little office refrigerator with a whole case of Kendi bottled water, allegedly taken from one of the plentiful artesian wells in the Anatolian mountains. All Westerners and all Turks who could afford it drank bottled water, never from the tap. Bayram was proud to be in the bottled water class.

6

*If you stared deep into a cat's
eyes, you would be able to see
into the world of spirits.*

English proverb

Sultana, the pure white Van cat, had her secret passages, which she only visited at night.

For a female cat, Sultana roamed a wide swath of Üsküdar. She knew and was known by the tough neighborhood tomcats, who recognized nobility and let her pass unmolested.

One of Sultana's favorite places was the fish market down the hill near the wharf. She only visited after the fishermen had left, so she rarely got a bite of fish. Still, the smells were attractive: rodent, fish, people. She was known and admired by the ladies selling flowers at the bus stop. One of them often gave her a tasty snack.

Tonight Sultana followed a different kind of woman. She walked as a non-Turk and bought a *jeton* to get on the ferry to Eminönü. Businesslike as she was, the woman gave off friendly vibes. Sultana tracked her for a few minutes, slinking quiet and invisible.

When the woman started to put her *jeton* into the turnstile, she turned and saw Sultana. "Why, kitty! Aren't you the beautiful one!" Language is no barrier between a cat and those who love them.

Sultana allowed herself to be petted, then slunk back into the shadows. Her judgment of people was impeccable. That didn't mean she felt safe being visible to everyone.

7

*"For heaven's sake, madam,
keep your voice lower…"*

Jane Austen, *Pride and Prejudice*

It was getting dark on the Eminönü pier, but a myriad of lights, ranging from neon to the chestnut roaster's dim coals, made the area glow. Feeling a little shaky, I lost sight of my woman companion and pushed along in the rush-hour crowd toward the taxi stand, slipping on the cobblestones.

I finally got a taxi, looking over my shoulder the whole time. The leather-jacketed man had faded into the crowded scene. Thank God! I breathed deeply and put him out of my mind.

Back at the Pera Palas, the desk clerk gave me a note along with my key.

I went upstairs to the haven of my room using the broad marble stairs rather than the ornate open iron elevator. I locked the door and threw the note onto the nearest chair, a heavy Victorian piece that sat like a prim old maid at a tea party. I'd have to find my glasses to read the note. Blast. Having enjoyed perfect vision throughout my youth, this annoyed me more than it should have, I suppose. At "a certain age" manifestations of age become as intolerable as they are immutable.

Rummaging through my purse, I glanced down. The rose-colored carpet had a pansy-shaped brown stain. A blood stain? Could it have inspired Agatha Christie or Ian Fleming? The Pera was proud of having entertained those authors, among others.

I bet Agatha Christie and Ian Fleming didn't have a leather-jacketed man following them. Or maybe they did, and that also inspired them.

At last the glasses were settled on my nose and I retrieved the note. It was on hotel stationery and had my room number on the envelope, no name.

"Be careful. Lock your door." Masculine writing, but neat, printed but sloping like italics. No signature.

I froze in place for a minute and sipped water from one of the little bottles in the mini-bar..

Tapping the note, I looked around. Not much to steal here. My travel clothes lay in a heap where I'd shed them before showering off the plane journey. I tucked the note into a nook in my black Eagle Creek travel purse, wondering what I'd do about it. No instructions. No timetable. Nothing to go on.

I re-checked the door lock. That part, at least, I could take seriously.

Then I put the dirty clothes in the laundry basket in the bathroom and got settled. Unwrap the bath soap; hang toiletry kit with its comfort supply: elderflower eye gel, skin cream, toothpaste. The familiar smells and tastes helped me shrug off my unease.

Agatha herself hadn't had an easy time in Istanbul, one had to assume. She'd sneaked away from London to Istanbul for twelve mysterious days in 1919. Perhaps she liked being free on her own. Or she may have sought anonymity as she pondered her unfaithful husband.

The bathroom had an old-fashioned free-standing tub and a balcony overlooking the street coming up from Galata Bridge—allowing for a peek between buildings down the hill to the Golden Horn. Yes, I could even survey the view while sitting in the tub. No one could see in from outside.

Now why did the shower scene from "Psycho" come to mind? Damn that note.

Glancing into the age-pocked mirror, I gave my unruly hair a few swipes with my fingers and then reached for a brush.

I took the note out of my purse and looked at it again. The longer I looked, the more ominous it seemed.

8

*I had come, as we all do when we
go to a city we have heard about so
much, to find an Istanbul I thought
I already knew—my city of presup-
positions—whispers and memories of
pashas and harems and sultans and
girls with almond eyes, the Orient
Express of Agatha Christie, the spies
of Eric Ambler, the civilized letters
of Lady Mary Wortley Montagu.*

Mary Lee Settle, *Turkish Reflections*

I'd showered quickly, to not waste the precious substance, and begun
to relax when the telephone rang.

"Hello?"

"Elizabeth Darcy? I am calling for Ms. Darcy." An American woman's voice. Thank goodness my rusty Turkish wouldn't be pressed into
service quite yet! I'd been quite good at one time, but that was several
years ago.

"Speaking."

"I am calling from the American consulate. Mr. Lawrence Andover
would like to speak with you."

In a moment, a man's voice came on. Articulate. Sophisticated. Under
the current circumstances, infinitely soothing. "Ms. Darcy? This is Lawrence Andover. I work in the American Consulate and was told you'd be
coming to replace Peter Franklin for the *Trib*."

"Well, I'm here for a while. I didn't know they'd sent my name." I
dabbed Estee Lauder cream on my face as I talked.

An appreciative chuckle. "Let's say I have my sources." Then his
voice turned empathetic. "Peter was a good friend of mine. I was very
sorry about his death."

"Yes. We all were." My voice caught. There was not much else to say.

Andover allowed a moment of respect to pass along the telephone
line before continuing. "We at the Consulate like to meet new journalists

as they arrive, especially American ones. Are you by chance free for a drink tomorrow?"

Was I free? Sure, I was free. Having been in Istanbul only long enough to shower, change clothes and take my obligatory refresher Bosphorus cruise, I was free.

"All right," I said, as though looking over a busy schedule. "When and where?"

"I'll pick you up at five-thirty in your lobby?" The consulate was right next door.

I jotted the appointment down on the hotel note pad.

Should I have mentioned the unsettling note to this diplomat? No. It would make me sound hysterical. Maybe when we were face to face on the morrow.

We signed off, great friends already. I had a plan and something on my social calendar. Until that happens, I don't feel my assignment has started.

Unpacking didn't take long. I don't carry a lot. Books, including a beloved, worn copy of *Pride and Prejudice* went onto the night table. I never travel without Jane Austen, and it looked as if this time I'd need her.

At the moment, I couldn't think of anyone to call about the note. Friends and family would get too upset. Things seem worse when they're happening an ocean away and loved ones are, as far as one knows, on the scene and in harm's way. I didn't yet feel comfortable enough with the hotel staff. The police would blow everything out of proportion. Maybe somebody at the U.S. Consulate next door could be approached, though not till tomorrow.

I went out on the bathroom balcony and tried to peer through to the Golden Horn, a poor sister to the elegant Bosphorus. A few elegant old Ottoman buildings raised newly-painted heads above a clutter of slums.

As in every city, slums hold murk below the surface. I go into them to broaden my horizons, to get the other side of the story. Like their residents, I also look forward to leaving.

A car on the street below honked an imperious horn. I looked down. A small blue vehicle made its way through traffic with aggressive intent. After pushing others to the side, it stood still near the hotel while other cars snaked along.

I stepped back into my room and shoved the warning note farther into my purse'. Then I dropped onto the inviting bed without taking off my jeans or pulling the shabby drapes closed and fell into the deep sleep of those who have spent miserable hours flying across oceans and continents in steel conveyances with uncomfortable seats and less comfortable bathrooms and only their own apprehensive thoughts to keep them company—if you don't count the loquacious water engineer sitting in your row.

The next-to-last thing I heard as I fell asleep was the insistent honking of a car horn under my window.

Sometime later, my door handle rattled.

9

*Tell me who your friend is, and
I'll tell you who you are.*

Turkish proverb

Ahmet Aslan was eating mussels in the historic hangout of artists and poets, Çiçek Pasajı.

The name meant Flower Passage. The aromas of carnations and jasmine and gladioli blended with the fishier smells of bluefish and shellfish from the far side of the alley.

Tonight he was alone. It was too bad Peter Franklin could not join him. They had enjoyed many evenings together at Çiçek Pasajı.

Here, the drink of choice was *rakı*, the anise-flavored "lion's milk" that turned white when water was added. It added to the masculine atmosphere of the Çiçek Pasajı, although here and there, at tables for four, a few avant garde women authors and artists enjoyed rebelling against the strict Muslim norms.

Peter Franklin, like Ahmet, had liked his *rakı*. They had come here together often. Ahmet missed Peter more than he had thought he would.

A black alley cat, beautiful as all Turkish cats are, waited politely near Ahmet Aslan's table, tail curled around its body, hoping for a bite of his seafood.

Absently, he tossed a shrimp to the floor.

10

"A lady's imagination is very rapid..."

Jane Austen, *Pride and Prejudice*

"Hello? Yes?" My voice sounded scared even to my own ears. The sound of the rattling doorknob, small, furtive, had wakened me from deep sleep and I leapt out of bed. I trembled, at once confused, alone, and vulnerable.

No answer. And I couldn't see anyone through the peephole. I checked the lock yet again, to be sure. And I looked to see if another note had appeared. It hadn't.

I plopped back on the bed, wide-awake and furious. I needed sleep after the trip. Who had dared to wake me up like that?

I took a deep breath. Get a grip, Elizabeth. No doubt some confused tourist was looking for his own room.

I dug through meds and took an Ambien to bring on the reluctant god of Morpheus—something I should have taken earlier to forestall jet lag. This way, I wouldn't even know if someone tried the door.

But the medicine didn't work the way intended. In a fitful dream I wandered lost through a snowy forest, shadowed by figures behind trees. Men? No. Wolves.

Heart pounding, I gave up, turned on the light, and pulled *Pride and Prejudice* to me. That's what it was there for, to provide balance.

The immortal, familiar first words were as calming as usual: *It is a truth universally acknowledged, that a single man in possession of a good fortune, must be in want of a wife.* The reader knows at that moment that she is in good hands. Safe hands. We all want truth universally acknowledged.

And in the midst of life's other trials, how comforting to be worrying that much about marriage.

I'd rather have slept, but in lieu of that, my old friend Jane held me as she's done in the past—transported to a different time and place, where finding husbands became the absorbing tale of a village—almost a matter of life and death.

Marriage is a little scary in its own right, but marriage made a better topic tonight than Peter. Murdered Peter.

And much better not to think of the slinking gray things in my nightmare. I do love wolves, but not in my dreams.

11

*At table keep a short hand; in
company keep a short tongue.*

Turkish proverb

Rays of early sunlight streamed across my newspaper in the dining room of the Pera. I sipped black, sweet Turkish coffee down to the grounds and then chewed the last bits, washing it all down with the bottled water on the table.

The jet-lag medicine had finally helped me get to sleep, but the night had been fitful. Was someone was after me? First on the ferry, then the note, and finally the movement of the door handle? How different things would have been if Peter were here with me.

And I don't mean in a romantic sense. Peter had that dangerous edge to him that attracts women, but he wasn't great in the intimacy area. We'd almost tried that once. Almost. And the reason it didn't work wasn't all Peter's fault. I'm a fine one to talk about intimacy.

About half the headlines in *Cümhüriyet* were intelligible to me this morning. I sighed. My Turkish had been so good when I lived here… first on the Moda coast along the Asian side, where ferries made watery tracks across to the Princes' Islands…on a good day, you could see across the Sea of Marmara all the way to the mountains of Bursa. Later in Bebek on the European side, where the glory of the Bosphorus lay at my feet, including ferries, tankers from Russia, Rumania, and Bulgaria, swift little American and Turkish spy boats checking on them, luxurious wooden *yalıs* along the coast.

Those had been days of free-lance correspondent work, commitment a foreign concept. Well, face it, commitment might never be a strong point with me. I could have enjoyed commitment a few years ago, when going to a restaurant alone felt strange and when I made an odd wheel at parties… At this stage of my life, when some of my friends were starting to worry over grandchildren, I found it exciting and stimulating to have no specific ties, no immutable partner. I rather liked my own company.

Still, it would be nice to have someone special again. I had plenty of girlfriends. It wasn't quite the same.

One of the *Cümhüriyet* headlines announced that police had arrested a *terorist* in Istanbul. A fuzzy picture showed a man being led away by uniforms. With my rusty Turkish, I couldn't understand the gist of his alleged crimes.

The unexplained term *terorist* probably meant the man was with the PKK, Kurdish separatists from the southeast. Because of the ongoing conflict between Turkish authorities and the PKK, for years the Kurdish group had used explosives to disrupt Turkish life. New linkages with Islamic extremists in recent years, however—and old linkages with communists or nationalists—made it hard to say just what the roots of terror were at any given point. Everybody seemed to have a cause they felt was worth blowing others up for.

Maybe because my Turkish was bad, maybe because apprehension lay under the surface, my attention wandered to last night's note. What did "be careful" mean? Too vague to be useful. Was someone trying to scare me? Why not just explain the problem?

Yet this morning my spirits were high. Hard to concentrate on fear with the distraction of chewy light-brown Turkish bread accompanied by wild cherry jam. Fresh piquant goat cheese with briny dry olives seduced me from another plate. I chased my coffee down with water and a tangy sour cherry juice.

A man sat at a table near me. He wore a tan suit and was handsome in a French sort of way—and he stared at me. Did I button my blouse wrong? Did I have a coffee grounds mustache?

I passed a napkin across my lips and ordered more coffee. Ignoring the strange man's stares, I retrieved the glasses I'd set aside and began looking through the file in my briefcase.

The polite waiter in his black and white penguin outfit brought the coffee. As I reached to help set it on the table, my files cascaded from my briefcase onto the floor. Mustering what dignity I could, I scrabbled around for the papers. The note with Andover's name, number, and the party meeting time had somehow gotten in with my file stuff and lay on top.

As I tried to stand up with what I'd retrieved from the mess, I realized I was not alone under the table. Brown shoes attached to tan-covered legs blocked my way. There were even arms and hands reaching under the tablecloth.

"Excuse *me*," I blurted out, furious at my situation and outraged that anyone would have the unmitigated nerve to offer, nay, insist on, helping.

Especially at breakfast, when one should always be alone.

"I am so sorry. Please let me show that chivalry is not dead." "Chivalry" had the accent on the second syllable. It was, of course, that man from the next table.

Tan-suit's charm was beginning to get to me, like a little rash that starts to itch. "I don't rely much on chivalry," I replied frostily, trying to push the hair out of my eyes and hold the strewn papers at the same time.

With the slipperiness of paper that has been refined, one little group detached itself from the main clump in my arms and slid to the floor. Where is nice, rough recycled paper when you need it?

The man picked up that bunch and handed it to me , looking kind but apprehensive. Did he fear my re-losing control of the situation? Or regaining control? I had to admit he was low-key about the whole thing. And I hadn't been nice to him.

In a flash, the humor of the situation hit me. I laughed, and Tan Suit grinned back in apparent relief. Grabbing the last of the papers and stuffing them unceremoniously into my briefcase, I sat down fast, leaving the guy standing beside the table.

"Thank you for your help," I said. Maybe that would get rid of him gracefully and let me organize myself.

But once you laugh with someone, you have a relationship, no matter how tenuous. I stifled a sigh. "Do please sit down."

Mr. Tan Suit reached into his wallet for a business card and handed it to me. The card said, "Jean Le Reau," and indicated he was some kind of engineer with a firm called Alcotec. His gray eyes smiled into mine.

The penguin had returned to ask whether the new person at my table wanted anything, and was told no.

"Excuse me, but I think you know Turkish?" My companion's eyes twinkled now.

"Well, yes. I know Turkish. I used to, anyway." I was digging through my purse for my own business cards, which never seem to be at hand.

"You have worked here before?" The eyes probed mine. Calm. Purposeful.

I grinned to show I wasn't hostile. "I am a journalist. I have worked many places." My heart raced a bit from scrabbling under the table.

"Perhaps you can, you know, help me?" said Mr. Le Reau.

"What is it you need?" I hoped it didn't sound rude. Ah, there were my cards. I got one out and pushed it toward him.

"I am trying to negotiate some business (he called it beez-ness) with a Turkish firm, and I need, um, advice?"

"Well, sorry, but I just got here myself and am not up on the business scene yet. Maybe you should try the English weekly, *Business Turkey*, for advice of that kind." I made writing motions toward the waiter for my check.

Jean Le Reau leaned toward me across the table. "Ms. Darcy. I think you are a person to help us. I see you are in a hurry now, but perhaps we can meet later? Here is the number of my room. Call me, please?"

He was off, like Fred Astaire in one of those Paris movies. Something lingered in his wake. Not an aroma; more of an aura. Something that didn't go with the pleasant, low-key exterior of Jean Le Reau.

Glancing at Le Reau's card, I saw his room was two floors up from mine, on the fourth floor.

12

*A wild mountain cat crept closer and
closer, and Ihsan began to pet it, and
give it bits of white cheese. It was
so quiet that we were surrounded
by the sound of the cat's purr.*

Mary Lee Settle, *Turkish Reflections*

In the midst of Cağaloğlu, the newspaper publishing area on the hill
going up from the Spice Market, Haldun Kutlu smoked and read, made
edit marks on a printout, and called for an assistant to take the copy to
the reporter.

The only other chair in the book-cluttered office was occupied by
a regal white cat, one eye blue and one green. Sultana had the run of
Cümhüriyet, but she claimed Haldun as her special friend and his office
as her personal (daytime) space. Every evening, Haldun put her back
into a basket to take the ferry ride to Üsküdar where he lived with Ayla
Hanım, his wife. Sultana thus lived in Europe by day and Asia by night.
People on both continents gave her respect—and treats.

Sultana's dignity befitted her royal heritage—that of the famous Van
cats from Lake Van in the east. White cats that could swim and had varicolored eyes.

Today Haldun was too engrossed to give Sultana her usual petting.
He had a few things on his mind.

Especially, he was worried about what had happened to Peter Franklin.

13

*The old-feeling neighborhood
climbing up a hill from the Golden
Horn into the New District is called
Galata, and has a seedier, less-
modern-European ambience than
Taksim Square or Istiklal Street.*

Rick Steves' Istanbul

In the hotel lobby I greeted the young, self-important-but-rather-sweet *Tribune* assistant who had met me at the airport the day before. Bayram Çengel, dark eyes aglow, sat on the wine-colored plush of an uncomfortable fake Louis XIV lobby chair.

"Hi, Bayram," I said, gripping my briefcase tightly to avoid further disasters. "I'm ready to see the *Tribune* office." Gentleman that he was, he offered to carry the briefcase, which I gave him gladly.

On the sidewalk outside the hotel, under the faded Pera canopy, Bayram shouldered aside the doorman to help me into the taxi to Cağaloğlu, the office address. He might be junior to me in the office; he was senior to the doorman and needed to make that clear.

The taxi waited while a small blue car inched past us in the narrow street. Glancing at the obstruction, I saw a Murat driven by a man both remarkable and familiar. He had curly black hair, a luxuriant mustache, and a hawk-like profile. On the seat beside him was a clean-shaven young man whose long eyelashes rested on olive-toned cheeks. Lashes any woman could envy.

"Could be a Greek god," I murmured. But no; no Turk wants to be called a Greek, even god-like. "Okay, a Hittite god." Had the central Anatolian Hittites had multiple gods?

Wait. I'd seen that mustachioed driver before. Yesterday, he had worn a leather jacket and been on my Bosphorus ferry.

14

I can see the first leaf falling
It's all yellow and nice
It's so very cold outside
Like the way I'm feeling inside.

Lyric to Turkish popular song

Leila Metin loved her work in Topkapı Palace and her identity as one of the respected curators, a specialist in Iznik tiles and ceramics. Nothing pleased her more than walking through the hallways and rooms of the old *harem*, where sons of the sultans were often held prisoner their whole lives, surrounded by spectacular blue-green or peach-colored tiles fired in Iznik, at the end of the Sea of Marmara. Tulips, carnations, scrolled Arabic letters…such beautiful tiles. Such a limited life for a prospective Sultan. For many of them, actually.

Every fall Leila worked on the dig in Iznik, ruining her perfect nails but enjoying the comradeship. Her other work with these tiles? No. She fluttered her fingers. She was an artist, pure and simple. Artists do not have to explain their work.

And they don't have to explain all their relationships. Peter Franklin was gone. Not forgotten, but gone. No explanations needed on any score. Except Leila would have liked more explanations from Peter Franklin.

15

*"You mistake me, my dear. I have a
high respect for your nerves. . ."*

Jane Austen, *Pride and Prejudice*

The streets in Cağaloğlu were even narrower and more congested than those in Pera. As we approached a four-story building covered with small billboards denoting publishing offices, Bayram signaled for the driver to stop, and paid the fare. We stood on the sidewalk while he argued over the last *kuruş*.

I glanced at the traffic inching past. There was that blue car again, with the same mustached driver and handsome passenger. I stood staring, but neither the driver nor his companion seemed aware of my existence.

One of those coincidences. Maybe they—or one of them—stayed at the Pera Palas, too. It's not against the law to go out on the Bosphorus to play your music or to drive a blue car. Still, why be interested in me yesterday and not at all today?

I shivered, then took a deep breath.

Back to business. We waited for an elevator in the cramped, terrazzo lobby of the building, scented with that lemon cleanser all Turkish janitors and housewives use. Bayram filled me in on what a good location the *Tribune* had.

"In these rooms, all around, are working the powerful newspaper writers from the whole political parties. The paper is lucky to get space here."

When I saw the cramped cubicle behind the door marked *Washington Tribune*, on the fifth floor, I wondered about the quality of the *Trib*'s luck. There were two desks, one bigger than the other, and Bayram and I would have to ask each other's permission to change position at all. All the space around, above, and below the desks was covered in paper, and more looked as if it had spewed out from a wire service teleprinter in the corner. When will the *Trib* catch up to the modern world?

Clearly, Bayram had not made this mess. His desk was as neat as his clothes. Even I would have had to work to accomplish this much havoc.

I gave Peter a mental salute and awarded him the Slob of the Year award, posthumously. His office in Washington had been on every employee's tour of the paper. "And he has it organized in his mind!" they would say, in amazement.

A pang hit my solar plexus. Pain of loss returned. Peter had been a close friend and associate for a long time. I wanted to joke with him about his housekeeping. I wanted to hear his raucous laugh.

"I hope you like the office," said Bayram, glancing at the mess. "Mr. Franklin told me never to throw anything away."

"Hmmm. Yes, Bayram. You've done a good job. When we get a chance, we'll toss the junk, and then I'm sure it will be perfect."

I shoved some files aside so I could sit in the rotating editor's chair behind the larger desk. Bayram wriggled into his own place, facing me. Except we couldn't see each other because of the mountain of paper between us.

I asked Bayram to reorganize my dumped file, and looked over Peter's desk.

From this vantage point, there was some order in the casual filing system Peter had established. The files on my right looked tempting, with that new-old look of off-white stiff paper that had the patina of having been handled some, but not too much. And Peter had kept them close at hand, ready for consulting.

Might be some good leads here. Let's see. Silver Wolves, the extreme rightist organization—a sub-head under "terrorism." Peter had them filed together with illicit arms trade and drugs. I picked up another file. Kurdish separatists. Different from the Silver Wolves, but under the same general heading. The same with the Islamist terrorists bent on restoring the Caliphate.

It was a tribute to Turkey that all these groups had not torn society apart. Not completely. The country's reputation and appeal to tourists remained solid.

I closed my eyes, but behind my lids paced the slinking gray figures of my dream. I stuffed the Silver Wolves' papers back into the file. They could be as dangerous as any wolf. Was I acting as one of those beautiful sheep dogs of Eastern Turkey—the great yellow-eyed guardians who wore spiked collars to allow them to fight off the wolves?

I threw those three files into my briefcase to be read back at the Pera. I left a very thin one marked "Misc." on the desk.

My sloppy habits will do me in one day.

16

*These are nothing like the remains of
great empires to be seen in western
cities, preserved like museums of
history and proudly displayed. The
people of Istanbul simply carry on
with their lives amid the ruins.*

Orhan Pamuk, *Istanbul, Memories and the City*

At the U.S. consulate in Pera, next to the Pera Palas, work carried on as usual. Junior officers, supervised by their betters, issued visas to the lines of hopeful applicants. "Are you coming back? How long will you be gone?" All the answers were carefully rehearsed. Like people from other countries, Turks wanted to go to America.

Upstairs, in offices with windows overlooking the Golden Horn, sat the men—and occasional woman—who ran the place. The consul-general, William Farrin, neared retirement. Istanbul was the prize last posting he had earned.

Farrin's deputy, Lawrence Andover, did most of the work, however. Andover had convinced the State Department to let him stay in Istanbul more-or-less forever. His knowledge of the language and culture was valuable in sorting out a complicated city and country. His networks were legendary.

And Andover lacked that driven need for a promotion that could have made life difficult within the Consulate community. He seemed quite happy being deputy to the Consul. A loyal soldier. And a diplomat who charmed everyone.

Farrin didn't know what he would do without Lawrence.

Lawrence had handled all the arrangements for Peter Franklin, the journalist, at the messy end of that tragedy. That work alone won him a row of gold stars in his boss's mind.

17

*Although only ten days had passed
since the news of the Commissioner's
appointment, everyone in town already
knew all there was to know about him,
where he was born, who his father
and mother were, his financial position, what sort of student he had been
at school, if he had a weakness for
women, if he drank and how much, his
likes and dislikes, every single thing.*

Yaşar Kemal, *Anatolian Tales*

Now to write the story. Today's story for the *Trib*. I assumed there would be one. First, I had to review the wire copy. It seemed a long time since I'd first gone out as a novice reporter. Senior editing, which I'd been promoted to some time ago, isn't the same thing.

When Bayram handed me back my now-orderly file, the note reminding me of drinks with Lawrence Andover lay on top. Bayram had clearly seen it, though he gave no hint. Clearly, he was the soul of discretion, well-trained by Peter as a reporter's assistant.

By one o'clock I was famished and suggested we eat lunch together. The young man's earnest face beamed with pleasure—something that always stirs up my demons for no good reason. I gave him a warning: "I'll need to get some information from you, Bayram."

Down we went to street level, in the same cramped elevator. There were two Turks (male) and another foreign woman riding with us. Most were journalists. You can just tell. Maybe it's the up-front ego that's a prerequisite for going into a news career; maybe the resigned look that says, "I've seen it all." Or maybe it's just the tense look that says, "I've got a deadline and I don't have any idea what I'm going to file."

Bayram nodded to the dark-suited young woman. Her red hair was sticking up in a style that was trendy but easy-care.

"Elizabeth Darcy, this is Miss Mollington, Faye Mollington of the *London News*. Ms. Mollington, ma'am, this is Ms. Darcy, who has come to take the place of, uh…to cover for the *Tribune* for a month or so." Bayram blushed.

My opinion of him went up a notch. He had cared about Peter and he didn't want to hurt my feelings.

Faye Mollington met my eyes with no-nonsense gray ones, stuck out a firm hand, all the while looking preoccupied. The hairs on the back of my neck stood at attention. Why? I sneaked a peak around the elevator.

Besides the three of us, there were the two Turkish men, who looked more like television types than newspaper reporters. One had a look that screamed "executive," spiffy all around. The other was well-dressed from the top of his head to the bottom of his jacket, declining in impressiveness past trousers that had a couple of spots and shoes run-down at the heels. Shoes never show on television. Must be an anchor. The men were conversing in Turkish, and neither Bayram nor Faye introduced them.

On the sidewalk, Faye Mollington took a hasty leave, saying she had to meet someone for lunch. She strode up the street, her raincoat sailing out behind her, a reporter's notebook tucked under her arm.

Bayram's gaze followed her, a slight smile on his face. "She and Mr. Franklin were good friends."

"Indeed," I said. "I must get to know her better, then."

18

*The introduction, however, was im-
mediately made; and as she named
their relationship to herself, she stole
a sly look at him to see how he bore it;
and was not without the expectation
of his decamping as fast as he could
from such disgraceful companions.*

Jane Austen, *Pride and Prejudice*

Bayram and I ate in one of those small, third-class restaurants that I would normally avoid in the developing world but embrace in Turkey, where food and cleanliness come next to godliness in the national creed. Crisp lamb *döner kebab* crackling with hot fat, sliced off the turning vertical spit onto warm, chewy pita bread…melted butter and tomato sauce, yogurt, and still more melted butter poured on…a nice little garnish of fresh broad-leaved parsley…. The smell of olive oil and lemon, of garlic sauted to the perfect "pinkness." It was hard to turn my mind to business.

But I had a job to do—the only job as far as editors at the *Trib* knew. "Who would you recommend as a contact on Turkish events?"

"Oh, you must go to Haldun Kutlu, famous columnist for *Cümhüri-yet* newspaper. He always a good friend of Mr. Franklin's. One of best sources, too. He can tell you where to look."

We'd eaten our food with minimal talk, our mouths full. Now Bayram made a ceremony of bringing his coffee to his lips and sipping it, almost sultan-style. Could the little man have a secret life, like Walter Mitty?

After we returned to the office I checked the wires. No story needed to be filed that day, so I sent a computer message to Washington saying a general "hi" to the bunch, knocked off early and headed back to the Pera. Bayram said he'd stay to monitor breaking news.

In the taxi back across the Golden Horn I relaxed back and closed my eyes. Once, when traffic was stalled getting onto the bridge, I roused myself enough to look behind us. Cars lined up as far as the old limestone Roman aquaduct looming over the crowded street. A black taxi revved its engine. Through its windows the car behind it, a blue one, was just visible. I turned back around, sank into the seat again.

I would not be paranoid. The world, after all, is full of blue cars.

19

*"...He leaves out half the
words, and blots the rest."*

Jane Austen, *Pride and Prejudice*

At the Pera Palas, I kicked off my shoes, pulled off most of my clothes, and lay on the bed, folders beside me. Just time for a nap before the meeting with Andover.

My eyes closed, but I couldn't sleep. What had happened to Peter? Was I crazy to think someone had killed him? Was he murdered? I wasn't sure I was ready to define my quest as a case of murder. My gut feeling was that Peter had not killed himself, either intentionally or not. And nobody but me seemed clear on that.

Peter's materials. They must contain a clue. Through the tiredness, sharpened nerves provided a little energy. Sleepiness dropped away like a cloak. I got up and pulled out the files from the office.

In the file marked "Silver Wolves" I found notations in Peter's almost illegible hand: "Aug. 7," followed by "Tpkpi," "Srkci," and the query "Ahmet?"

A bit like a crossword puzzle. Topkapı Palace housed the old Sultans. Sirkeci Station was the train terminus on the European side of the Bosphorus—the end point once for the famed Orient Express from Paris. "Ahmet," a common name in Turkey, could refer to anyone.

Peter's scratched notes seemed to have been written in a moving vehicle: "Tpkpi," again, then "Çengelköy." Okay. One of the villages along the Asian side of the Bosphorus. A charming place. It would be a pleasure to check it out—if only I knew the object of my search.

Jet lag caught up with me. I must have dozed. Thuds from the carpeted hallway woke me. Heart lurching, I pulled myself from sleep to consciousness. Muted cacophony rose from the street below: the steady roar of motors stalled in traffic punctuated by horns and shouts from street vendors. *"Aygaz!"* Bottled gas. *"Simit, simit!"* Delicious, chewy, sesame-covered, bagel-like rolls. The calls soothed me.

The racket in the hall ebbed away. I cracked the door and caught a glimpse of a black uniform rounding the corner toward the elevator. Must be one of the staff.

I checked my watch. Yes, time to get ready. I dashed on lipstick and eye shadow and checked my green silk dress for wrinkles (which I found, but ignored). I glanced in the mirror to see if things were pulled together. In the low-wattage Pera lamplight, the green silk sort of matched my eyes. Everything looks better by lamplight, one of those truisms advancing age has taught me. Impression, not reality, is the more essential attribute. I grabbed my trench-coat and headed down to the lobby.

Even in the dim Victorian lighting of the Pera Palas lobby, I singled out Lawrence Andover. His sleek thinning blond diplomat hair, the immaculate raincoat over his arm, hat carried in his hand—above all, his lack of self-consciousness—gave him away.

When I stepped out of the fretted-iron elevator, Andover arose from a rose-velour stuffed armchair and came toward me. I got the full force of his personality.

I extended my hand. "Elizabeth Darcy…and you must be Lawrence Andover."

"I am, indeed." Andover's gaze traveled over me from head to foot. More like a military inspection than a sexual appraisal. His eyes were light blue and friendly, but masked. Could he be a covert member of the CIA, known overseas as "The Company?" They're trained to be hard to read.

Out in the autumn drizzle, we pulled our raincoats around us and waited for the gray diplomatic car called by Andover. A stone-faced Consulate driver sat behind the wheel. He looked like he doubled as a bodyguard.

"I thought we'd go to my place for drinks," said Andover. "Is that all right with you? Do you have time?"

Under ordinary circumstances I don't run off to a strange man's house with him. Especially an attractive man. But Andover was a foreign service officer of my own country. A taste of home. Since we were going to Andover's house, maybe he'd introduce me to other diplomats.

Never say no to an invitation on a journalistic assignment. All contacts can be useful.

20

*The purity of a person's heart can be quickly
measured by how he regards cats.*

Anonymous proverb

Haldun Kutlu glanced unseeing at his cluttered desk. The *Cümhüriyet* newspaper office in Cağaloğlu had a strategic location. Out his window he could see bits of the Topkapı walls and the tip of Ayasofya museum. He'd had lunch a few blocks away at the Fountain Restaurant at the Covered Market.

It was time to go home. Ayla would worry if he missed the usual ferry. What a good wife she was! Always thinking first of her husband. She would have been a wonderful mother. Both of them felt pangs of regret over their lack of children.

He pushed that regret to the back of his mind. Peter Franklin. A man who could not be pushed to the back of his mind. The very night he died last week, they were supposed to meet at a party in Bebek. Peter had indicated he had something to tell him. They'd worked together, as much as journalists ever work together, on some interesting leads. Their newspapers were not in competition with each other.

Haldun had many questions regarding the death of Peter Franklin.

* * * *

Sultana the cat stretched as Haldun gathered his papers. Then she walked purposefully toward the basket under his desk and jumped in. Together they exited the office and took the tram to Eminönü wharf to catch the ferry to Üsküdar.

After the short ride, they disembarked at the busy wharf at Üsküdar and Sultana pushed her way out of the basket. She would soon be up the hill at Haldun's house for Ayla's fish and rice. But he understood the cat's need for freedom.

21

*"Young women should always be
properly guarded and attended,
according to their situation in life."*

Jane Austen, *Pride and Prejudice*

The sleek diplomatic car drove down Barbaros Boulevard, named
after the famous Turkish pirate known to the West as Barbarossa. Yıldız
Park lay up the hill in mist on the left. The shore road led past Dolma-
bahçe Palace, where rain dripped through the remaining vegetation on
plane trees. Big orange and brown leaves that had fallen earlier became
a slippery mass on the pavement, made even more gloomy by the dusk.
They matched my mood, on which nameless fears and apprehensions
had become a slimy mass of their own.

As we drove, we spoke of Peter Franklin, the link between us. I asked
Andover what he knew of Peter's death.

"Not much, I'm afraid. The police called us to say a body they thought
was Franklin's had turned up, and asked for our formal identification."

"Were you the one who identified the body, then?" Fate had taken me
much closer to the scene of the crime than I'd expected.

"Yes."

"Can you tell me about it?" I suppressed the desire to take out a notebook.

"Franklin was due at a party. He didn't show up, but we all assumed
that was because he had a deadline to meet or something. You journalists have a penchant for missing social functions, you know!" Andover
chuckled deep in his throat. A pleasant chuckle.

"And?" I prompted.

"In the middle of the night, the police commissioner called me to say
one more American had succumbed to drug use, and could I identify the
body. That's about it."

"Were there marks on Peter's body? Evidence of violence?" It seemed
intrusive to Peter to be asking all this, but how else was I to find out?

"No. No marks except for the needle pricks in his arm." Andover's
face twisted.

"But I don't understand. If he died of an overdose, how did his body end up in the Bosphorus?"

"The police said he fell off a boat where he had been shooting up. It was just bad luck that the boat was upstream from the restaurant where the party was being held." Andover stared ahead. "The body caught on pilings under the restaurant verandah. The police could not find the boat's owner, so no information there."

The graphic details made me sick to my stomach. Peter was dead. How could Andover speak so calmly? He obviously hadn't known Peter as I had.

He might have read my thoughts. "Sorry, my dear. Oh, I'm sorry!" He patted my hand. "I forgot you were his friend. Didn't mean to offend."

"I'm fine." I looked at his hand resting on mine. Lawrence Andover. Kind, as well as sophisticated.

22

*Now I began to fear that spit would
suddenly climb out of my throat and
land on the ground without my even
willing it. But as I knew, spitting was
mostly a habit of grown-ups of the
same stock as those brainless, weak-
willed, insolent children who were
always being punished by my teacher.*

Orhan Pamuk, *Istanbul*

Erol Metin got off the ferry and made his way by circuitous routes to
the Silver Wolves' safe house in Üsküdar. It would be a long night. He
was getting oriented to the group's rituals. First, the meeting of five or
six members. They always arrived separately, did not give their names,
and kept the curtains of every room closed.

The safe house was one of many buildings clustered behind the big
mosque overlooking Üsküdar wharf. When the evening call to prayer
resounded from the minaret, the group performed their ablutions in separate bathrooms and then prayed together in the main room. They were
protecting both Turkey and Islam from vile influences of the West.

After prayers and a quick meal, they began their lessons for that night.
No announcement was made of what the topic would be. Or of what
their individual assignments would consist. Assignments were handed
out orally by Hamdi himself, the Wolves' leader, and they were done in
absolute privacy.

When the curtains were raised, the safe house was an excellent location for observation without being observed. Most of the time, however,
it was a secret world inside. A magnet for young men like Erol.

23

*"Indeed you are mistaken. I have
no such injuries to resent. It is not
of peculiar, but of general evils,
which I am now complaining."*

Jane Austen, *Pride and Prejudice*

"I want to see the restaurant where Peter missed the party," I told
Andover. At Beşiktaş wharf, the car slowed and nosed its way into line
with other vehicles dropping off ferry commuters.

"That can be arranged." Andover reached for the door handle on his
side.

"And where did Peter live?" I grabbed my purse and my own door
handle. Bayram could give me that information, but I wanted my own
government to tell me.

"He lived up the Bosphorus from here, in Yeniköy."

We were out of the car now and Andover walked around to my side
to extend a gentlemanly arm. Yeniköy. I'd go soon.

The driver drove away. Saying we'd take the scenic route to his house,
Andover led the way across the rain-slick road to the wooden building
where he bought two coin-like *jeton*s. We waited on hard wooden benches for the next ferry. The wait was made more interesting by a basket
of multi-colored kittens in a corner of the room. The calico mother cat
watched warily as I petted her offspring, but when I found a cookie in
my bag and offered it, she accepted with grace, watched indulgently by
other passengers.

Should I have waited a day or two before accompanying a stranger to
an unknown address in the evening dark? Especially on a rainy night. I
breathed that thought back.

It turned out the ferry ride made sense. Andover's old wooden *yali*
was across the Bosphorus from the ferry pier at Beşiktaş, in Çengelköy,
a village on the Asian side. Çengelköy. I'd run across that name before.

During the twenty-minute passage, blurred lights of fellow ferries
crossed our path in the dusk, sounding their combination whoops and
wails to warn small boats with no lights. Once in a while came the deeper

boom of a Russian tanker plying its careful way past hidden obstacles in the narrow waters that comprise the northern giant's only all-weather escape by sea.

When I'd been here last, the Soviet Union was the big enemy of the West. Now Islamist terrorists filled that role. Turkey'd had its own share of terrorism, often aimed at intellectual, secular Turks. Most of it was rightly blamed on Kurdish separatists, but terrorists often weave spider-web networks that are hard to trace.

Inside the smoke-filled ferry cabin, Andover and I exchanged the usual small talk of the wandering expatriate: Who was posted in Dubai or Karachi in which years? Did you know the Ambassador in Tashkent? Over the years, I've found that almost everyone I encounter outside America knows at least one person I do. The global world of professional expatriates is small.

"Did you know Peter Franklin before Istanbul?" It was a natural question given our conversation.

Andover looked thoughtful. "Well…yes, come to think of it, I guess we overlapped a little in Cairo. Back in the '80s, it would be. Didn't know him well until we both came here, though." He had an air of sad reminiscence.

My feelings, exactly.

24

Bodrum folk cut harvest early,
And Fate has cut her harvest early
Making martyr with golden scissors
Of Bodrum's judge—a woman.
Oh, lady judge, beloved judge,
Whyever did you hang yourself?

Lyric to "Hakim Hanım" folksong (translated in *A Turkish Odyssey*)

Professor Oktay Fener slipped gratefully into clean clothes after his shower. Life at the archaeological dig near Iznik was delightful, though not always comfortable.

This trip was a special treat for Oktay because his daughter, Aytem, had accompanied him from their home on the Asian side of the Bosphorus. She was studying ceramics, just like her *baba ciğim*, as she affectionately called him. Daddy dear.

Also on the dig was Perihan Kıraz, an old friend. Oktay and Perihan had worked together for more than a quarter century, having attended university together and gone into the same field. Perihan was more of a female don than a woman who played up her attractions. Still, Oktay remembered moments of sexual tension with Perihan. Using a time-honored male approach, he had usually tried to ignore it, to pretend it didn't exist. They'd never broken the bounds of discretion. He'd never even been tempted to do that.

Food at the tent was delicious: oval-shaped lamb *köfte* balls; crispy *su boreği*, the oven-baked pastry laced with white cheese and broad-leafed parsley. Rice *pilav* with bits of lamb liver and raisins.

Perihan, as always, had had a role in supervising the chef. They had found a few broken pieces of the old Iznik tiles today. Each glimpse of the vivid reds and blues and greens made his heart beat faster. It was a pleasure to wipe off the dust from each plate or vase. It was also a pleasure to work with his students on finding and preserving the nation's treasures. Everyone knew about the jewels in Topkapı. About the great emerald in the Sultan's belt featured in the old movie, *Topkapi*. Many fewer realized what intricate work the craftsmen of Iznik had wrought.

It was the usual case of foreign things being valued above the local. The Sultans had used this exquisite ceramic work for their everyday meals. The porcelain from China was for state occasions.

There was, of course, one problem with eating off the Iznik ceramics: lead was used in the glaze. Oktay Fener often wondered what role the lead had had in the streaks of insanity that flashed through the history of the Sultans and their families. Lead, added to inbreeding.

His next article would address that issue. Controversy again, he supposed. But someone had to expose the past.

25

"Oh, yes—I understand
you perfectly!"

"I wish I might take this for a com-
pliment; but to be so easily seen
through I am afraid is pitiful."

Jane Austen, *Pride and Prejudice*

The ferry slowed and came to a stop, grinding its string of worn rubber tires along the wooden wharf at Çengelköy.

Çengelköy. Now I remembered where I'd seen that name. It had been
in Peter's notes. I'd keep my eyes open. Or at least try to think why Peter
had jotted it into his files.

As I jumped across the space between the boat and the shore, a few
sharp raindrops hit my uncovered head. Andover hailed a taxi whose
driver seemed to know him well, and we bumped over narrow cobblestone streets for ten minutes until the car stopped. Lights welcomed from
windows as we stepped from the street to a little set of stairs. High walls
loomed on each side of the lighted portion of the traditional wooden
yali. But tree branches visible against the city-hued night sky promised
garden delights in warmer weather.

"Welcome to my house," said Andover, with a smile and a grand gesture of his well-manicured hands.

26

The call to prayer seemed to him, as
it would later to me, addressed to the
"mute, blind, and deaf houses fall-
ing here in silence and solitude."

Orhan Pamuk, *Istanbul, Memories and the City*

In Üsküdar along the Asian side and down a few villages from Çengelköy, Erol Metin was back in his cell-like room, thinking. The meeting had consisted of an inspirational talk from Hamdi about the past glories of the Ottoman Empire and the need for a Pan-Turkic Empire today. This time, Hamdi emphasized, the Turks would not turn themselves into a multicultural hodgepodge in which they played a relatively minor role. You could hardly tell Ottoman Istanbul from the capitals of Europe! Or even China.

Thus, the invidious influence of modern-day intellectuals drawing from global philosophies had to be stopped. Foreigners became suspect.

Islam could be one tool in the Wolves' playbook. People liked to think of themselves as religious. You could play on their sympathies that way.

Another tool, regrettably, would have to be the violence they had been experimenting with. Hamdi had gestured sadly as he announced this.

And the tools for violence required money. Lots of money. The Silver Wolves had some irons in that fire, too. Drugs, arms. Trade in anything was acceptable in order to carry out their objectives.

Erol hated some of the tasks they were asking him to do. He sighed. What would this do to his sister, Leila?

27

I had a sudden chill of recognition
that I was in Asia Minor, on the
shore at last of a holy land where
three great religions had helped to
form me and everything I knew.

Mary Lee Settle, *Turkish Reflections*

Lawrence Andover's house was, in a word, perfect. Its uneven floors were polished so that the wood gleamed in lamplight. Scattered around the living room lay exquisite rugs, some Turkish, some Persian, in muted tones of red, blue, green. Bookcases lined the walls, a collector's library on the shelves. The scent of roses infused the room from two slim vases that boasted Ottoman designs.

On every piece of antique furniture sat some startling work of art: richly-decorated Iznik-style plates and bowls; statues Greek or Roman in inspiration; old manuscripts in the flowing, pictorial Arabic script, adorned by intricate miniatures. I couldn't take my eyes off the ceramics, swirls of blue and orange, red and green, with tulips or carnations.

Andover caught my amazed, admiring gaze at the room: "Yes," he said wryly. "I am a collector."

"It's beautiful," I breathed.

Out the six vertical windows at the back of the *yalı*, the Bosphorus glided by, wide and dark and silent between this continent and Europe. A passing ferry switched on its lights, becoming in an instant a jeweled princess' slipper.

Drinks were served by a well-trained, white-uniformed servant.

"Have some *rakı*," urged Andover, pointing to a bottle of the deceptively-innocent-looking, colorless liquid.

The memory of the burning, anise-flavored national drink made my mouth water. Turkish *meze* in all its glorious variety is meant to be nibbled as one sips, just sips, *rakı*. And one, of course, gossips while sipping. I might get Andover to talk more freely over *rakı*.

The *meze* was laid out on a large glass-covered coffee table: charred eggplant and green pepper and two or three kinds of beans, each fried in olive oil and garlic and served with yogurt with still more garlic; tiny Black Sea anchovies, fried to a crisp; buttery-leaved *börek* filled with goat cheese or bits of lamb and spinach; Persian melon called *kavun* in Turkey; and flat, hot *pide* bread.

Only the food could have taken my mind off the ceramics and art works on the walls. I dug in with gusto.

Andover clearly enjoyed entertaining amazed guests. "It's good, isn't it?" he said. "I have the best chef in Istanbul!"

"You do indeed!"

Even the distant sound of a doorbell didn't slow me down. A shame that my mouth was full as I turned to meet the newcomer.

28

*"...I am in no humour at present to
give consequence to young ladies
who are slighted by other men."*

Jane Austen, *Pride and Prejudice*

Before me stood the handsomest man I had ever seen. Pure Mediterranean—curly dark hair sprinkled with distinguished gray. Strong, craggy features lined with an indeterminate number of years.

"Ahmet Aslan," said the head-turner, holding out his hand.

I caught the flash of something in his expressive dark eyes. The glimmer's meaning was clear to any woman who has cut her eye-teeth. It surprised me and put me on guard.

"Aslan here was due to have a meeting with me, and I said he should meet you. By the way, Elizabeth, Mr. Aslan is one of Turkey's biggest businessmen." Lawrence—no, I couldn't call him that yet—Andover-turned to discuss something with his butler.

"What sort of business?" I asked.

"We make dishes and tiles, for the domestic market and for export," said Aslan. "And we do some cement projects."

"Saying Aslan makes dishes is like saying Wedgwood makes plates," remarked Andover, turning from his butler and offering me another glass of *rakı* and water. "His name is the signature brand of Turkey."

I said no to more *rakı*. After all, I had a significant trip returning to the Pera. Ahmet Aslan took a glass and added water from the bottle the servant had brought.

At this point, Andover excused himself to take a telephone call, leaving Aslan and me to do the *homo sapien* equivalent of dogs sniffing around each other.

"Does your family live along the Bosphorus, too, Ahmet *Bey*?"

"My family roots are in the southeast of Turkey, in Diyarbakır."

Interesting. Coming from there, he could be Kurdish.

He continued. "And you, what does your husband do?"

Oh, for heaven's sake. Would the world never get past this kind of sexism? I decided to throw it back at him. "I am not married. Does your wife work?"

"If I had a wife, she would take care of my children and cook my meals. That is the way of the East." The smug, infuriating words were accompanied by such charm I couldn't take them seriously. I didn't think Aslan did, either. He was trying to rile me.

So I laughed. "Well, it may once have been, but, after all, Turkey has beaten the United States in having a woman head of government. Aren't you overstating the case?" I licked butter off my fingers as I spoke. The same old boring argument, the role of women. When would we get past it?

When it's no longer an issue, I guessed.

Andover returned and glanced at the table.

I had already had far too much and wanted to get back to my primary mission.

"Did you know Peter Franklin?" I asked Ahmet Aslan.

"Of course! Terrible thing. Awful." Aslan's thoughtful frown morphed into concern for me. "You also work for the *Tribune?*"

Andover confirmed this with a sympathetic nod. "Elizabeth knew Peter well, Ahmet. I gather they were friends."

I composed my face. "Yes. We were friends and long-time colleagues. All of us at the paper miss him very much."

All of us looked at the floor and there was a moment of silence in the room. A tribute to Peter. I turned to Andover. "I suppose Peter was pretty much a novice when you knew him in Cairo...."

"Peter and I were both novices!" Andover's pleasant laugh broke the solemn silence and went well with the perfect room. "I was in the consular section and he was reporting freelance. But we at the Embassy knew Peter was a good source for finding out what was going on." Andover gestured us into the comfortable chairs arranged in a conversational ell around the carpets, facing the windows toward the water. He sat in a sleek leather chair. I shared the couch with Aslan.

"Yes," I agreed. "He was always first with a story! Tell me more about what he was doing here." I addressed the question to both men, trying to sound nonchalant.

Ahmet answered first. "Istanbul's a complicated city and Peter was one of the few correspondents who got past the surface. I always read his pieces. Sometimes I, as a Turk, learned things from his writing. In fact, I saw Peter at parties. I knew him. I would say we were friends. Nice. He was nice."

"Nice" was not a word I'd ever heard used in relation to Peter Franklin.

Andover uncrossed his trim legs. "I didn't know him well. Of course, I read his stories in the *Trib* clippings at the Embassy every morning. Sometimes we had drinks...."

I knew I was skating on thin ice, but went ahead: "There wasn't any police follow-up to his death? I haven't heard much about that."

Andover answered. "I guess you probably saw the official cable we sent to your paper. The police assumed it was an overdose. They didn't want to get dragged into another country's affairs. They were only too happy to have us arrange to cremate the body."

Why hadn't I organized a group from the *Trib* to meet the plane carrying Peter's ashes? We should have done that, out of respect.

"Where did you send the ashes? To his parents?" It occurred to me I knew absolutely nothing about Peter's family life, even after working with him for years, after being friends with him.

"His sister. Lives in New Hampshire, apparently." Andover got up again and headed for the kitchen.

So Peter didn't have much in the way of family. I sighed and dug once more into the *meze*, dropping *börek* crumbs on Andover's beautiful Hereke carpet.

29

*"The more I see of the world, the
more I am dissatisfied with it..."*

Jane Austen, *Pride and Prejudice*

Haldun Kutlu's wife, Ayla, waited every evening for both her husband and the white cat they called Sultana. Sultana always came last, as she wanted out of the basket as soon as Haldun stepped off the ferry. Ayla had no idea where Sultana spent the next hour. But she would come by for supper, as regular as clockwork.

Ayla worried about Haldun. The newspapers were full of dramatic headlines about this terrorist group or that. And Haldun, as a journalist, was a target. He was also a target as a liberal, Western-leaning intellectual.

And he was all she had.

The door opened. Oh, good. He was home safe.

"*Allah korusun,*" she whispered, as she did every time Haldun left or came back. "God protect him."

30

*She listened most attentively to all that
passed between them, and gloried in
every expression, every sentence of her
uncle, which marked his intelligence,
his taste, or his good manners.*

Jane Austen, *Pride and Prejudice*

The atmosphere in Andover's home was charming, both inside the old-fashioned windows and outside, where flickering lights had appeared in many places on the water. A laziness stole over me—maybe a combination of jet lag, *rakı*, and excellent food—and I yawned.

But I had to get back to work. Andover was still out of the room. I turned to Aslan.

"Tell me about being Kurdish in Turkey—you are Kurdish, I assume, since you come from the Southeast?—and how you have managed to succeed." The *rakı* must be taking effect. I'd abandoned diplomatic skills. I didn't actually take out a notebook and pen, but I'd remember crucial elements for future stories on Turkey's most volatile minority, should Aslan choose to confide.

I received a sharp glance from my handsome companion at the bald-faced assertion that he must be a Kurd. But whether Aslan would have told me anything became a moot point when Andover re-entered the room. Picking up his drink, after checking to see if Aslan and I were still supplied, he draped himself artistically in a third armchair near where we sat looking out the windows. A huge tanker flying a lighted Turkish flag in front and the Russian flag aft made its ponderous way by.

"Now, Elizabeth. Tell us about yourself. How long have you worked for the *Tribune*? How well did you know Franklin?"

Andover's fluid voice and face went well with the room. Had he decorated around himself? His eyes, as before, gave few hints of his thoughts.

Talk about myself, with Andover sitting there like a sphinx and Aslan's impeccably-tailored legs crossed over each other? They'd get the abridged version.

"I've been at the *Tribune* for several years, since I stopped teaching journalism at George Washington University. I knew Peter well, of course. We worked together on several stories—and he was also my friend, as you know." I left out the prize Peter and I had won for investigative reporting. But I wanted to keep the focus on Peter. "What can you tell me about his life here?"

I was rather proud of switching to offense. I didn't intend to be interrogated. The diplomat's appreciative gaze indicated he was aware of my tactic.

"Oh, Franklin was a loner," he said. "We at the Consulate offered to help him out on occasion, but he usually preferred to go his own way. Ahmet *Bey* here, saw more of him socially than I did, I suspect."

The legs uncrossed, and Aslan put his elbows on his knees. "Franklin had a good name as a journalist, so he was courted by influential people. I believe he was quite a man for the ladies, too—but I imagine you would know more about that, Ms. Darcy?"

Another change from defense to offense. I ignored the comment, as it richly deserved. And I didn't think Peter had been a loner, either. I filed Andover's comment in the back of my mind.

"What about the police report that he died of drugs?" I asked. "That doesn't sound right to me."

"A lot of Westerners, Europeans and Americans, get into drugs here, when they find out how readily available good stuff is," murmured Andover. "Our consular section spends half its time visiting people in prisons who insist they'd never touched drugs until they came to Turkey."

"Look, Lawrence." There, I'd called him by his first name. I half-glanced at Aslan to see if he reacted. "You and I both know Peter wasn't an innocent and wasn't a criminal, either. I can't see him jeopardizing his career for anything as stupid as drugs." I bit around the pit of a black olive as I spoke. Aslan's face had not adjusted its expression one iota.

"Well, maybe not." Andover's smile let me know he was teasing. "I agree with you. I like playing devil's advocate."

I gave him a grin.

At this point, Ahmet Aslan chimed in as he stood. "I never heard that Franklin took drugs. Doesn't sound like him."

Warmth bloomed behind my ribs. "My thoughts exactly!" Aslan, at least, seemed to believe as I did. Couldn't tell about Andover.

Aslan held out his hand to Andover. "Much as I would like to stay, now I must leave for an appointment."

I stood, too. I'd only been invited to drinks; it wouldn't be right to stay longer.

Andover protested politely, but then courteously saw us both to the door. The butler stood there with an impassive expression and our coats. Andover held mine for me and turned to Aslan.

"Are you going her way or shall I call the car?" he asked.

With typical Turkish hospitality, Aslan offered me a ride to the ferry.

I had to admit I enjoyed the luxurious custom leather seats in the red BMW. In a few minutes we were at the Çengelköy wharf.

"Take a taxi on the other side," Aslan said with a devastating smile. "There are lots of them. And don't pay more than six liras!"

Ahmet Aslan seemed a man who liked to take control. That never has and never will work with me.

"Certainly," I said meekly. No harm in letting him think it had.

31

*The tumult of her mind was
now painfully great.*

Jane Austen, *Pride and Prejudice*

When we got to Eminönü, the ferry stop at Galata Bridge, I caught a bus going up the hill and walked the rest of the way to the Pera under old-fashioned, tulip-shaped street lights. Ha! So much for a man telling me what to do.

I looked over my shoulder as I hurried down Istiklal Caddesi from the bus stop. No need to enter the darkened side streets until I had to. But I didn't feel afraid. There were plenty of people on Istiklal Caddesi tonight. Well-dressed young couples. Small groups of young men. A few clumps of chattering young women. Young, young, young. Had Istiklal forgotten its diplomatic roots, when carriages drew up to the embassies? When envoys carrying precious gifts to the Sultan were received in Topkapı Palace on the other side of the Golden Horn?

The scene was different now. Shops were mostly closed, but trendy restaurants boomed popular music out their doors. Loud laughter indicated well-heeled patrons were enjoying their *rakı* and good Turkish wine as well as the music. Disco displacement of history.

I stopped at one of the small shops to get two large bottles of Ayvaz water for the hotel room and stuck them in my bag. Those tiny bottles in the minibar were never enough.

When I turned off Istiklal Caddesi, the streets grew narrow and dark. This was once, after its elite diplomatic heyday, the red light district of "new" Istanbul. Recent prosperity had changed that—or at least made it so high-class it wasn't obvious to the casual walker.

Here there were smatterings of people, most of whom I couldn't see clearly. I kept my eyes to the cobblestones to avoid tripping.

Once, someone ran past me the other way, slipping a little as he went. I glimpsed a young face. A handsome face. No. It couldn't be the passenger I'd seen in that blue car. It looked something like him, though.

I walked faster.

With relief, I reached the street of the U.S. consulate and the Pera Palas. Whew. Safety.

I walked closer to the wall than I usually do. Since my eyes were downcast, I didn't see the black-clad figure ahead of me until it was too late. I bumped into him.

The man crumpled against the wall, falling to the side where street lights didn't reach. He landed heavily, a dead weight. I let out a scream.

32

*"They have none of them much
to recommend them…"*

Jane Austen, *Pride and Prejudice*

Something was very wrong. The man crumpled down the wall when I brushed against him, though the bump hadn't been hard.

The Pera concierge stepped onto the sidewalk at my cry. Both of us stared at the huddled form in the shadows.

"Dial for help!" I demanded. The concierge ran inside. A taxi stopped to let out passengers in front of the hotel, so I wasn't alone on the sidewalk. I rushed back to where the still form lay, waving for help from the taxi passengers as I ran. They jumped out and ran over.

Without a flashlight, I could see only the man's outline. I grasped his shoulder and turned him over carefully.

"Please move." The voice from behind me carried authority. I was pushed aside. A flashlight beam lit the scene.

"Hold this." Hands shoved a briefcase into my arms.

Was it a night for peremptory men? Still, I had bumped the poor man and cried out. I held the briefcase as commanded.

The flashlight-wielder was my unwelcome breakfast companion, that Frenchman. Jean Le-something. Le Reau? He leaned over the crumpled figure, held his finger to the man's neck, felt his torso, then straightened slowly.

"I am afraid there is nothing to do," he said.

"You mean he is dead?" I tried very hard to keep my voice steady.

"Yes. I fear so."

"But why? How?" Istanbul wasn't exactly a murder capital like Detroit.

"There is a knife wound," said Le Reau, wiping his hand on a handkerchief he pulled from his pocket.

At that moment, the emergency vehicle and police arrived. Jean Le Reau and I gave our preliminary witness statements, as did the concierge. We didn't have much to tell.

Cautioned by the police that they would need to speak with us again that evening, Le Reau and I headed as one toward the old-fashioned bar of the Pera. We both seemed to need a drink.

33

Hey, who's there? Who laughs?
No one, I guess. Dark, empty halls.
Yet laughter rings in my ears.

Güngör Dilmen, "The Ears of King Midas" (play)

Erol Metin vomited in a shadowed gutter. He had followed orders. He had gone out on his own to uphold the honor of glorious Turkey. He should feel proud.

He did not feel proud.

Erol had not killed before. Perhaps this was a normal reaction. He was glad his sister could not see him.

The victim—why did that word come to mind?—had broken with the Silver Wolves. Altan had taken an oath and then had been lured away with money. Someone's money. That was a capital offense in the group. New members were required to prove allegiance by carrying out the execution.

So he had followed Altan to the Pera Palas, where he apparently had non-Wolves business. While Altan waited in the shadows, Erol's knife had come out and done its work.

Work. Just work. Remember that… It was all for the glorious cause.

He vomited again, wiped his mouth, and made his way back to Eminönü and the ferry.

The companion who had been training him for several days, Yusuf, fell into line behind him at the ferry. As their eyes met, Yusuf gave an almost imperceptible thumbs up.

So Erol was being followed and checked on. He wasn't surprised.

34

It wasn't my first dead body, but I was shaking. The man, when Le Reau shone his flashlight on his face, was young. Too young to be lying against a wall, dead. Unless, of course, he was a drug addict. Youth is no proof against addiction—the opposite, actually. The two are often found together.

His clothes were unremarkable. Jeans. Sweatshirt that proclaimed his loyalty to the Fenerbahçe soccer team. Baseball hat saying "New York Yankees."

What was remarkable was the amount of blood on the sidewalk, pooling now in a slippery mess. Since he had been standing when I inadvertently knocked him over, the murder must have happened just before I bumped against the guy. I may even have met the killer as I approached the hotel, since I'd come from the darker side of the street. Apparently the guards at the American consulate the next door had not heard a thing. Running to the site, their representative appeared shocked that anyone would have the nerve to commit a crime so close.

Having taken charge at first, Jean Le Reau became an innocent-looking bystander as soon as the police arrived. The team of six policemen, including two in plainclothes, came quickly and took preliminary statements from all three of us—Le Reau, the concierge, and me. We sat in lobby seats for the process, in front of the little desk. Out the window I could see the body being loaded onto a gurney. These guys were nothing if not efficient.

Jean Le Reau and I sat a long time in the bar area of the Pera waiting to give more detailed statements. A watchful officer kept an eye on us while questioning the desk clerk, who remained on duty. Few people seemed to have been disturbed by the incident. There was no crowd. A couple of hotel guests wondered aloud why police cars were there and were told, "*Bir şey değil*—it's nothing to worry about." The Pera was far from full, so there weren't many guests.

"Get you something?" asked Le Reau, as he headed for the bar.

"A glass of white wine—*Çankaya*, if they have it. And a bottle of water, too? Thanks."

The velvet chairs and the warmth of the room, plus the wine, helped me pull myself together. For quite a while, we didn't speak.

"Do you have any idea who that man was?" I finally said.

"None at all. I think he was a drug addict."

"I assumed so. But why was he killed? Why here?"

Silence from Le Reau. Then, "I'm not at all sure. It is odd." He looked troubled. "Not so odd that an addict got killed as that it happened here, right in front of the Consulate guards."

I admit it: we each had two glasses of wine. By the time the plain-clothes detective whose nameplate said "Durmaz" returned to us, we were feeling pretty relaxed.

"Do you have anything to add to your earlier statements?" Detective Durmaz asked, looking at the business cards we had handed him. When we shook our heads, he smiled enigmatically and politely and said he would like to speak with each of us. "Separately, please. Ladies first, Mizz Darcy."

He led me through French doors to an isolated part of the old lobby, where a small round coffee table separated our chairs. A third chair was occupied by a police translator, though I didn't think Durmaz needed him. Occasionally we spoke a few words in Turkish, which I could follow fine. I explained the incident and told him I was in Istanbul on an interim assignment for the *Washington Tribune*. I couldn't help the regret in my voice when I said the word, "interim."

"Yes, I know about your paper's former correspondent," Detective Durmaz said. "I worked on that case."

"You did?" I had a thousand questions, but this was not the time for any of them. As soon as I was released, I waved goodnight to Jean Le Reau, shook hands with Detective Durmaz, and went upstairs.

I locked the door to my room and undressed, tossing clothes onto the armchair. How tenuous life seemed in this city of mystery! Who was that dead man? Was I being pursued? How much could I trust Le Reau? He had been a godsend tonight. Almost too quickly on the scene...

I pulled yesterday's note from the back of a drawer where I'd put it. Was this a piece of solid evidence that I was someone's target? "Lock your door. This is from a friend." Was it really from a friend? Did I have any friends?

I crumpled the note and threw it in the wastebasket.

35

With patience, mulberry leaves become satin.
Work as if you were to live forever; live
as if you were to die tomorrow.

Two Turkish proverbs

The next day was as gray as the solid multi-storied building in Cağaloğlu with the newspaper's name, *Cümhüriyet*, down a corner in big letters. I folded my umbrella and shook rain off my coat as I stepped into the gloomy reception area. Walking, it had taken me seven minutes from the *Tribune*'s little office. By car in all that traffic, it would have taken twenty.

"May I see Haldun Kutlu, please? He's expecting me." A spindly, downtrodden clerk asked me to wait on an old wooden chair, one of several. The others were occupied, I guessed, by nervous job applicants, or in some cases, young writers trying to sell their free-lance work. The trousers of one young man's suit didn't quite match the jacket. I hoped he had better coordination between his verb tenses and nouns.

Digging into my bag, I found Tony Hillerman's *Dark Wind* and started reading. The red mesas of New Mexico lent their familiar and comforting presence to this dreary waiting room. Navajo officer Jim Chee had often felt out of place, too, caught between his native culture and the white man's world. It's not easy to live in two universes at once.

Chee and his boss, Joe Leaphorn, had barely finished their first argument when the clerk returned to escort me to Haldun Kutlu's office.

The room was shabby but spacious. Kutlu ranked high within the tough world of Turkish journalism, especially here at the country's largest newspaper.

The room had another attraction: an elegant white cat with varicolored eyes, one blue, one green. The cat occupied the chair facing the desk. I went over, presented the tips of my fingers for approval, and petted the beautiful creature. She looked exactly like the cat I'd seen at the Eminönü wharf.

"Sit down," said Kutlu, looking up from his writing to give me a professorial inspection.

The cat deigned to let me have the chair. Jumping down, she sat on a stack of papers on the floor, cleaning her whiskers. Entranced, I asked what her name was.

"Sultana," he said.

Kutlu was balding and paunchy and looked as though he had slept in his clothes. He lit one brown *Yeni Bahar* from another, scattering ashes over the red-brown carpet that had clearly been used for that purpose before.

"Do you take one or two sugars in your tea?"

Feeling a little like Alice with the March Hare, I held up one finger, and wriggled into place on the reclaimed chair. After searching through the papers on his desk, Kutlu found and rang a bell. A tea boy responded, and was given the hospitality order.

The cat exited when the assistant opened the door.

I started by identifying myself as a friend and colleague of Peter Franklin's.

Kutlu gave me a hard look and nodded brusquely. "That was a blow about Peter."

"It certainly was to those of us in Washington!" I wondered how much I should share. "Did you know Peter well?"

Kutlu nodded through a haze of cigarette smoke. "Yes. Pretty well. Very well, actually. We worked together on some stories."

"So did I! Do you believe the police story about his death?" I was jumping in pretty fast, but I had no idea how long this busy journalist would put up with my questions. Why did I trust him? Was it the cat? I tend to give animal lovers the benefit of the doubt.

After a long pause, Kutlu gave me a piercing look, as though he were weighing my trustworthiness, too. At last he said, "No."

A timid knock came on the door.

"*Evet?* Come in, and put the *chai* in front of us. There. Close the door as you go out!" A semi-smile softened the harshness of the words.

No sign of Sultana. I guess she had left for good.

"So you agree with me that Peter would not have overdosed on drugs." For the moment, I'd forgotten all about being a journalist. I was just a friend.

"Not a chance. Somebody did this to him." Kutlu took a couple of long puffs on his *Yeni Bahar*. Each of us lifted a glass of tea to our lips.

"Any idea who?" I asked.

"I'm working on it," was the brusque reply.

For some time, we sat without speaking. "Are you going to tell me anything more?" I ventured.

"Soon," he promised. "I think we should meet again. I'm working on an angle." He got up, gave me a quick smile, and politely indicated the door. "But right now I have a deadline. Tomorrow?" he asked.

Not satisfactory, but I had to respect a deadline.

36

Tell us, giddy goats, the tale of Midas.
Tell about the awful thing
That happened to our noble King
The day he stepped between two gods.

Güngör Dilmen, "The Ears of King Midas" (play)

Faye Mollington sat in the Altın Küpe, her favorite little restaurant up the hill from Cağaloğlu. The owners knew her preference for an anonymous corner half-hidden behind a screen and saved her that seat every day.

Another set of regular customers played *tavla*, backgammon, at a table in the front. She could hear the roll of the dice and subsequent click of the wooden pieces counting down their moves on the inlaid board.

It wasn't time for dinner, but delectable smells seeped out from the kitchen not too far from her table. *Köfte*, lamb patties, vied with deep-fried potatoes and simmered eggplant *mousakka*.

Faye enjoyed the smells and the presence of distant waiters who gave her warm smiles when she came in. Here, she could be alone but not alone, able to work in privacy without retreating into isolation.

In many ways, working in plain sight was safer than hiding in a room, anyway. People don't see what's right before their noses.

37

*After leaving Galata you ascend
to Beyoğlu or old Pera. The most
direct approach on foot is via Yüksek
Kaldırım, a lively street which climbs
up the hill from the main square
before the bridge, passing close to
the Galata Tower halfway along.*

John Freely, *The Companion Guide to Turkey*

Jean Le Reau rose early and went for a walk to the edge of Pera, from where he could see the Golden Horn. He hadn't slept well. He'd never seen the dead man before. The modus operandus of the person who knifed him did, however, have a familiar feel. It looked professional. Trained.

Why did the incident happen at the Pera Palas? Surely it had nothing to do with him. Or Elizabeth? He hoped not. He was beginning to like her, in spite of her snoopy inquisitions.

As long as the murder didn't interrupt his own plans, which had very little to do with AgroBusiness.

He didn't have time for extraneous murders.

38

Let it play with your hair, this gentle breeze
Blowing from the seven seas.

Nedim, 17th Century Turkish poet

Perihan Kıraz had mixed feelings as she tramped around the dig at Iznik. The old enthusiasm always returned when the work restarted in the fall. The hot summer months she spent in the university classroom made anthropology seem hazy and distant, full of facts or surmises but nothing hands-on.

Here she inhaled the scent of freshly-cut wheat and soil dry from the rainless summer. The smells of Mother Earth. Her students' eyes sparkled as they came across a bit of column or statuary—or even a piece of Iznik ceramics—after hours of fruitless digging, sifting, and hoping. Perhaps the brightest spot in this assignment was working with Oktay Fener, her university colleague. He was on the other side of the dig, laboring as hard as any of his students.

Oktay. She smiled, savoring the warm glow that always accompanied his name. Did he feel the same way? If he did, he was far too loyal to his wife to say anything intimate to her, Perihan. She was satisfied with the bond she knew drew them together.

He was a subject of attack by certain right-leaning newspapers who viewed with suspicion his close ties to universities in Hamburg and Chicago. The Turkish academic community was outraged at the newspaper attacks—especially since they were often followed by violence. Being an intellectual was a goal for many in Turkey. And it had become dangerous.

She glanced over at him again, the cold bite of fear dimming her enjoyment of the day. She was even afraid for herself, at times.

Oktay had been shot a few months ago—right here at the dig. His shoulder wound had healed. But the atmosphere of fear in the archaeologist community had not.

Perihan shivered. She still could hardly believe it, a gunshot breaking the quiet at the dig. They had stopped work for more than a week as the police investigated.

They had not found the perpetrator.

He was out there somewhere. He, or she.

39

The sun moved the shadows over me.
Power and its crimes are remembered,
the revolts against the decisions of
the powerful all too easily forgotten.

Mary Lee Settle, *Turkish Reflections*

I wrote as fast as I could while my New Best Friend, Haldun Kutlu, filled me in on what was happening in Turkey and the stories I'd be covering. After the abrupt end to our conversation yesterday, I'd asked if I could come back at what amounted to the crack of dawn the next day, nine a.m. I'd said I needed a longer talk and advice about things other than Peter Franklin.

To make sure I didn't lose any of it, I was taping our session. Haldun's concise and well-informed review indicated that his mind was more orderly than his office—and he gave unstintingly of his stored information.

"As you know, the Kurdish question has vexed Turkey since independence in 1920. It's not easy having a fierce, nomadic minority that spills across your borders into Iraq and Iran. Unfortunately, our army has usually tried to deal with Kurds by stamping out their individuality by force—I do not defend the tactics."

I was nodding and writing as he went on: "The result of a very complicated scenario is that now we have Kurdish extremists who receive training from other radical groups and set off bombs in our cities. They kill innocent people, just like the leftist groups back during the Cold War... And like more recent rightists... And, of course, like the secret police, that shadowy presence that has helped to give Turkey a bad name on human rights for many years."

I hated to break in but feared that Haldun would get tired or busy and send me away.

"On the Kurds. Was Peter by any chance doing a special story on that?" His notes showed some urgency.

"Hmmm. I see what you are thinking." His voice came slowly, almost hesitantly, not at all like his confidence a moment ago. "I'm not sure. Of course the Kurdish extremist question ties in with some of the drug and arms smuggling, too. With Iran and Iraq to the east, Chechnya and Armenia to the north, and Bosnia, Bulgaria and Rumania to the west...." He jabbed a nicotine-stained finger up, down, right, and left as he spoke. "And all those former communist mafias lurking in the area—you are going to have tie-ins. Terrorist groups need money and arms. Drugs often are the way for getting them."

Haldun lit another *Yeni Bahar*. Its aromatic smoke filled the air and added a layer to the smudge on the window. I choked in as polite a fashion as possible.

"And Islamic fundamentalism...does that tie in, too?"

Haldun stirred his tea and sipped. "Of course, the Islamist movement should be helping to curb the drug trade. The country is a lot more religious than it used to be. You've probably seen more women wearing scarves than they used to—my own wife has started doing it and people in villages have always been conservative. It's a swing of the pendulum after the years dominated by Atatürk and his secularism. But extremists enter every movement, good or bad, and when they do, all bets are off."

"Especially when Iran is your immediate neighbor," I murmured.

"Yes. Yes! Then, of course, there are the ultra-nationalists to think about. The right-wing neo-Nazis."

"You mean the terrorist groups that target professors and intellectuals they find too liberal?" They'd been doing that back when I lived in Turkey.

"Exactly. The biggest group is the Silver Wolves."

I was writing as fast as I could. "Quite a cast of characters... But you still haven't answered my question about Peter. Did he ever talk to you about any of these stories?"

Haldun stood up, stretched as he lighted yet another cigarette, and signaled for me to turn off the tape recorder.

40

*"And do you know what I'll do,
Resul Efendi? I'll go straight to
Ankara, to the Ministry and tell
them what I've seen with my own
eyes. I won't give up the fight."*

Yaşar Kemal, *Anatolian Tales*

"I suppose it is time to talk about Franklin," Haldun Kutlu muttered. He went to the window and scowled out at the sodden day.

"You probably think Franklin learned too much and was, shall we say, disposed of," Haldun said, turning back to me.

"Of course I think he was murdered!" I was surprised at the conviction in my voice. Journalists are like cops—they hate to see one of their own get taken out. And they can't stand to see false evidence tainting a good man's reputation after he can no longer defend himself.

Kutlu sat back down, his broad gestures rumpling his hair and suit even more. "I happen to agree with you," he growled. "Franklin was a good journalist and was getting close to some stories plenty of people could have taken exception to. My guess is someone took violent exception. Now is that person—or group—Turkish or foreign? Or some kind of mix? Without the police behind us, it won't be easy finding out. I have a couple ideas regarding people we need to see."

We? Looked like I was getting a colleague. Or being deputized. Haldun had obviously planned a strategy that predated meeting me.

"One of our first contacts should be a woman by the name of Leila Metin who works at Topkapı Museum. She's an expert on Iznik tiles and ceramics. There are rumors that her brother might be a member of the Silver Wolves."

Aha. That was in Peter's notes, too.

Haldun's voice was matter-of-fact and his expression bland. "She probably will not tell us about that."

41

*A cup of coffee commits one
to forty years of friendship.*

Turkish proverb

I jotted down the name: Leila Metin at Topkapı Museum. I'd go see her very soon. People were starting to demand Haldun Kutlu's attention in the *Cümhüriyet* office, so I stood to leave.

I'd found a companion in the cynical, weathered journalist. Our search could be unpleasant, at best, and dangerous, at worst.

"Haldun *Bey*, I think we have a deal." Our gazes met for a moment. The kindly intelligence reassured me.

"Before I forget, let me give you these papers," he said. "Franklin dropped these by my house a couple days before he died. I have theories. It may be better I not have them at the office."

And they were safer with me? A murder had taken place last night on the sidewalk of my hotel. Should I keep valuable documents there? I hadn't even told Haldun about that incident. But he was clearly ushering me out. There would be time later.

He handed me the small packet of papers, which I received with the solemnity it deserved. It's rare for journalists to share something as vital as information. This indicated trust.

"I appreciate this," I said. "I'll call you when I've finished." Then I left with my briefcase bulging and a set of new theories in my head.

There was something gallant about Haldun Kutlu. It touched me. He knew we were wading into an unknown morass better than I. If he didn't flinch, neither would I.

I caught a cab back to the Pera Palas. I didn't want to walk the streets with valuable papers. It was good to get going on my basic missions, of covering the news while searching for the truth about Peter.

I went straight to the *Tribune* office, greeting Bayram and doing my morning read-in. I kept the papers from Haldun Kutlu in my briefcase, resting against my leg. It would be good to get those back to the hotel this afternoon. It would also be good to get back to Jane Austen. You

wouldn't find terror cells or murders of friends or even strangers anywhere near her settled village life.

42

*He will kill mice, and he will be kind to babies when he is in
the house, just as long as they do not pull his tail too hard.*

Rudyard Kipling, on the cat

Sultana sniffed the garbage at the house in Üsküdar not far from where
Ayla fed her. Pink nose framed by delicate whiskers, she resembled an
attractive coed doing a research project—probably one in a lab.

She had followed the young man who leaned down to pet her at the
wharf. Sultana was a princess. She accepted homage from any source.

And, like cats of all castes, she was curious.

Most garbage in Üsküdar smelled rather good—some fish, a pile of
chicken bones, left-over fruits and vegetables or rice pilav, a little oil
or gas, odds and ends. This garbage smelled different—almost like almonds, though Sultana didn't eat almonds.

Sultana didn't know the word for ammonium nitrate, either. People
used fertilizer in their gardens, where she dug holes for her own purposes. This fertilizer didn't smell like donkey dung, however.

ተ3

*Nothing is more deceitful than
the appearance of humility.*

Jane Austen, *Pride and Prejudice*

The day was uneventful. Back in my room, I tucked the papers from Haldun *Bey* into a drawer and covered them with a couple of newspapers. In my mind Haldun had gone from "Mr. Kutlu" to the more Turkish honorific, *Bey*, used with his first name. It sounded friendlier.

No sense leaving the papers out for the room staff to see. And I didn't want to waste my time reading them before I could take proper notes and arrange them.

I washed hands and face, dabbed a little moisturizer on my skin, and pulled on black tights. Dressed in a woolen skirt and blazer, I went down to the Pera Palas restaurant. The meal was a delectable mix of green beans, eggplant, garlic, tomatoes, and green peppers sauted in olive oil, served with yogurt and accompanied by the *piece de resistance*, succulent roast lamb. Garlic and onion sauted in olive oil scented the air.

I liked the old-world atmosphere of the place at night, its shabbiness masked by gentle lighting making little yellow pools on the almost-white tablecloths.

I'd filed a story after seeing Haldun Kutlu. An everyday sort of news story—knives in the back from one political leader toward another. Figuratively speaking, of course.

Knives. Not a comfortable topic since the incident in front of the hotel. Because it wasn't international news, I hadn't included the actual knifing in my news story. If I told Mac back in Washington, he'd just worry. The very thought of knives made me a little queasy. I used a fork instead of a knife on my white cheese.

Other than the murder—and never forgetting the tragedy that had brought me here—I was enjoying getting back to actual reporting. It's more fun being on the scene than officiating as an editor in a swivel chair. I tend to forget that when promotion time comes around—like when I let them make me a senior international editor.

This assignment had turned into a good exercise in priority-setting. I doubted I'd go back to editing when I finished. By "finish" I meant learning the truth about Peter, as well as covering for the *Trib* while they found a new correspondent.

Baklava dripping with honey and nuts, and thick black Turkish coffee, just the way I like it—*orta*—medium-sweet, completed my meal. Ah, balance.

And ah, Peter. I wish you were here to share this. That drug series we researched together was dirty and dangerous work. It was also satisfying. We'd earned the awards. You taught me so much.

And there was the night we thought we were going to die at the hands of a particularly nasty drug trafficker. Peter had grabbed me in the dank hole where we'd been imprisoned and had said, his lips searching mine, "What a woman! What an exciting woman!"

I'd responded without thinking, but then pushed him away and said, "Thanks, Peter. I needed that." We hugged for a long time.

"I'm sorry, sweetheart. I didn't want to die without doing that, just once. We could have had something, you know." That was Peter; always the gentleman—almost.

My face buried in his jacket, I'd whispered, "Peter, you are my friend, and that's more lasting than lust."

"A typical woman's point of view," he muttered. Then he'd started to laugh, and I joined him, and we kept hugging each other and somehow, by a miracle, we were rescued to go our different paths. We remained friends.

And now, Peter was my "dear departed" friend. I hated the thought. I hated thinking, period. All I desired was a night of blissful unconsciousness. I went upstairs.

The knob on my door opened easily—too easily. I hadn't even turned the key, and sure enough, it was unlocked. Did I leave it that way? Or the room staff? Maybe.

I saw no signs of the housekeeping staff and no indication that anyone had entered. Nonetheless, I checked for the sheaf of papers Haldun *Bey* had given me. They were there, but they might not be if this happened again. I had to find a better place for them.

I shed my clothes, soaked for a while in the tub that would have had a view of the Golden Horn if its balcony door had been open, and crawled into my long, white, Travelsmith cotton nightgown.

I read the in *Pride and Prejudice* where Mr. Darcy humiliates Elizabeth Bennet at the ball. It helped pull me together before sleep. Nothing more relaxing than seeing someone else uncomfortable and remembering that she came out all right.

In spite of Jane, that night the dream was back. I was running down a hillside, hair streaming back from my face...calling to someone, but getting no answer. As I lost control of my feet on the steep slope, I had the sudden grotesque knowledge that who I was calling for was wrong. The name was wrong...the face blurred. Running, running but unsure of my object, I screamed silently, over and over.

Morning finally came. I got up to brush my teeth, hoping to ease the leaden mood left by the nightmare. For a long time, I stood in my robe on the covered bathroom balcony. Rain fell mistily over the crooked wooden and square concrete buildings running downhill in three directions toward the Golden Horn. Just next door was the American consulate, and a few streets beyond, the edge of Istanbul's infamous red light district.

Somewhere in this labyrinth lay the answer to Peter's death. I shivered, and came in from the rain.

☩☩

Again I must remind you that
A dog's a Dog—A CAT'S A CAT.

T.S. Eliot, *Old Possum's Book of Practical Cats*

Sultana stretched and rose from her warm spot near the heater in the Üsküdar ferry waiting room. On days when Haldun didn't carry her to the office in the basket, she waited for him at the wharf. He was late tonight.

When the kind woman who always petted her left to catch her boat, the cat slipped between her feet and exited, too. Sultana was one part dog to three parts cat. She didn't wait around forever. Her destination, as always, was Ayla *Hanım's* kitchen. Haldun would eventually arrive there, too.

After nibbling on tidbits of fish, rice, and meat, mixed with rice *pilav*, Sultana rubbed her head on Ayla *Hanım's* hand, washed her fur and headed out again. Ayla *Hanım* understood she had work to do.

Night work. Cat work.

♄5

*"Do not consider me now as an
elegant female intending to plague
you, but as a rational creature speaking the truth from her heart."*

Jane Austen, *Pride and Prejudice*

I'd finished breakfast and signaled the waiter for my check when a familiar voice intruded.

"Good morning, Ms. Darcy. *Bon appetit!*"

Where had his affected accent from earlier gone? I didn't miss it.

Jean Le Reau, and I had to call him "jhahn,"dapper and attentive as usual, was at my service.

"Oh, hello," I said. Our shared experience of the murder evening and long drinks in the bar had improved our relationship.

I wondered casually where he'd been last night.

"Is this a good time to talk?" The man was unfailingly polite.

"Well, I have a few minutes. Won't you sit down?" The waiter, heading in my direction, detoured to bring a menu rather than the check I'd asked for.

If Jean Le Reau had something to say, he didn't get around to saying it. We steered clear of the trauma night before last ,except to wonder what the police had learned. We talked of Turkish food and Turkish music and the Topkapı Museum and of the perils—and pleasures—of staying in a grand old hotel that had seen better days. He asked me whether life as a journalist was busy, and I said yes.

When I asked for my check, I found to my chagrin that Le Reau had somehow managed to pay it. Well, he might think this amounted to an obligation, but he had another think coming.

I thanked him coolly, excused myself, and headed to my room to do some work.

* * * *

It was a gray but dry morning and I had no immediate appointments. I addressed myself to the files. There were two clumps of news clippings, tied with string. Franklin's notes adorned each article.

One set dealt with Turkey's foreign relations, especially with the ex-Soviet states where a form of Turkish was the native language: all the "Stans" except Tajikstan. Complicated factors there, like the drug mafias in Turkmenistan, Kazakhistan, and Uzbekistan, already in place before Communist regimes were overthrown or changed their names. The interweaving of the KGB, though it, too, had changed its name. All the old components of the Soviet Union gathered in Istanbul, it seemed.

Spies, underworld activities. Big, nebulous relationships that I couldn't hope to understand on a short assignment. Possibly relevant. Wasn't it true that people who learn the secrets of spies often die mysteriously?

I set that group of papers to one side.

The other set of clippings dealt with unexplained acts of terrorism in Turkey over the past eighteen months. The tops of some of the sheets had the initials, "SW"—southwest? SE would make more sense, since the majority of Turkish Kurds lived in that area. Silver Wolves?

On others were notations like "drugs" or "smuggling, gen."

There were too many possible reasons why Peter had been killed. It looked like he'd been in the midst of several dangerous stories.

One story, about a Turkish archeologist hurt while working around the town of Iznik, across the Sea of Marmara from Istanbul, intrigued me. "Police are checking into possible sabotage," according to the report in Haldun Kutlu's newspaper, because the archeologist claimed he'd been shot at while at the dig. This story was borne out by students and other archeologists at the site.

The man, Professor Oktay Fener, had been shot in the shoulder but had recovered. Regular members of the archeological team at Iznik had been questioned for possible leads.

Why kill an archeologist?

Among the team members were a Professor Perihan Kıraz and Dr. Leila Metin. The second name leaped out at me. Peter Franklin, or Haldun Kutlu, had highlighted it, too.

Seeing Leila Metin's name made me think of a touristy expedition I needed to make. I hadn't been to Topkapı Palace yet on this trip. Disgraceful neglect. There was an off chance I could meet this Leila Metin, as Haldun had mentioned she worked there.

The woman's name was a rash infecting half the things I researched around here.

46

I felt proud of myself as I stood there
in front of the tanks. I had gradu-
ated from Khaldan and now I was
on to something much bigger...
Clearly, whatever lay beyond the
checkpoint was worth guarding.

Omar Nasiri, *Inside the Jihad, My Life with Al Qaeda*

Despite vomiting after his mission, Erol Metin was as a tough guy. After all, Turks were traditionally warriors, and he was the very embodiment of a Turk. It was worth repeating every day. And he faithfully worked out to make sure he was strong enough, despite being on the small side. Not a big hulking man like Yusuf, who was assigned as driver on all kinds of tailing operations.

When the Silver Wolves' leaders had asked who would volunteer for dangerous missions, all of them had raised their hands. It was for Turkey, after all. For the fatherland.

"Send me," they had begged. "Let it be me!"

It was all so clear, what was right and what was wrong. The opposition were enemies who deserved to be killed.

After his success last night, Erol was now being given a bigger chance. The details of the mission didn't matter, because he was loyal and would adhere to the rules absolutely. He would succeed, whatever it was.

Still, his gut churned with fear. And, though he hated to admit it, with guilt.

ЧᲖ

Many will show you the way once your cart has overturned.

Turkish proverb

Leila Metin chain-smoked and gazed out her sitting room window. The Bosphorus spread out below, a winding dark surface surrounded by hills whose pink sunset haze had turned black some time ago. A bottle of Çankaya white lay on ice in its wine cooler. The crystal ashtray was full of cigarette butts.

Where was Erol? What was he doing? No word from him. No phone calls for him from his friends. He had simply disappeared.

Should she call the police? She hesitated. No. If the police could help her brother, Leila would have contacted them. But she didn't know for certain. She had her own reasons not to involve the police. No, her brother probably didn't need—or want—the authorities.

Leila looked around the empty room. Who would know if she lived or died? She reached for her glass of white wine. She'd probably finish the bottle.

Peter Franklin would have provided company and drunk some of that wine. She missed him.

48

*Every object in the next day's
journey was new and interesting to Elizabeth; and her spirits
were in a state for enjoyment...*

Jane Austen, *Pride and Prejudice*

I took my favorite route from Pera district to the other side of the Golden Horn: zig-zagging down cobblestone streets to the shortest underground system in the world (a five-minute ride), emerging at the bottom near the Golden Horn, walking across the lower level of Galata Bridge, where fishermen served their catch at little restaurants, and finally catching a tram for the short trip up the hill to Gülhane.

My commute in Washington is green and charming, but this was far more dramatic,and it included exotic aromas—everything from fish to roasting chestnuts and corn, to that indescribable smell of grease mixed with paper.

The tram left me off at the corner of the magnificent *Aya* Sofya mosque—the Byzantine Saint Sofia cathedral in disguise. *Aya* Sofya is lovely in any color, which tends to change every few years. Formerly it was a worn yellow; now it's a faded ochrish brick red. Built by Justinian in 537 A.D., after two of its predecessors had been burned to the ground in riots, it's massive and overpowering, with great wide buttresses literally holding it up—a lumbering elephant, beautiful in that special way of elephants.

Hard to walk past without stopping in, but I had to guard against getting distracted from my principal purpose—meeting the omnipresent Leila Metin. She seemed connected to almost every part of my investigation.

I'd scarcely entered the great stone outer gates of Topkapı, just past what the *Lonely Planet Guide* calls the "grandest and most handsome of all the street-fountains in Istanbul," the Fountain of Ahmet III, when sun burst through the lowering clouds. It spotlighted the grand scene below and past the railroad: the intersection of the Bosphorus, the Sea of Marmara, and the Golden Horn. Big cargo ships plying a course to or from the Black Sea interspersed with white slipper-shaped ferries criss-crossing in the foreground. The first bridge over the Bosphorus looped majestically across the waterway near the closest curve.

Inside the outer walls, I headed toward the great kitchens where today the pots, pans, and dishes from the Ottoman Empire reside. The Chinese and Ottoman porcelain collection in the old kitchens of Topkapı is the third richest in the world, behind only those in Beijing and Dresden. Its plates and bowls date from the Yuan, Sung, and Ming dynasties and were originally presents exchanged by powerful rulers three or four centuries ago.

There are also a few wonderful old Iznik pieces, as lovely in the form of dishes as they are in tiles. The Iznik ceramics are, ironically, much rarer than the Chinese because the latter were better cared for during at least ten devastating fires that swept through old Istanbul between the fifteenth and nineteenth centuries.

I thought of Lawrence Andover's collection of Iznik ceramics and wondered what it might be worth.

49

Remember she follows the law of her kind,
And Instinct is neither wayward nor blind.

William Wordsworth, on cats

At exactly six that morning, Sultana meowed at Haldun and Ayla's kitchen door. She received, as always, a breakfast of milk or yogurt, a little rice, and a taste of meat from left-overs. She was petted by both her people, washed her fur with a pink tongue, and went back outside.

When Haldun left for the office, about seven, she followed him, as she always did. Not like a dog, of course. She followed while pretending not to, looking into boxes or barrels, checking for mice in the alleys.

Usually, the cat went to the office on the other side, boarding the ferry in a basket on Haldun's arm. Today she wasn't in the mood. She lifted her head for a final pet and then dashed behind the flower ladies' water containers to indicate she wasn't going with him.

Having sent Haldun off, Sultana headed back up the hill toward the house where the garbage had smelled strange. Cats hate unsolved mysteries. This almond-scented garbage was a mystery. It didn't belong in Sultana's neighborhood. It had not been there before.

50

She saw all the glories of the camp;
its tents stretched forth in beauteous
uniformity of lines, crowded with
the young and the gay, and daz-
zling with scarlet; and to complete
the view, she saw herself seated
beneath a tent, tenderly flirting with
at least six officers at once.

Jane Austen, *Pride and Prejudice*

I walked down the shelf-lined aisles of the stone-floored kitchens, admiring the delicate tracery of blue and peach on white ceramic. A woman sat at a desk in the corner of the room, talking with a man whose chair faced her desk. A small lamp on the desk created a pool of warmth in the chill atmosphere of thick stone walls inside and crisp fall air outside. The woman needed no light to enhance her features. Dark, shining hair was pulled back from her face into a roll that combined sophistication with intellect. She wore a black angora wool cape. I couldn't see what she wore under the cape, but clearly it would be both stylish and becoming. Sharp-cut dramatic cheekbones were marred by an equally sharp set to her jaw. Her eyes failed to reflect the warmth of the lamp.

I put out my hand. "Are you by any chance Leila Metin? Haldun Kutlu suggested I come to see you..."

"Well, yes, I am." Dr. Metin half-stood, extending a languid hand. Either she didn't like my looks or she hoped not to contract a communicable disease. I handed her my card, which I managed to locate in the depths of my capacious bag.

Without enthusiasm, Leila indicated I should sit in the chair beside the occupied one. The man, of course, had stood as I approached.

I turned with my hand out. "Elizabeth Darcy." Before he could speak, Leila Metin introduced him as Professor Oktay Fener.

Wonderful! Two of the people I most wanted to interview—two thirds of the archeologists from Iznik. I was batting a thousand—or at least seven-fifty.

Oktay Fener was quiet and attractive. Somewhere in his early fifties. Not very tall. Intelligent eyes. A little anxious.

Leila Metin fidgeted with one intricate filigree earring, picked up a pen, and put it down again.

We exchanged the obligatory small talk about the weather and how I liked Istanbul. I asked for more information on the collection of ceramics at Topkapı.

Leila *Hanım,* to give her the feminine honorific equivalent to *Bey,* enthusiastically launched in. "In days gone by, huge royal households lived on this point of land. Intrigue was an element of every Sultan's rule. The young princes, sometimes caged in the *harem* section of Topkapı for all their growing-up years, at least had beautiful tiles to look at."

She explained that like their mothers and other women of the *harem,* the princes were guarded by maybe two hundred Black Eunuchs. Which prince actually became Sultan depended largely on whose mother was the most unscrupulous.

"I doubt all the luxury made up for not having freedom or even a semblance of normalcy in their lives," I observed.

Leila's laugh was short and dry. She seemed to be warming to her subject. "Many potential Sultans were removed from the sumptuous palace in ornate coffins when their mothers fought. Maybe the excitement helped make up for being one of hundreds competing for the favors of the Sultan."

Life at Topkapı didn't sound all that attractive, when explained this way. I mentioned the dig at Iznik, and explained I was with the *Trib,* filling in after the death of Peter Franklin. They both appeared to know Peter, and offered the usual condolences. But the already chilly atmosphere in the ceramic section went down a degree and something flashed in Leila's eyes.

Paydirt. Careful, now. Keep the conversation general. How could I capitalize on the woman's discomfort?

Leila offered a glass of hot sweet tea, and I accepted.

"I read in the paper that you were attacked at Iznik," I said to Professor Fener.

He seemed to retreat into greater stillness. "Someone shot at me, yes. That was some time ago." He didn't seem eager to discuss it further.

Time to take another tack. "Dr. Metin, I wanted to ask you about the rumor that Turkish antiquities are being sold on the international black market." I had my notebook out and looked expectant.

Silence. A definite silence. Call me fanciful, but the question hit home with one or both of them, just as my mention of Peter had. Perhaps I was just being too blunt.

"Certainly some disturbing things have happened in the past," said Leila Metin. Her voice flowed like a smooth stream across the glass-topped table.

Dr. Fener resembled a cornered mouse. Why? Was Fener up to something, and Leila was onto him? Did Leila herself pose a threat?

Or was I just being paranoid? My mother used to warn me about letting my imagination run away with me. The conversation was leading nowhere, so I gracefully excused myself. I shook hands with the two eminent archaeologists and made a mental note to contact Oktay Fener soon to probe a little further. He'd be an easier target than Leila. All too easily, I could picture her as one of the scheming Sultan's wives in the *harem* a few centuries ago, casually killing off the sons of other wives to ensure the succession of her own. My suspicions did not arise from jealousy, though no one could deny Leila was beautiful.

After the unproductive interview, I buttoned my raincoat and walked around the Topkapı grounds, soaking in layers of mystery evoked by the tiled passageways. The crowds were sparse, reflecting the inclement weather.

In spite of the chilly day, I studied the superb little open pavilion from which royal residents in past times could watch the ships landing at the bottom of the Pera hill, a few crooked streets down from Galata Tower. The scene looked like a faded Monet.

Only two other people stood on the pavilion balcony, both men, looking the other way. Something familiar about them made my skin prick. Or was this imagination, too?

I sloshed my way down the footpath under the avenue of trees to the main gate and hurried to the tram. I didn't look back to see if anyone followed.

51

"I would not be so fastidious as you are, for a kingdom!"

Jane Austen, *Pride and Prejudice*

After dark the next day, in the cozy back lobby bar of the Pera, my new friend Faye Mollington and I were drinking our wine (me) and Scotch (Faye). We had hit it off since our first meeting. I enjoyed our girl talk.

We sat on Victorian sofas arranged in a conversational square, with our feet up on the sturdy wood coffee table; a fire blazed in the old-fashioned fireplace. In the corner, the bartender polished glasses with a dishtowel, softly whistling a modern Turkish song. I knew the words. They were, as usual, plaintive:

> *I'm a big big girl*
> *in a big big world*
> *It's not a big big thing*
> *if you leave me*
> *but I do do feel*
> *I will miss you too, too much*
> *miss you much...*

The air held scents of Turkish tobacco and *limon kolonyası*, lemon cologne. The smells mixed with those of old velvet and dust. We were probably sitting over a mouse nest, but mice are adaptable.

My budding relationship with Faye helped me feel more comfortable in the Istanbul routine. We'd had lunch at a restaurant near the office a couple of times. Faye was different from me—a few years younger, for one thing, with a driven personality—but we respected each other. I found her invaluable in helping find contacts and discussing news events.

She seemed to like talking about life. Hers in England had apparently been more focused, and thereby restricted, than mine. I think she felt she'd missed something, just as I wondered if I'd been too diffuse in my interests and attachments.

Jobwise, things were going well. Writing to deadline and to the allotted space was coming back to me, and I reveled in the active assignment. So far, I'd sent in stories on a smuggled arms shipment intercepted by Turkish police, a cabinet power struggle, and a holding piece on security preparations for Turkey's Independence Day on October 29—two weeks off.

I didn't mention to headquarters that I was working on Peter's murder. Mac would just worry. And he might forbid it on work grounds, which would put me in a ticklish situation.

Early on, I'd asked Faye if she had any theories about Peter's sudden death. She'd become very intent, as everyone seemed to on the subject.

"Drug story, maybe?" she suggested. "He always had that investigative streak."

Faye seemed to have known Peter well. I didn't ask how well. Didn't want to know.

She agreed with me that drugs had been used to make Peter's death appear suicide. But Peter had worked on stories about drugs before; he knew the dangers. Could he have run afoul of some of the shadowy terrorist groups, left, right, or religious, that lurked behind Turkey's charm? Of those groups, I'd put my money on the right-wing Silver Wolves—maybe because, if truth be told, I dislike rightists more than leftists. Except that in the news there should be no left or right. And killing civilians is unsavory from any direction.

I took a sip of wine. We both stared into the fire, silent for a long moment. I'd decided not to discuss the Leila Metin or Oktay Fener angle until I had something more concrete, so I turned to her and reached for a general topic.

"What's the most important story in Turkey today?" I asked. "Economic deregulation's mixed effects?"

"That might be the story for the *Wall Street Journal*," said Faye. "Personally, I find Turkey's balancing act between Europe and Asia fascinating. Today, that act has more importance for the rest of the world than ever before—except maybe in the days of the Ottoman Empire, when things were being run from here. Will Turkey emerge as a full-blown European power, with democracy an unchallenged way of life and a set of values in tune with Germany and England and Italy? Or will its Moslemness, its Asianness, whatever that is, prevail? Can it do both, as I think it's trying to do? Hell, I sound like a commentator on CNN!" Faye's stocking-clad toes wiggled toward the warmth of the fire as she stretched like a cat.

Just then, the waiter came over and said there was a telephone call for me. I walked to the bar to answer.

"Miz Darcy? Bayram here. A bomb has exploded in Kadıköy over on the Asian side."

52

The tumult of her mind was now painfully great.

Jane Austen, *Pride and Prejudice*

"Any casualties?" I asked, grabbing a napkin and pen from the counter.

"First reports say house of famous archeologist Professor Oktay Fener has been damaged. Reports do not say if anybody was hurt."

"Oh, my God, I met the man yesterday! I'll be right over to the office, Bayram. Collect everything you can on those terrorist groups, and on Professor Fener. And keep tearing the wire copy!"

"Yes, Miz Darcy. 'Bye."

By the time I returned to our chairs, Faye, who'd obviously been listening, had her shoes on and was headed for the door.

"Wait for me!" I called. I just had to run upstairs for my raincoat and the files I'd been reading.

She waved. "I'll meet you there!"

See what I mean? Driven. Neither of us had to write an actual story for at least a few hours, and who knows whether we'd learn anything at Fener's house. But if there was something brewing, Faye had to be there, and she had to be first. In this case there might be a time zone excuse, since it was the London newspaper she worked for versus my own Washington *Trib*.

I sighed as I dashed upstairs. I didn't distrust Faye…not really. She was a bit hyper, perhaps. And it would have been nice to ride together to the bomb site.

Bayram had things neatly arranged when I got to the office. Wire copy. Background material. Names to call. After glancing at the copy, I asked Bayram for the number at *Cümhüriyet* and dialed Haldun Kutlu. Though it was past 7:30, Haldun was in his office. The nicotine rasp of his voice cut through the newness of our relationship.

"You going? Want me to pick you up?"

Bless the man!

* * * *

The bomb scene was not a pleasant place. Impassive police guarded the area and only under pressure from Haldun allowed us near the Fener house. The small concrete house had a large garden. One corner of the building looked lopsided in the darkness, lit in crazy patterns by police squad lights. Chunks of concrete and broken glass lay everywhere. A smell of cordite and charring filled the chilly air. Some of the charred smell was organic. Very disturbing. A few dazed neighbors gathered outside the garden gates.

We stood near a clump of three medium-sized cypresses, planted, I presumed, by Fener's wife. Cypresses are a mainstay in Turkish cemeteries. Surprising she didn't think of that when making her garden plans. Would she wonder from now on whether planting the cypresses was an omen?

Faye Mollington was already there, taking notes furiously as she talked with a police officer. Haldun *Bey* knew the officer, too, so we joined the little group. I nodded to the homicide detective, Inspector Durmaz, whom I had met earlier. Durmaz, gave us a quick run-down: "Professor Fener had gone out to his car to run an errand. The bomb exploded when he turned on the engine. He was killed instantly."

"Anyone else hurt?"

"No, but Fener's wife and daughter are being treated for shock. They were taken to hospital a few minutes ago." Durmaz's dark eyes rested on me for a moment, registering the fact that we'd already met. To him, I guessed, I was now the new kid on the block of pesky reporters the police have to deal with.

I asked the next question: "Do you know what kind of bomb it was?"

"It seems to have been a simple bomb. We think it was placed there between five p.m., the last time Mrs. Fener used the car, and six-thirty. During the evening rush hour. Someone took a chance of killing other family members."

Faye jumped in. "Do you have any suspects yet?"

"Not yet. We are looking. And now, you must all go. There is an investigation to be done here."

53

Hey, who's there? Who laughs?
No one, I guess. Dark, empty halls.
Yet laughter rings in my ears.

Gungor Dilmen, "The Ears of Midas" (play)

Leila Metin was watching TV in her house along the Bosphorus. The nine-o'clock news had a disturbing flash: "Possible deaths in Kadıköy bomb. Police are still on the scene."

She shivered. Got up to look out the window. A sense of dread invaded her torso and reached to her bones. Where was Erol? With whom was he staying these days?

Leila had been like a mother to that boy. For about a year, he had been pulling back from the relationship—acting like a resentful teenaged son. She must arrange to meet Erol very soon, if he didn't come back. She hoped he wasn't getting into real trouble.

Erol was the only family she had.

5Ψ

*"To oblige you, I would try to believe
almost anything, but no one else could
be benefited by such a belief as this…"*

Jane Austen, *Pride and Prejudice*

After a quick exchange of business cards outside the Fener house, Faye, Haldun, and I went back to our respective cars and drivers. We said goodnight in the cursory way of journalists who are off to write the story and who know they'll run into each other often in the ensuing days, or even hours.

"See ya!"

Still writing frantically, Faye got into her taxi and left, probably for the office via the nearest, and oldest, Bosphorus Bridge. Why was Faye taking down all the details? She seemed in such a hurry to file the story. Odd. International news outlets didn't really care, unless one of their own nationality was slain. I viewed my own job as getting down the big picture and putting events into perspective for my readers.

The taxi ride back took us through Kadıköy's modern but twisted streets to the ferry landing. It was across a little inlet from the Germanic-looking Haydarpaşa train station. Here we paid the driver and boarded that fusty bureaucrat of ferries taken daily by commuters from Kadıköy to Galata Bridge. The fancier new ferries held much less charm for me. Enroute, Haldun and I talked about Oktay Fener.

"He was one of Turkey's finest archaeologists," said Haldun. "His speciality was ceramics from the Ottoman period in its heyday, the fifteenth and sixteenth centuries."

"Yes, yes, I know," I said. "But didn't I read that Fener was the archeologist who was shot at the Iznik dig?" I was beginning to get interested in Professor Oktay Fener.

"Yes, that was an unexplained incident. I don't suppose it has anything to do with anything, but it is a strange coincidence." Haldun scratched his straggly chin. "We should do some checking."

"And I think we should talk to Mrs. Fener and her daughter, if they'll share what they know." By this time, I was so into the current story, I'd put Peter's murder—I was sure it was murder—on the back burner. Just for the moment.

As we neared the pier at Karaköy, I ventured further. "Haldun *Bey*, any ideas on the bomb?"

"Well, it certainly looks like terrorism. That's about all we know. Perhaps those papers I gave you are more relevant than we thought."

"But which group, and why?"

"Probably the Silver Wolves. They are most likely to kill intellectuals. I don't know what Fener has to do with them, though."

"I met Mr. Fener yesterday at Topkapı. He was with Leila Metin. I was going to call you when I'd done a little research. I planned to contact Fener, too." Too late. I shook my head at the unpredictability of life. And death.

Haldun *Bey*'s calm voice was more soothing than his words. "Fener, of course, knows Leila Metin. They are both experts in ceramics. Fener digs them up, and Leila cleans and takes care of them for the museum."

"Didn't you say something about Leila's brother being in the Silver Wolves? Would that be significant?"

"Since you say you saw Leila and Fener together yesterday, it bears looking into."

We stood by the edge of the boat, preparing to make the jump from the ferry to the pier, risking, as everyone did, falling into the churning narrow slit of water below. The creaking, dull crunch of worn rubber tires added drama as the ferry nuzzled against the pier. It conjured unpleasant thoughts of what could happen to a human caught between.

"How about Leila Metin?" I asked from the safety of the Karaköy pier. "When do we go to see her?"

Haldun had flagged a taxi for the trip back to his office at Cağaloğlu, while I was headed back to my hotel.

"I think it would be better to see her at her house," he said. "She is not going to talk in a public place like Topkapı. Shall I call her and ask for an appointment?"

"Haldun *Bey*, yes! I'll be ready when you are."

55

Then think of her beautiful gliding form,
Her tread that would scarcely crush a worm,
And her soothing song by the winter fire,
Soft as the dying throb of the lyre.

William Wordsworth, on cats

Sultana didn't like the smell of the garbage outside the house near the great mosque in Üsküdar. She checked it every night, sniffing, pausing, sniffing again.

She saw young men going in and coming out of the house, often carrying bags, but never in a group. One or two stopped to pet her. Most walked by without seeing her. In spite of her shining white fur, Sultana was good at being invisible.

This house was different from the rest in the neighborhood. Very different from Ayla *Hanım's* welcoming kitchen.

Sultana sniffed, tried to bury the smell with her dainty paws, and left. She felt the need to patrol around Haldun and Ayla's house. Cats like to protect their people.

56

*What could be the meaning of it? It
was impossible to imagine; it was
impossible not to long to know.*

Jane Austen, *Pride and Prejudice*

The clerk who had originally checked me in was on duty. Not my favorite. I missed my friends from the other shifts.

"Two letters for you, Miss," he said, handing them over along with my key. As usual, he seemed to sneer—or maybe my current state made me paranoid.

I opened the envelopes in my room. One contained an engraved invitation from the American consul-general for a party on the eve of Turkish Independence Day. The other was a note from Ahmet Aslan, the Kurdish businessman, suggesting dinner two days hence. The handwriting sprawled all over the small piece of note paper had the same electricity as its creator.

I decided to accept both invitations, and dropped them on the night table beside the telephone.

After faxing a story to Washington on the Fener bombing, with what details I knew, I got ready for bed. Even mushing the pillows to give my head and neck support didn't help me relax.

I'd taken to reading part of Haldun's papers each night before falling asleep, in case something leaped out in my subconscious to help me make sense of them. Tonight was no exception. But after poring over the documents, I was no closer to understanding what Peter had been working on. I thrust the package back in the drawer. It was frustrating!

I took out my personal remedy for all chaos, including nightmares: Jane Austen. Getting drawn in once again to the comforting microcosm of Longbourne, where earthshaking drama involved the question of whether Lydia flirted too much with soldiers, I read a few pages. Better than meds to produce soothing sleep. Perhaps it was her elegant and comfortable sense of order. Jane Austen doesn't put up with untidiness for a moment. She provides balance in the midst of confusion.

I slept.

It wasn't the nightmare. I was sure of that. I bolted to a sitting position in bed, wide awake. Tiny slivers of orange light where the curtains met the edge of the windows still proclaimed street lights, not daylight, outside. Something was amiss in my room, and for a moment I couldn't determine what.

My first instinct was to grab the robe I'd tossed on the floor. As I reached over the side of the bed to pick it up, I felt a stiff breeze blowing into the room, apparently from the bathroom.

Bathroom. Balcony. Oh, my God. My bathroom balcony door was open. I couldn't remember locking it, and probably hadn't. Had it blown open by itself?

My toes were about to hit the floor, when I pulled them back under the covers. I sensed rather than saw a shadow in the bathroom doorway.

57

I have not betrayed you, Midas.
Only know this: I was true to the last.

Gungor Dilmen, "The Ears of Midas" (play)

In his home in Üsküdar, Haldun had trouble sleeping. He rose and padded to the living room to read so he wouldn't disturb Ayla.

The Fener case disturbed him greatly. An archaeologist? Who had been after that eminent man? What was the purpose of killing him? Had Oktay Fener known something, or was this just a terrorist statement aimed at intellectuals generally?

If it was part of the anti-intellectual movement, he had better watch his step. Journalists were more dangerous than academics. At least, they usually were.

After a long interval, he lay down beside his peacefully-sleeping wife. She was in so many ways his center. He didn't know what he'd do without her.

58

When the earth's asleep in the heavy sun
And the forest is empty of sound
And nothing quivers, nothing shakes
Yet a fear in your heart awakes
As if embraced by a thing unknown...

Gungor Dilmen, "The Ears of King Midas" (play)

Under pressure, one either does the safe thing or something rash. I vary my approach. In this case, I rolled as quietly and quickly as I could toward the window side of the bed, away from the bathroom door. At the edge of the bed, I lowered myself, slowly, down to the carpeted floor, pushing blankets into a pile on the bed as I went.

I held my breath and waited a moment. This wasn't doing my night-gown any good. Then I scrunched under the high bed. Quietly, I hoped.

It was not at all comfortable. Dark legs were outlined against the indistinct street light from the bathroom balcony door. Whoever belonged to the legs stayed as quiet as I did, apparently getting his bearings in the dark room. The wool carpet roughed my cheek. *Please don't let dust bunnies make me sneeze.*

Footsteps crossed the room. Now my eyes closed. Would the intruder notice that the pile of bedding didn't contain a solid core? Could he feel the vibrations of my thumping heart? My right hand searched for something, anything, to grasp.

The footsteps passed the foot of the bed, headed toward the dresser. Was this an ordinary burglary or something else? What about the papers I'd hidden in the locked suitcase in the closet? Just because I could make little of them didn't mean someone else didn't want them.

Surprising how calm I was, lying there. Adrenaline must have taken over—the mind and body's defense mechanism in times of stress and danger. Certainly I'd have a neck ache from being so tense.

Soft noises now around the dresser, as one drawer after the other was pulled out, rummaged through, and closed. I opened my eyes and caught the occasional glint of a pinpoint flashlight. Which precise second would the intruder discover the bed was empty? No time to figure that out.

As the legs stole away from the dresser, I reached out and grabbed an ankle, jerking it as hard as I could. A shin cracked against the end of the bed. A whoop of pain and a stream of Turkish invective. Then a thud as body joined ankle, hitting the floor with a crack.

59

Surprise was the least of her feelings on this development.

Jane Austen, *Pride and Prejudice*

I rolled out from under the bed, snatched the first hard object that came to hand—in this case the glass ashtray from the low bedtable—and swung it in the direction of the rising head. I felt rather than heard the blow—a sickening thud.

The head went down and became silent in mid-curse.

Thank God for that adrenaline. At any moment it would start to wear off.

Switching on a light, I found the telephone and dialed zero.

"Help!" I yelled. "Someone is in my room!"

Suddenly, I shook all over, more from the horror of my own violence than fear. But curiosity was as strong as revulsion. I stepped over my victim's legs and pulled aside a bandana mask. Good God, the hawk-nosed driver of the blue Murat I'd noticed on various occasions!

He was definitely breathing. Blood trickled from a wound behind his temple, so I ran to the bathroom to get a towel, which I wrapped firmly around his head. He no longer looked like a macho hunk. More like someone in a gruesome Halloween costume.

I wasn't about to hit a person while he was down, so I went to the closet to look for a belt to tie around my prisoner's wrists. As I bent over the low closet shelf, a creak sounded behind me. I whirled to see Hawk Nose leaping out the balcony window, exiting the way he'd apparently come in. He still had the bloody towel wrapped around his head.

I ran to the balcony. He clambered down the vines along the hotel wall. A car of indeterminate color waited at the curb. It would presumably swoop him away.

As though staged by a master dramatist, loud thumping rocked the door. "Hotel security," came a gruff voice.

"It's about time," I muttered, and suddenly lost all the strength I'd gathered. The adrenaline rush was over.

The man who came in looked unpromising as a sleuth. He wore baggy, dark blue trousers, a non-matching dark blue coat, and shoes that looked like bedroom slippers. He needed a shave. His appearance indicated it'd been a long time since the night security guard at the Pera Palas had had his sleep disturbed.

"*O tarafa*—He went that way!" I shouted at the guard, and ran toward the bathroom to show him the open balcony door, its net curtains blowing inward from the night wind. The guard took his time getting there. Then he peered over the balcony railing.

"*İşte, gitti.* He's gone, right enough," he muttered. Then he came back into the room, looking at me as though I'd caused an unnecessary fuss.

I showed the guard the bloodstain on the carpet. He didn't seem impressed. Maybe he thought it was a good match for the pansy-shaped stain on the other side of the bed, since he'd been poking around the room nearsightedly.

By now, there were sounds of agitation in the hall outside. The guard went out to the corridor and told several guests who were looking out of their rooms, "*Yok bir şey.* Nothing. Nothing."

A break-in characterized as nothing? I had had enough and grabbed the door, ready to slam it shut in the guard's face. A familiar form—not suited, but in pajamas and a Turkish robe—appeared in time to block the door with his foot.

"Meez Darcy. What has happened? Can I perhaps help?"

So Jean Le Reau was prowling around outside my room. His room wasn't even nearby. I gave him a cursory glance. A less prepossessing hero would be hard to find. When you tried to remember what he looked like, he faded into mist. Hard to describe. A real Everyman. He blinked his blue-gray eyes behind glasses I hadn't seen him wear previously.

"No. I'm fine. Really. Nothing is wrong." Summoning inner strength, I firmly pushed the door shut in Le Reau's face, managing to encompass the useless guard in the same movement, so that I was once again alone.

I took a deep breath. Alone was a little uncomfortable. Should I call Haldun? No, unkind to wake him. Faye, too, would be sleeping.

What would I do if I were home? Police, of course. I searched my bag for one of the cards I'd picked up during the Q and A session at the Fener house bomb scene. Ah, there it was: Inspector Mehmet Durmaz, with both home and office numbers. I tried the office. The Inspector had gone home. I would not share the intruder information with Inspector Durmaz's colleague. And I would not bother him in the middle of the night with my small incident.

Slowly, like an automaton, I straightened the room. I picked up the bloodstained ashtray and looked at it for a long time. I might have killed a man with this. Pure chance, really, that I hadn't. I washed the ashtray in the bathroom, feeling like Lady MacBeth. True, I hadn't betrayed anyone or engaged in a plot to overthrow the king. I had been defending myself, after all.

Wait. Washing the ashtray was not a good idea. There would be DNA. It wasn't used in trials in the U.S., but it might help the police identify my intruder. I set the ashtry down in the bathroom and crept back to my rumpled bed. There, I curled up in a tight ball, my arms wrapped around my legs. I pulled the blankets over my head and lay there for a long time.

At last, I took a deep breath and stretched out. I hadn't killed the guy. Even if he might come after me again, I was glad I hadn't killed him.

I just wished I knew who to trust.

60

But self, though it would intrude, could not engross her.

Jane Austen, *Pride and Prejudice*

As I dressed for the day, I tried to unravel threads tangled in my mind. Swallowing pills for my unsurprising headache, I recited the mantra, "Peter, Peter," as I pulled on trousers and shirt. Had I learned anything that could be useful in identifying my colleague's killer? I had to focus.

So far, everyone I'd met was polite—in several cases, friendly. But life in the Orient is never simple. Politeness can mask a lot of things.

Daubing on lip gloss and a light blush, I went over the cast of characters: Ahmet Aslan could be anything. Rich and handsome and Kurdish were all I could swear to at this point. Plenty of room for subversive activities, and the money to carry them out. I'd keep my eyes open during the dinner date he'd suggested.

Leila Metin also had money, and if my instincts were right, a complex personality that could encompass a wide range of activities. I must try to find out more about her alleged terrorist brother. Thank God for an insider like Haldun! And what had been Leila's relationship with Peter, if any? Any hope Peter might have ever had of privacy was now moot. I hated snooping around his life. But that wasn't going to stop me.

Andover was a bit eccentric, perhaps, but well within the limits of a major power's Foreign Service. Maybe a little secretive, which often goes with the territory. How could I find out if he was a spy, in this capital of spies? Again, I could ask Haldun *Bey*, who probably knew the top police officials intimately and would be familiar with the local gossip.

And speaking of Haldun *Bey*, could I assume he was as trustworthy as I wanted to believe? Journalists like to think of themselves as pure. They aren't always so. My instincts were more in Haldun's favor than Aslan's or Andover's, but I had to consider my own prejudice in the case.

And if I had to include Haldun on my list, I suppose I'd also have to consider Faye. Faye was a loner, a lot like Peter had been. What was their relationship? I must ask, diplomatically. Somebody must know.

Before I could even consider bit players like Jean Le Reau and Bayram, I was presentable enough for breakfast and headed down.

Nobody I knew was there.

61

They are alike, prim scholar and perfervid lover:
When comes the season of decay, they both decide
Upon sweet, husky cats to be the household pride;
Cats choose, like them, to sit, and like them, shudder.

Charles Baudelaire, on cats

Sultana had stayed a long time outside the Kutlu house that night. Her usual nap spot was a protected alcove into which Ayla *Hanım* had placed a wooden box with rags. This usually sufficed, as anytime after six in the morning Ayla was up and ready to open the door for the cat.

Like most cats, Sultana liked to temper her freedom with a reliable butler.

This night had been unusual. Someone—a stranger—had stood outside the house. Waiting. Watching.

Almost like a cat.

Sultana never took her eyes off him. When she had first sneaked behind him, she'd smelled almonds.

As long as he stood there, she did not approach the house. Sultana knew where she had seen him before. She uttered a low growl.

62

She knew not what to think, nor how to account for it.

Jane Austen, *Pride and Prejudice*

After consultations with Bayram and reading the wire copy, my follow-up story on the bombing for the *Trib* was, pretty much, "Nothing is known. Police are investigating." No obvious American connection, so this story probably wouldn't make it into the paper at all.

I didn't share my night's adventures with Bayram or anyone else. I needed to tell Haldun, but he wasn't in the office yet.

Most of the actual story was so boring nobody would have printed it. Bureaucrats at the police department told us how thorough the investigation would be. We had gossiped among ourselves about possible culprits. It wasn't very useful.

* * * *

The liveliest reporting was from frustrated groups of students from Istanbul University who marched in protest at Professor Fener's memorial ceremony. Groups of protestors carried signs blaming the incident on a series of favorite demons: "Uncle Sam Takes Hand," "Kurdish Rage Reaches Istanbul," "Iran Strikes at Turkey?"

Clearly *someone* had struck at Professor Fener and, in a way, at Turkey; no one had evidence yet for a motive. I tucked the information I'd gathered into a stack to be folded into background stories.

And, over there, was Haldun. He had made it to the interesting part, at least.

"Need to talk to you," I signaled from a distance.

He hurried over. In the crowd at the memorial service, it was possible to share a few secrets.

"Someone came into my room last night," I whispered.

His eyes widened.

"What happened?" He lit another cigarette, fingers shaking.

I provided a quick rundown. "I wounded the guy, at least a little, though not enough to stop him from climbing out my window."

Haldun was thoughtful. "How about the papers? Did he get them?"

"No. The papers are here in my briefcase. What can I do with them?" Someone wanted them badly. They'd become dangerous.

"Does the hotel have a safe?"

"I think you have to hand things in at the desk and they'll take responsibility. Yes, I suppose they have a safe of some sort."

"Then let's put the papers there. In a very public way. I'm worried about you."

After what had happened to Oktay Fener, I was worried about Haldun, too.

63

Like partisans of carnal dalliance and science,
They search for silence and the shadowings of dread;
Hell well might harness them as horses for the dead,
If it could bend their native proudness in compliance.

Charles Baudelaire, on cats

Sultana and Haldun were a regular sight on the morning and evening commuter ferries between Eminönü and Üsküdar. Haldun had the basket over his arm; elegant white cat ears poked out from the top. When the ferry landed, Sultana liked to jump out of the basket. As Haldun arrived at the *Cümhüriyet* office and was let in by the guard, Sultana slipped in just ahead of him. The guard invariably laughed, petted her, and complimented Haldun *Bey* on his companion.

They took the elevator together to the fifth floor, where Haldun unlocked his office door, Sultana situated herself on her assigned chair, and Haldun called for the tea-boy to bring his second glass of the day.

Sultana viewed the basket trips as her sleep ritual, since she slept all day on the chair, paws curled around her eyes, completely relaxed. When she needed to go out, Sultana would rub Haldun's leg with her face. He opened the door. They understood each other perfectly.

On the return ferry trip, Sultana once again jumped out of the basket, this time onto the Üsküdar wharf. Sultana was attached to her people. But she needed to patrol the area.

Nights were when cats could sneak around, even white cats like Sultana, and no one noticed them.

64

One enjoyment was certain—that
of suitableness as companions; a
suitableness which comprehended
health and temper to bear incon-
veniences, cheerfulness to enhance
every pleasure, and affection and
intelligence, which might sup-
ply it among themselves if there
were disappointments abroad.

Jane Austen, *Pride and Prejudice*

A little shaken by the events of the past few hours and by Haldun's concern, I returned to the hotel to rest and take another couple of aspirins. As I reached the desk, I pulled the file of papers out of my briefcase.

"I wonder if you have a safe I can put these into?" My voice was loud.

"Yes, of course, madam. Can you please sign these papers for us?" The clerk today was a cheerful young man with an open countenance.

As I slipped the papers over to him, a voice came from over my shoulder. "Meez Darcy, are you all right today? I think you had a problem last night."

Only the desk clerk and I could hear the question. Of course all the hotel staff must know that something happened. No doubt the pitiful night guard milked the story for everything it contained. Which wasn't much, in facts. Just lots of suppositions.

"Uh, yes," I admitted. Le Reau looked almost as worried as Haldun. Perhaps I had misjudged him. "I am fine now, though. Thanks for asking." I rubbed my forehead. I just wanted to get to my room.

"Perhaps we can talk later?"

"Yes. Maybe we can have a drink or something this evening."

"Done. I expect to get back by seven."

* * * *

In my room, I lay down a few minutes with a warm compress over my eyes and my legs straight up against the wall in a useful yoga pose.

There wasn't time for a headache. I gave myself twenty minutes, got it under control, and got back to work.

I consulted my list of suspects in Peter's death, beginning with finding out what I could about the Silver Wolves. Someone—Haldun?—had said Leila Metin's brother had ties there.

I picked up the phone to call my principal source of info. He had, after all, promised to help.

"Haldun? Elizabeth Darcy here. Any luck getting an appointment with Leila Metin?"

The gravelly voice spun audible circles around a cigarette. "In fact, yes. Are you coming?"

"Think you could stop me?"

I was coming to love this man more every day.

* * * *

The ferry from Beşiktaş was almost empty. Haldun and I sat in the front, glassed-in section, sipping glasses of sweet, mahogany-colored tea. I could feel the liquid building up a layer on my teeth. I'd stopped attaching *Bey* to Haldun's name. We were becoming equals, and friends.

"Looks like a storm," muttered my companion, waving a cigarette in one hand and his tea in the other. The cigarette gestured toward black clouds shadowing the hills of the European side. The tea swooped perilously toward groves of cypress trees on the Asian shore. "Up there. The red house. That's where we're going."

65

"I am afraid you have been long desir-
ing my absence, nor have I anything
to plead in excuse of my stay, but real,
though unavailing, concern. Would to
heaven that anything could be either
said or done on my part, that might
offer consolation to such distress."

Jane Austen, *Pride and Prejudice*

Leila's red house sat in decorous dignity on a point above Çengelköy village, where I'd come earlier to visit Lawrence Andover. A cypress tree grew beside it. From the ferry it looked like a small gem in a box. I fell in love with it on sight.

The boat creaked and groaned against the rubber tires along the pier. A wizened boatman tied a great frayed rope to the pilings and slid gangplanks across. Lots of passengers, like Haldun, didn't wait for the walkways, choosing the riskier method of stepping or jumping across the churning water between the ferry and the wharf.

The power of the water reminded me uncomfortably of Peter. With a frown and an inner nod, I promised him—again—I'd find out what had happened. He deserved no less.

As we emerged from the little gate where outgoing passengers gave used tickets to a seedy official, I glanced up at the cars on the little village street. I often don't notice cars but this time I gasped. A blue Murat. It was parked near a little stand selling roasted chestnuts under the spreading plane trees that shaded the market area on sunny days, and whose last few leaves offered a bit of protection now from a brisk fall wind gusting around the shops. The chestnut man had his plastic windbreaker wrapped around him to stave off the cold. As we watched, he moved into the lee of the ferry building.

I didn't mention this to Haldun. Didn't want him to think he had a hysterical woman on his hands.

Haldun and I waited for a taxi, but apparently the combination of off-hours and threatening weather had convinced drivers to stay in a warm coffee house somewhere. As usual, Haldun had no patience.

"Let's just walk." He pulled his worn raincoat around him, adjusting a neck scarf. "It won't take more than ten minutes."

Not thrilled with the prospect of being caught in a downpour, I nonetheless went along with the plan. Haldun knew Istanbul's moods better than I. If he thought it would hold off until we climbed the hill, okay. I flipped up the hood of my trench coat, buttoned the top button, and started trudging with my head down against the wind. For all his smoking and sedentary lifestyle, Haldun set an impressive pace.

I was not as impressed with Haldun's fortune-telling abilities when the rain started halfway up. But since up or down were the only two options, we kept going.

As we neared the top of the steep incline, feet slipping on wet cobblestones, the sound of a motor intruded on the wailing wind. I reached out to pull Haldun away from the road. We both stopped and turned to wait for the car to pass.

The car, wipers still, headed straight toward us. Maybe the driver couldn't see us because of the rain?

I screamed. "*Dıkkat!* Look out!" and waved my arms. The car didn't slow.

My heart sank. It was blue, it was a Murat, and with my recent luck, its driver would be the macho fellow who had played music at me on the ferry and who so unexpectedly shared my hotel room for a while last night.

Haldun shoved me so hard I stumbled out of the road into a bush. He had turned to jump when the car reached him. There was a sickening thud. Haldun fell heavily into the mud on the roadside verge and lay crumpled like a pile of rags. The driver of the Murat gunned the motor and took off, disappearing around a bend at the top.

"Haldun, Haldun, are you okay?"

I scrambled out of the bush as fast as I could. My friend hadn't moved from where he'd fallen. I gently turned his face. His eyes were closed. A good sign. I checked for a pulse. Faint, but there. No obvious bleeding, but his left leg extended unnaturally away from his body. He could also have internal injuries.I gently aligned his leg and body, then took off my raincoat and placed it over Haldun, face and all.

The symbolism was terrible, but the practical need for keeping rain off his face prevailed.

"What happened?"

A woman's voice, sharp with concern and, it seemed, irritation, came from up the hill. Leila Metin carried an umbrella and slid down the road toward us.

"Oh, thank God," I yelled. "Call a doctor! Now!"

66

Astonishment, apprehension, and even horror, oppressed her.

Jane Austen, *Pride and Prejudice*

It seemed hours before help reached us, there on the side of the road. I held off well-wishers who had by now gathered to lend assistance, even in the rain.

"No, he must not be moved. *Yok, yok.* Please just bring more blankets."

Leila had obliged with this and stood guard with me. I held a sheet of plastic contributed by one local over Haldun's unconscious form, grateful that even over my wet clothes, I had my own raincoat back on.

The emergency squad, when it arrived, was well-prepared. Three young men carefully placed Haldun on a stretcher and then into the ambulance, where a woman doctor waited. Leila stood beside me, her face still.

The ambulance was full, and I decided not to ask to travel in it. Instead, I slogged up the hill with Leila to use her telephone. We shared her umbrella.

The interior of Leila's red house fulfilled every promise the romantic view from the ferry had engendered. Antiques. Carpets everywhere. A charming window seat from where one could watch the ferries and huge cargo ships ply the Bosphorus. But I didn't have time to appreciate the scene. I took off my wet shoes at the door and picked up the phone Leila had indicated, reachable from the window seat and an easy chair.

"Bayram? Listen carefully. Haldun Kutlu had an accident and is being taken to Üsküdar Hospital. Telephone *Cümhüriyet* and ask them to call his wife and tell her. No, no more details right now. I'm on my way to the hospital. 'Bye."

With Haldun cared for, I turned to Leila Metin. "May I make one more call?"

With a cold, graceful nod, permission was granted. Was the card still in my purse? I dug frantically. Yes. Now to hope my rusty Turkish would suffice. I didn't want to ask Leila to translate.

"*Merhaba*. May I please speak with Detective Mehmet Durmaz? My name is Elizabeth Darcy."

While I waited for Durmaz to come to the phone, I shivered. What should I say? Leila rose from her position on the window seat and fetched me a large towel. Did hearing me ask for the police bother her? I nodded my thanks, then rubbed my hair and chilled legs with the towel.

"Inspector? I met you at the Fener house the other night. Yes. Yes. Inspector, I have an incident I would like to report. Can you meet me at the Üsküdar hospital? I will be somewhere near wherever they have Haldun Kutlu. Yes. Haldun Kutlu. The journalist. He's had an, uh, accident."

I looked at Leila as I said "accident." Her face remained inscrutable.

Durmaz said he'd meet me at the hospital. He sounded intrigued. And alarmed.

I asked Leila for the number for a taxi, and she made the call herself. We parted at the door, me trying to express once more my gratitude, she being the perfect lady. I handed back the towel, thanking her again.

En route to the hospital, I shivered and my teeth chattered. What were Haldun's chances for survival? I could not lose him. Could not.

67

*When the fish were not running we sat
by the fire in Nazmi's back room and
listened to Riza as he catalogued the
winds and storms of the Bosphorus,
each in its passing season. The fierce
wind now howling outside Nazmi's,
dashing salt spray on the windows
and whistling through the cracks
in the walls, is Karayel, the Black
Wind, blowing from the cold northeastern quarter of the compass.*

John Freely, *Istanbul the Imperial*

Leila Metin's frozen expression as she bade me adieu stayed in my mind. I could relate to the adjective frozen, as my wet clothes had soaked the lining of my raincoat.

Haldun was still alive when I reached Üsküdar Hospital. He'd been moved from the Emergency Room to Intensive Care and could not be visited. That was all they'd say. I sat down in the dreary, pale green waiting room until someone would give me more information, or until Inspector Durmaz arrived.

Thank heavens it was warm, at least. Overwarm, actually, but nice to sit there steaming.

Pride and Prejudice was back at the Pera Palas, so I took out the Hillerman mystery, *Dark Wind*, I had been reading earlier. Hillerman described enough blood in the Southwest mesas to preclude any need for me to watch admissions to the ER. At the same time, I enjoyed the irony and imagined the smell of sagebrush while sitting in Istanbul. It felt good to escape mentally with Joe Leaphorn and Jim Chee, two of my favorite protagonists.

Durmaz arrived by himself. I gave him full marks for dropping whatever he was doing to come. A tribute to Haldun Kutlu, not me, but I was grateful.

So far, to my surprise, the press hadn't arrived. Apparently Bayram's call to the newspaper and mine to the police had been handled discreetly. Had Haldun *Bey's* wife arrived?

She had, Inspector Durmaz found out in one minute. Not surprisingly, the nurses on duty were more forthcoming with the police than with a bedraggled foreign woman. Durmaz's good looks may have also had something to do with it.

The doctor who'd been in the ambulance came out to give more details: While Haldun had a broken leg and a concussion, there was no reason to think he wouldn't pull through. The break was bad, though, and would require further operations. The doctor mixed her Turkish and English, as many educated Turks do when talking with peers. The policeman didn't seem to mind my standing at his elbow, listening. Perhaps he enjoyed it.

After the doctor left, Inspector Durmaz sat beside me and watched as I tucked *Dark Wind* away in my bag. He had his notebook out before I started to talk, and that man could scribble at an amazing pace.

I told him how the car approached us in the rain, how Haldun pushed me to the side, how frightened I'd been. I told him Leila Metin had come to help. And then I mentioned that I might have recognized the Murat that hit Haldun.

"I think the license number ended with 'JB.'"

Finally, hesitantly, I told Inspector Durmaz about the incident in my room the night before, with one of the men I'd previously seen in the blue Murat.

"Why did you not call me?" Durmaz's friendliness evaporated. "Perhaps Haldun Kutlu would not be injured if you called me."

I hung my head. "I tried to, but you had already gone home. Then I thought it wasn't important."

Durmaz issued a few curt orders on the cellular phone he removed from his waistband. They would look for a blue Murat with a license ending with "JB," and a handsome young driver with a large mustache. "But don't forget, he may have shaved," said Durmaz to his men, voicing my own thoughts.

After setting action in motion, he relaxed again. "Please, next time call me at home. Here is the number." His smile was wry, regretful, and quite charming.

I agreed.

"It is lucky you remember JB from the license of the Murat. We will seek for this car."

Yes, it was lucky I remembered that much. But poor Haldun still had been badly injured. Not so much luck for him. He would have to make do with what had been "written on his forehead," as they say in Turkish. *Kismet* is written on one's forehead at birth.

68

*"I am sorry to have occasioned
pain to anyone. It has been most
unconsciously done, however, and
I hope will be of short duration."*

Jane Austen, *Pride and Prejudice*

By the time we saw Haldun, he was conscious but sleepy, and his leg was in traction. A determined-looking, middle-aged woman in *jilbab,* the Moslem scarf, sat beside his bed, guarding him like a Doberman.

"How do you feel?" I asked Haldun, as I turned to shake Mrs. Kutlu's hand.

"I have been better." Haldun tried to smile. His eyes widened when he saw the policeman with me. "Did you get him?"

It was an unfair question this early in the investigation. Durmaz took it in the spirit intended.

"Not yet. But we will."

I hoped for all our sakes the Inspector was right. Plots and plans swirled around us. If I only knew whose plans those were....

69

*Counting ships passing through the
Bosphorus might be a strange habit,
but once I began discussing it with
others, I discovered that it's common among Istanbullus [residents of
Istanbul] of all ages. In the course of
a normal day, a large number of us
make regular trips to our windows and
balconies to take account, and we do
so to get some sense of the disaster,
deaths, and catastrophes that might
or might not be heading down the
strait to turn our lives upside down.*

Orhan Pamuk, *Istanbul, Memories and the City*

"Don't worry, Haldun. We'll get him," I said, almost to myself. Then
I added, "Or her." Anybody could have been driving that car.
Detective Durmaz looked at me. "We?"

* * * *

Exhausted, sore, and muddy from head to foot, I was more than ready
for a bath and meal when Inspector Durmaz dropped me at the hotel in
his plain black car well after dark. He came in with me to ask the manager for information about the break-in.

My stock soared in the eyes of the bullet-headed desk clerk when he
saw the solicitude I received from high-ranking police. The manager,
whom I'd not met before, nodded over and over in his eagerness to express cooperation.

I just wanted a bath and bed.

"I want you to call me if anything, anything at all, happens," admonished Inspector Durmaz. He handed me a card. "Here is a pager number.
It will find me at any time of day or night."

"*Teşekkür ederim*, thank you," I said. It was inadequate, as ritual
thank yous so often are.

Durmaz left. I made my way to my room. In the crisis atmosphere surrounding Haldun's injuries, I'd forgotten to mention my suspicions that there might be ties between Peter's death and all that was going on. Who knows how they would be received? It had been, after all, the Turkish police who called his death an overdose.

This time I indulged in a good, hot bath in aromatic oils, keeping the water level low in the tub. Wrapping myself in the wonderful Bursa robe the hotel provided, I decided I would sleep on whether to talk to Mehmet Durmaz about Peter Franklin. The tea from room service came faster than usual, due, I imagine, to my new stature in the hotel as victim-cum-friend-of-the-police. Hard on its heels came a telephone call.

"Elizabeth? Lawrence Andover here. Are you all right?"

"Oh, yes. Fine, thanks. How did you hear I might not be?"

"You must understand people like me get paid for knowing things. What happened, exactly?" It was comforting to hear the accents of my home country.

"The short version is somebody tried to run us down. In Haldun Kutlu's case, they succeeded."

"Yes, I heard. It's terrible! I gather he's okay. Did you get a good look at the car?"

"Small and blue, that's about all. A Murat. The license number ended with JB. I couldn't see who was driving." With all I'd been through, the conversation began to pall—though it was nice to know my government cared about me.

"I'll see what we can do about this," said Andover. "Any impressions at all about the driver?"

"Look, Lawrence, I already said I didn't see who was driving. Do you think we can get together to discuss this tomorrow or the next day? I'm a little bumped and bruised and would like to get to bed."

"But of course, my dear! Thoughtless of me. Just wanted to find out how you are. Shall we meet for drinks in your lobby tomorrow?"

"It depends on the news situation, but in principle, yes. And Lawrence, thanks very much for calling. It was nice of you."

"Not at all, Elizabeth. Just doing my job. See you tomorrow—shall we say five?—unless you call."

That's what I call good service from a Consulate. Maybe I wouldn't tell my new-found Turkish policeman about Peter, after all. Maybe I'd just talk it all over with Lawrence.

Despite all the kind support I'd received in the last few hours, I slept fitfully, just on the non-screaming side of The Dream. Something seemed to be hovering in the wings of my mind. Something I should have noticed, or should have done. It didn't come to me, of course. The mind has a mind of its own, and will release information when it wishes, no sooner.

I suppose that, too, might be *kismet*.

70

*"Society has claims on us all;
and I profess myself one of
those who consider intervals of
recreation and amusement as
desirable for everybody."*

Jane Austen, *Pride and Prejudice*

My first destination in the morning was Üsküdar Hospital, by the convenient ferry from Eminönü, near Galata Bridge. I nibbled a chewy, sesame-covered *simit* and drank strong tea on the boat. Morning tonic.

Haldun was in a fierce mood, which made me feel much better. "When are they going to let me out of here?" he growled through tobacco pieces that had fallen from a cigarette he was trying to chew.

"Well, I imagine when you can walk." I tried to be diplomatic.

"The way I feel today, I may not want to walk ever again."

"You will. You will. Just think: we're both alive. What's a little mud and a broken leg?"

The patient was not soothed, but a nurse came in and said visiting hours were over, so I was forced to leave him as grumpy as I had found him. I'm sure nicotine deprivation wasn't helping his frame of mind.

As I opened the door, a white shadow entered. Sultana! She acted as though she were in charge, and jumped with one graceful swoop onto Haldun's bed. He winced, then patted a place for her and smiled. She lay beside him and purred.

It was a little unorthodox having a cat in a hospital, but Turks wouldn't care—especially in a rehab unit. They love cats and tell the story of how the Prophet Mohammed, God be merciful to his soul, had cut his own cloak to avoid disturbing a cat sleeping on it.

Haldun seemed to feel that way. "Here's my therapy," he said, stroking Sultana's ears. But then he frowned. "You will keep me informed...." A request in the form of an order.

"Haldun, I'll call you every day. And I'll come by whenever I have something good to share."

I stepped on some loose tobacco on the way out the door. He must be chewing the stuff. At the little flower shop around the corner from the hospital, I placed an order for a fresh bouquet daily to Room 217. Haldun would hate that, but tough luck. Had to do something to assuage the guilt at being the one with the unbroken leg. And Ayla *hanım* could take the flowers home. Along with the cat.

* * * *

Bayram and I were still finishing a story at 7:00 p.m., so drinks with Andover had to be put off til the next day. Dashing as fast as possible (i.e., at a snail's pace in rush hour traffic) from the office to the hotel, I hoped to be dressed and ready by the time Ahmet Aslan arrived for our dinner date at eight.

I'd thought about cancelling, but Haldun had said he was too tired for visitors (Ayla's edict, I suspected) and I needed to learn all I could, on all fronts. Of course that's why I was just a little flustered and anxious.

21

*The rooms were lofty and hand-
some, and their furniture suitable
to the fortune of their proprietor;
but Elizabeth saw, with admiration of his taste, that it was neither
gaudy nor uselessly fine...*

Jane Austen, *Pride and Prejudice*

A quick shower, a brush-through of hair, and it was time to slip into
an all-purpose off-white cashmere sweater, not too wrinkled, and the
only woolen skirt I'd brought. A brief struggle with the clasp on my
Colombian necklace of jade and coral, and preparations were finished
almost on time.

I glanced in the mirror. Maybe I'd put on too much rouge; my cheeks
looked flushed. Elizabeth, Elizabeth. Just because Aslan is what any
woman would call a "hunk" is no reason to fuss over looks. I threw
my camel-hair jacket over the outfit, hoping that layering would do the
trick both for comfort and style. The jacket didn't clash with either my
medium-heeled beige shoes or the purse that's my over-arm office.

"Almost matched" is pretty good for a Pisces. Fish-people always
have trouble with color coordination—particularly shoes, I've read.

Aslan was more casual than when I'd first met him at Andover's.
Khaki pants, a polo sweater, a black leather jacket in place of the London
Fog.

Handsome couple. I caught our reflections in the big, gilt-framed mirror near the old-fashioned elevator in the lobby. The old mirror with its
chipped gilt and distortions caught a fleeting image of a ghost. A tall, thin,
intelligent man with kind eyes. Dad? What are you doing here? Checking on me? Worrying about me? Years after his death, I still missed him.

Ahmet Aslan said we were going to Çiçek Pasajı, the Flower Passageway, not far from the Pera Palas Hotel. We took his red BMW and
were conspicuous in the crawl of evening traffic. A herd of self-appoint-
ed eight-to-fifteen-year old guards accosted Aslan as we parked, and he
gave a small bill to the strongest-looking tough.

"More where that came from, if the car is untouched when I return."
The boy gave him a cheeky salute.

Çiçek Pasajı has lost some of its seedy, artistic charm in renovations. A meeting place, where artists, writers, professors, self-styled philosophers, and less savory types sit around simple tables drinking *rakı* or beer, eating fresh seafood and *meze*. A Haldun Kutlu kind of place—where intellectuals can drink, spout poetry or political dogma, drink and let down their hair.

"Did you ever come here with Peter?" I asked Ahmet.

He smiled. "Often. Peter was a great drinking buddy."

The real ghost of my entire Istanbul visit was turning out to be Peter Franklin. He seemed to have known everyone and everything.

We smelled the *pasaj* before we arrived: the sweet smell of flowers and spices blended with fresh fish laid out on wooden planks, ready for choosing. In the warren of alleyways around Çiçek Pasajı, semi-open fruit and vegetable markets formed a cornucopia of temptation: mounds of smooth round oranges vying for attention with small, plump, purple-black eggplants and green zucchinis; heaps of salty, shriveled black olives; brine-filled vats with creamy goat's cheese. And everywhere the raucous, good-natured tumult of selling small things, lots of small things, so some could make a living and others enjoy the good life.

In the brisk autumn night air, with a half-moon peeping over the canvas shop-coverings, walking with a handsome man, smelling roses and carnations from the flower shops, I assessed my situation. Apparently, I'd dropped into one of Sheherezade's stories in *The Arabian Nights*.

When I said this to Aslan, he grinned. "Never confuse Turks and Arabs," he scolded. "We live next to each other, that's all."

Interesting that when presented with an outsider like an Arab, this Kurd considered himself a Turk. I bristled. Did Aslan really think I was that ill-informed?

"Well, of course Turks are not the same as Persians or Arabs! But Turkey has the magic of Asia, with some European architecture and culture."

He took my arm to escort me to one of the restaurants. We sat at a table near the outside corner, protected from rain if it came, yet feeling the chill of the outdoors on one side. A charcoal brazier nearby kept the other side uncomfortably warm. Because of the arrangement, I shifted in my seat, moving from chill to heat.

We ordered wood-skewered, deep-fried mussels for our main course, with a tomato-and-olive shepherd's salad and the inevitable rice *pilav*. When the waiter came by with trays of *meze* from which to choose, I pointed to white beans in olive oil, garnished with fresh green parsley, *pilaki*. Aslan picked out delicate chunks of *Arnavut ciğeri*, Albanian liver. The well-trained waiter kept his eyes on Ahmet Aslan's face, not mine. The Turkish code dictates that a man doesn't look at another man's woman.

However, in this case, the waiter was very intent. Did they know each other?

72

Mrs. Gardiner and Elizabeth talked
of all that had occurred, during their
visit, as they returned, except what
had particularly interested them both.

Jane Austen, *Pride and Prejudice*

Haldun hadn't talked to his wife about the political situation much since the car hit him. Ayla *hanım* would just have worried. She sat now beside the hospital bed, leaning over to pet Sultana from time to time. At first the hospital staff had objected to a cat in the ward, but Sultana had won them over. Turks love cats, anyhow, and Van cats are considered so special you can't even take them out of the country.

"How does the leg feel?" Ayla asked.

"It hurts." Haldun was grumpy with the nurses, the doctors, and his wife. He was gentle only with the cat, who didn't nag or fuss over him. She lay near him, but not near enough to cause pain.

Elizabeth called twice every day. The staff had discouraged visitors for the first days, until the initial shock had worn off and his concussion healed. Haldun frowned and rubbed his brow. Who was after him? The same people who killed Oktay Fener?

The police had asked for an interview today. How strange. Police and artists and intellectuals had had a long, tense relationship in modern Turkey. Now, in addition to possible police repression, intellectuals had to fear for their lives from fringe groups like the Silver Wolves. Before he left for Rome to try to kill the pope, one of the Silver Wolves, Mehmet Ali Ağca, had killed Abdi Ipekci, a prominent journalist.

Haldun stroked Sultana. She was his good luck charm and had a sharp eye for strangers. In the collar around her neck, she wore a *nazarlık*, a blue bead to protect from the Evil Eye.

73

*The food was some of the best I ate
in Turkey. The flies and the men
gathered around the huge round flat
baking dishes of borek, a meat or
vegetable pie, and lamb stew, or piled
high with the salad that is a part of
every Turkish meal. There was a scent
of spices and newly baked bread.*

Mary Lee Settle, *Turkish Reflections*

In the Çiçek Pasajı restaurant, Ahmet Aslan's eyes were hard to read, except for the occasional appreciative twinkle. And yet…his gaze wandered. Something else was going on. Was he playing a game? From time to time, he nodded at an acquaintance. Most often, he gazed at another restaurant across the narrow walkway. The brazier's uncomfortable warmth gave me an excuse to move my chair a little. Now I could see the restaurant.

Two men lounged at a table. Their waiter hovered over them. Surprising, since they wore rough clothing and didn't look well-to-do. They looked, in fact, as though they were getting drunk. At one point, their waiter and our waiter nodded to each other.

Did Aslan know these guys? Or was it their waiter he watched? I glanced around casually and caught a familiar profile a couple of tables away. Could it be my erstwhile breakfast companion, Jean Le Reau? He ate alone and didn't seem to have noticed us.

Once our *garson* left I smiled at Aslan. "What's it like being Kurdish in a country like Turkey?"

Aslan laughed. "If you believe everything you hear from Turks, there are no Kurds, just something called 'eastern Turks' or 'mountain Turks.' But our languages aren't even related. There's some repression; always has been. I decided a long time ago I wasn't going to let it stop me from doing what I want, and it hasn't."

"For you, maybe. What about your ethnic cohorts who plant the bombs? Do they think this is the way to solve their problems?" Could

I switch on my tape recorder in my purse? No, that wouldn't be ethical without getting permission, and asking would seem strange on a "date," of sorts.

"There are so many groups, you cannot generalize. Some are idealistic and some are interested in money-making or power. Either can lead to terrorism."

"Money-making or power? You mean drugs and arms, I presume."

Our *garson* approached with the main course. After a pause for receiving food and the departure of the *garson*, Aslan answered my question.

"Of course. It's a pattern with groups like this. All it takes is one charismatic leader to run off in some direction, leading hundreds of wild-eyed youngsters, who have little to lose from illegal activity. There's a lot of infighting, of course."

Aslan certainly was being frank. And he didn't appear emotionally involved with the welfare of his own ethnic group. I guess if you're rich enough, idealism comes in a poor second. Did he send money surreptitiously, or openly, to his Kurdish brethren? The Turkish government had begun some impressive development projects in the Kurdish areas to encourage assimilation. What did he think of that?

Aslan's gaze continued to rove, and at one point he raised his hand. To my knowledge, he didn't know Le Reau, so I assumed he was not waving to him. Then he looked at me. "You know, this place has two levels."

"You mean Istanbul, or Çiçek Pasajı?"

"Istanbul, of course, has many levels. I'm talking about where we are right now, Çiçek Pasajı. It's a contest between the intellectuals who have been in jail versus the intellectuals who haven't. Artists of all types are considered intellectuals in Turkey, and most of them have leaned leftist at one time or another. They think of themselves as revolutionaries."

I nodded. Many intellectuals and journalists had gone to jail for their defiant writings. It was an ongoing obstacle to the country's democratic push. Up to now the obstacle had kept getting overcome.

However, violence took its toll. Look at Haldun. Someone had tried to kill him. The Silver Wolves? I'd been researching them, but it could have been Kurdish extremists. Or even Russian thugs.

Aslan continued. "Of course, now, with so many people in Istanbul from the former Soviet countries, with cash from someplace—who knows where?—we have a whole new element in Istanbul—and right here in Çiçek Pasajı: common criminals. International or domestic, who cares?"

As if to punctuate Aslan's words, a loud rat-tat-tat broke out across the little passageway. Everybody dropped to the ground and crawled under the tables. Someone fell heavily, hitting tables and chairs.

My heart pounded wildly as I crouched beside the table. I didn't dare raise my head to look.

٢٤

Everyone talks openly about math-
ematics, success at school, soccer, and
having fun, but they grapple with the
most basic questions of existence—
love, compassion, religion, the mean-
ing of life, jealousy, hatred—in trem-
bling confusion and painful solitude.

Orhan Pamuk, *Istanbul, Memories and the City*

Courage! I raised my head and glanced around.

The two young men across the alley from our restaurant jumped up from their table and ran. A crowd gathered in the passage, hovering around a person on the ground. Less than a minute later, several police-men came into view. Some checked the fallen figure while others darted down the passage. Chasing the young men? The incident was so quick, no one moved until hares and hounds had passed. I couldn't see who had been injured.

All of us in the area were out from under the tables and on our feet, now. Police sirens and an ambulance whined their way through narrow alleys to the crowded Çiçek Pasajı.

My dinner partner's face was composed, as always, but I glimpsed something beneath the surface. Anger? Dismay? Fear?

I sat and stared hard at Aslan. "So what was that all about? Why did those men run? Did they shoot that person? And who was the victim?"

Aslan's handsome face tightened. "An example of repression," he said. "Those young men were Kurds. They were doing nothing, yet the police immediately suspect them. And now, I think, we go."

"But who was shot? How is he now?" The ambulance crew had loaded someone into the vehicle and taken off again.

"I think…" Aslan paused. "I think that was an accidental hit."

How did he know?

75

As anxiety overtook me, I hit on a
frantic stopgap measure that would
become a habit: I applied my full
mind, sharpened as it was by memo-
rization, to the Soviet ship, committed
it to memory, and counted it. What
do I mean to say? I did the same
as those legendary American spies
rumored to live on hilltops overlooking
the Bosphorus, who photographed
every passing Communist ship. .

Orhan Pamuk, *Istanbul, Memories and the City*

"How do you know they weren't terrorists?" I asked Ahmet.

Abruptly, without answering, Ahmet Aslan paid the bill and we stood. The Arabian Nights adventure had been cut short by real-world violence. As we left, I checked for the man sitting alone. The napkin lay among dirty plates, but the chair was empty. Our waiter, too, had disappeared.

Ahmet took my arm brusquely. His thick brows drew together, his jaw was set. When we reached the BMW, it was unscathed. Ahmet's mouth relaxed and he paid our self-styled youthful guards a handsome sum. We heard a delighted shriek as we left the group.

The drive back to the Pera was short and silent. I gazed out the window. The man seated beside me was more than an urbane professional; he seethed with raw resentment. I shivered.

Had Jean Le Reau been at the restaurant before shots rang out? Had my handsome escort turned from Dr. Jekyll into Mr. Hyde?

Le Reau could be anyone. Aslan could be anyone. Could they be working together? Not something I wanted to imagine. Had I seen Le Reau? Ahmet Aslan had waved in that direction.

Who could I trust?

76

"Since writing the above, dearest
Lizzy, something has occurred of a
most unexpected and serious nature;
but I am afraid of alarming you..."

Jane Austen, *Pride and Prejudice*

At the archeological dig outside Iznik, Perihan Kıraz's head throbbed. Psychological repression, she called it. Knowing what she was repressing didn't help. Oktay, dead. Friend and classmate. Admired friend and maybe something more. Quite a lot more for Perihan. Working at the dig would never be the same.

Perihan had paid his wife a condolence visit, of course. His wife remained ignorant about the feelings between Oktay and Perihan. Well, the feelings Perihan had about Oktay.

He had been a discreet man.

She would carry on his mission. That was all she could do.

??

*"My love, should not you like to see
a place of which you have heard
so much?" said her aunt. "A place
too, with which so many of your
acquaintance are connected."*

Jane Austen, *Pride and Prejudice*

At the office, we read every day about Haldun Kutlu's "accident" and still followed the shooting at Çiçek Pasajı. Protests had died down, but an uneasy mood remained around Istanbul University. Faye Mollington and I climbed the hill to the campus in Beyazit to interview some students and professors. It was one of those bright October days when you can get by with a sweater. The sun shone on white-barked trees that had lost most of their leaves, and on old stone walls, rain-washed and mossy, golden in the sun.

As with most university campuses, scraggly young people crowded the buildings that crown one of Istanbul's oldest hills. Lounging in the courtyards and the big plaza in front of the main gates, they appeared dedicated to a lifestyle most of us could only envy. Needless to say, it's a lifestyle that relies largely on someone else's income. But we all understand. It's a world-wide phenomenon.

University is a phase in anyone's life. Time enough when one must place nose to the grindstone and press on. I'm sure the students are learning. *Something.*

The girl we approached first was neater than some of the others, her hair pulled back in a severe bun.

"Excuse me," Faye asked. "May we talk to you for a minute?" She identified us as journalists.

The girl paused. Faye pressed on: "Is it possible to ask you about your views on terrorism?"

Blunt, but it seemed to work.

"Terror?" the girl repeated. "I'll tell you what is terror. Terror is letting the people of Bosnia go down the drain. Terror is the great big Turkish army fighting the Kurds in southwest Turkey. Terror is the U.S.

army going into countries like Vietnam. Terror is letting Israel send commandos to Arab countries to kill innocent people."

"And who do you think killed Professor Fener?" Faye's question was immediate and personal.

"It could have been any of them," she sniffed. "Violence is the reason." She thought for a moment, and came up with an answer: "I am sure it was done by the secret police."

The exact answer I expected.

Her lecture on the ills of the world was full of idealism, but it was also predictable and ideological. It's boring to have one's predictions turn out true.

Other students had different ideas, of course.

"The fundamentalists want to turn Turkey back," said one.

"Too much nationalism," said another.

"A foreign plot," was the view of a third.

We called on one of Professor Fener's colleagues, the archeologist Perihan Kıraz. Statuesque and staid; the epitome of a female don. Her cluttered but comfortable corner office boasted a spectacular view of Süleymaniye Mosque, the finest imperial mosque complex in Istanbul.

Caught up in the precise, proportioned lines of Süleymaniye, I let Faye ask questions.

"You were friends with Professor Fener. Who do you think killed him?"

Now that, perhaps, was a little too blunt. I turned back. Perihan *hanım's* face was ashen. This was a colleague she had lost, and it had obviously hit her hard.

I leaned forward, smiling. "What we mean is, was Mr. Fener—Oktay *Bey*—involved in any political group that you know of?"

Faye glared.

"Oktay was not a political type," Professor Kıraz began slowly. "All he cared about was ceramics. That was always his duty on digs that we did together."

Her eyes filled with tears.

Faye tilted her head, eyes narrowed. "Do you have any suspicions about who set the bomb at the Fener house, Perihan *Hanım*?"

There was another long pause.

"Well, not a suspicion." Dr. Kıraz looked down at her neatly-shod feet. "Not quite."

"An idea maybe?" pressed Faye.

"There are unscrupulous art dealers," said the archeologist, chin on hand. Her warm brown eyes looked troubled. "People often asked Oktay to look at their collections, to see if the items were genuine. Of course, with Turkey's strict laws against selling antiquities and taking ancient things out of the country, Oktay's views could be sensitive."

Perihan Kıraz continued. "You might want to talk to a woman named Leila Metin who works at Topkapı Museum. She's almost as expert as Oktay was. Go and talk to her."

Oh, boy. Leila again. I couldn't wait.

Perihan intrigued me, though. The interview had felt more like one with a widow than one with a colleague of a murdered man.

78

*The passion of scholars for tracing
sources is up, literally, against a
stone wall there. They tend to leave
out the element of play, and the north
door of the mosque is nothing but
play, as if the carvers had woven an
embroidered tapestry and turned it
into stone cat's cradles of designs,
vines, an exuberance of flowers.*

Mary Lee Settle, *Turkish Reflections*

We said goodbye to Professor Kıraz, who nodded briefly as she dug through masses of books and papers on her desk. What was she trying to find? Or did she simply not want to look at us? Well, she could gaze out her window at that great mosque of Sinan's, Süleymaniye. If she could see through her tears.

Was her grief just that for a colleague? Or was there something more?

Since there was nothing else on the roster at the moment, Faye and I decided to go straight to Topkapı for lunch. The restaurant was on the side of the museum overlooking the entry to the Bosphorus. After lunch, we would stop in to see Leila Metin.

Faye snapped at me once or twice on the way. Was she still irritated by my interruption of her questioning of Professor Kıraz? If I had known Faye better, I would have called her on it. As it was, I let it go. I had no illusions, though. Faye would never let anything—or anyone—get in the way of her digging at the story. In that sense, she might be a better journalist than friend. But would she miss the big picture in her zeal for details? In any case, she agreed that both of us needed to talk to Leila Metin.

How had Faye and Peter interacted? To date, she had been far from forthcoming on the subject, though I'd tried subtle lead-ins. The usual response was a shuttered look in her gray eyes. She either loved or hated Peter; I preferred the former. It was easier to forgive Faye's little annoyances that way.

Since it was a gorgeous day, we decided to walk from the university to Topkapı, past some of Istanbul's colorful history: the grand and mysterious covered market, or Kapalı Çarşı; the Column of Constantine erected in 330 A.D. to celebrate that ruler's dedication of the city as capital of the Roman Empire. Near *Aya* Sofya was the entrance to the Underground Palace, where Byzantines and Ottomans had well-defended cisterns.

Called Yerebatan Sarayı, the sunken palace, in Turkish, the cisterns are an eerie experience. Deep underground. Smelling of water and moss. You watch your step down the stairs. Golden carp swim silently in lights trained on them. It's so extensive you can't see from one end to the other. Once when I was visiting the cisterns, an Italian tenor burst into song, his rich tones echoing across the shallow pools of water, hitting the walls at the back and tumbling back like surround sound. An unforgettable moment.

For quite awhile, Yerebatan Sarayı was closed to the public for fear of terrorism; I wasn't sure whether it was open now or not. But the day was too sparkling to entertain somber thoughts long or even to descend below the ground. It was perfect for dining at the Konyalı Restaurant at Topkapı. As we wended our way past the Ahmet III fountain through the imperial gates to the outer courtyard—still big enough to contain the Byzantine cathedral of St. Irene—I tossed my trenchcoat into the air and caught it.

A pair of well-dressed tourists looked scandalized. Faye just looked at me. Then we both laughed.

We had to walk through Topkapı to get to the restaurant, through familiar courtyards and arched passageways leading from one wing of the palace to another. Ah, the Treasury, with all those jewels.... No. Faye would never allow a diversion. We headed around the end of that building and down the steps to the Konyalı.

There might be a nicer place to have lunch than the Topkapı Museum's Konyalı restaurant on a beautiful day, but I don't know of one. I ordered *ayran*, a salty mix of yogurt and water; Faye asked for a beer. Blue sky made the dark waters of the Bosphorus bright and vivid today. White ferries wove their way from Europe to Asia, Asia to Europe, interspersed with the odd cruise ship or lumbering cargo vessel.

As we waited for our drinks, I let my gaze stray from the busy water scene at the bottom of the hill to the tables around us, arranged lengthwise so that everyone could see out the picture windows. At the end table, almost hidden by a column, sat Lawrence Andover, having lunch with a man I hadn't met—and the woman we were planning to see later.

79

I was drawn to the boy, and felt sorry
for him; he seemed so lonely. I tried
to talk and joke with him, but he was
terribly earnest and never smiled...
it broke my heart that these children
were forced to sacrifice their lives
so early, before they had eaten an
ice cream cone or kissed a girl.

Omar Nasiri, *Inside the Jihad, My Life with Al Quaeda: A Spy's Story*

Erol lay on a thin pallet in the safe house in Üsküdar with the curtains drawn. He had done it. Within a few days he had gone from just a believer to an activist in the cause.

Nazim, the Wolves' bombmaker, had been right. It was easy to make a bomb. A few pounds of ammonium nitrate, used as fertilizer. Easy to get. Several packages of sugar. Also easy to get. And he hadn't known it could be so effective. A couple of blasting caps stolen from a construction site. Wires to lead from the car's battery to the explosive mix.

Boom. No more Professor Oktay Fener.

The hardest part had been putting the ammonium-sugar blend through Turkish coffee grinders—a painstaking process that Erol, as a new member of the Wolves, had had to work on for hours.

At least his task had just been to place the bomb in Fener's car. He hadn't had to detonate it and watch the effect.

The other members of the brotherhood had been very impressed. "*Yaşa!*" they had shouted to him. "Long life!"

It was not long life for Professor Fener, though.

30

*"...and as for her eyes, which have
sometimes been called so fine, I never
could perceive anything extraordinary
in them. They have a sharp, shrewish
look, which I do not like at all..."*

Jane Austen, *Pride and Prejudice*

At lunch, Leila Metin, our target interviewee for later, wore a red wool dress that accentuated her figure and held a cigarette between slim fingers tipped with a red to match her dress. Her eyes, as usual, were stony. The little group appeared to be discussing serious business.

I glanced over at them casually. Interesting. Andover spoke the most, his words accompanied by elegant gestures. Leila appeared to be listening while fiddling with something on her lap. The Western businessman with them entered into the conversation from time to time.

I turned to Faye. She nodded.

"So, our prey comes to us. Or at least to dine from the same plates."

I couldn't let that pass. "I wouldn't exactly call Leila Metin our 'prey.' But since she's with someone I know, I'll go say hello when we've ordered our food." Faye shouldn't think she could order me around like a novice reporter.

But then came the delightful job of choosing entrees and I almost forgot to watch Leila and her group. Faye decided on skewered long meatballs called *köfte*, fixed the spicy Gaziantep way and arranged on pieces of fresh warm *pide* bread with tomato sauce and Turkish cousins to roasted jalapenos lying in wait beside a garlic-yogurt mixture. I was hungry for *köfte* too; I chose mine arranged on a bed of mashed eggplant, in the manner of an Ottoman dish.

As soon as we had ordered, Faye rose and headed toward Leila. I hurried after her. Damn the woman, I told her *I* would do this.

Andover looked up as we approached, stopped talking, and gave a friendly wave. The man with him opened expectant blue eyes. Leila just stared for a moment, then looked away. Not very Turkish. Who was Leila Metin?

Andover and the other American—somehow, I just knew he was American—were on their feet by the time Faye and I reached the table.

"Hello, hello," said Andover, genially. "I see all your work doesn't preclude finding the good food in town."

"There is good food everywhere here." I smiled and nodded at Leila, shook hands with Andover, and held out my hand toward the other man.

"Howard Black," he said, before Andover could perform introductions. Yes, it was an American accent.

"I'm Elizabeth Darcy."

I wondered what tack Faye would take to make an appointment with Leila Metin.

She met the challenge head-on: "Ms. Metin, are you going to be in your office later? Perihan Kıraz suggested we talk to you about ceramics."

The frozen, impassive look on Leila's face did not thaw. "I am sorry. I will be busy today. Perhaps another time?"

I studied her. Was she trying to speak in code, so that someone at the table would not understand her real meaning? Either that or she was having a difficult enough day without being interrogated by two brazen hussies from the press.

Andover had maintained a well-bred silence. Both he and Howard Black remained standing. They shifted a little. Uncomfortable?

It was time for a mature, decent withdrawal.

"May I call you?" I stepped toward Leila, gently touching her arm. "I would like to talk to you, but your coffee is growing cold. So we will leave you now."

The still tableau came back to life. "Good to see you," said Andover to me. "I owe you drinks, don't forget!"

"Pleasure to meet you," said Black.

The man was an enigma.

Leila seemed far less than enthusiastic, but she put out her hand when Faye and I offered ours. "Goodbye."

* * * *

Conversation between Faye and me waned after the foray to Leila's table. Still, the *köfte* was delicious. It always is. By the time we finished lunch and headed toward our office building in Cağaloğlu, her annoyance at my ending the meeting with Leila and Andover had faded and we chatted amiably. She and I had not yet had a girlish tete-a-tete regarding Peter. Would we ever have a chance? Did either of us want to do that?

31

"Care of him!—Yes, I really believe
Darcy does take care of him in those
points where he most wants care."

Jane Austen, *Pride and Prejudice*

When I called Haldun from the office, his voice sounded weak.

"My doctor is on my case about smoking, and I can't even get up and leave the room!"

"Don't worry, Haldun. They'll have you out of there before you know it." Easy for me to say. Tomorrow I would visit him. In the meantime, though, maybe I could take Haldun's mind off his discomfort as well as gather more information.

"I saw Leila Metin at lunch," I said. "That woman interests me. Who and what in the world is she?"

"Leila is interesting," he admitted. His voice already sounded stronger. "Daughter of an old family. Used to have lots of money and own property all over the place, but then her father gambled too much with some stocks, and ended up losing most of their fortune. He committed suicide about ten years ago, a broken man. His wife couldn't take his loss—or maybe the loss of money and prestige—and she had a total nervous breakdown. Had to be put in an asylum. Leila took charge of her younger brother, but the kid has been a disappointment. A combination of his mother and father, they say. And bitter as hell." Haldun's voice continued to grow stronger.

"Is Leila still rich?"

"She still owns some property—like that red house. But she's way too good a businesswoman to sit in genteel poverty on valuable land. She got that job at Topkapı and runs some kind of design business out of her home on the side. I think she works on-and-off with one of the big clothiers. I'd bet she makes most of her money from that angle now. The Topkapı thing just gives her a venerable old institution in which to hang one of her hats. And she goes to conferences and all that…" He broke off abruptly to talk to someone else. "*Ne söyliyon?* What do you say? I need to get off the phone? What kind of service is this, anyhow? You're going to give me a *what*? Elizabeth, I must sign off and defend myself against this sadistic nurse."

I couldn't help chuckling. "Do you need anything, Haldun?"

"No, goddamn it. I just need to go home."

"Well, you'd better do something about that mood before you ask your wife to have you at home. Or even Sultana, though I know she visits."

Haldun was easy to talk to, and I liked the man. His poor wife was the supportive kind—the sort one can depend on. Long ago I'd dreamed of being that kind of wife. Hadn't managed it very long, though.

Haldun had given me Leila's telephone number at home, so I tried it that night. She answered on the third ring.

"Dr. Metin? I'm sorry to bother you, but I wondered whether I could make an appointment to see you. Tomorrow, maybe? I need to find out something about ceramics for a story I am doing, and Professor Kıraz and others say you are an expert." Some little white lies, but what's a reporter to do?

Leila Metin didn't sound very enthusiastic. "I am quite busy tomorrow," she said. "Also, I will be working at home for the next two days, not at my office."

"I won't take much of your time," I assured her. That, at least, was true. "And I am able to meet you wherever most convenient, at your home or Topkapı."

Her voice was curiously apathetic. "I suppose I can meet you at home, then. Come about four o'clock, not tomorrow but the day after. I will expect you." And she hung up.

An abrupt end to a telephone call. At least I had an appointment.

Should I invite Faye to join me? I liked Faye, but her competitiveness, while admirable, rubbed me the wrong way at times. However, since we had tried to get an appointment together, we should complete the process together. I rang her immediately, before I could change my mind.

"Yep. I'll be there," said Faye. "Don't wait for me to start, though. I'll meet you at Leila's about four."

Well, that was fine with me. I had a hospital visit to make on that side of the Bosphorus, anyway. I wanted to see Haldun before interviewing Leila.

There were several more things I needed to know about Leila Metin and her mysterious young brother.

82

...the Kangal dogs, who stand as tall
as Irish wolfhounds, and who wear
iron collars with spikes six inches
long that you can buy in country
hardware stores. It is to protect
them from the wolves that they are
bred to attack on sight. They are
half feral and completely loyal to
the shepherds who train them.

Mary Lee Settle, *Turkish Reflections*

At the office, Bayram and I had been working on the final touches to a Sunday background piece, using a current debate in Europe as a peg. Turkey was continuing its effort to be accepted into the European community, and human rights questions were coming up, such as who was being jailed and how was the Kurdish question being handled. While there was plenty of reason for concern on that score, as well as others, the outsider view could be simplistic and self-righteous—just like the Crusader tales centuries earlier. Turks had suffered bad public relations for a long time. Being nomadic horsemen originally, p.r. was not their strong point. So I was determined to try to tell the whole story, not the inaccurate but popular one in the West.

Truth be told, I love these broader stories where you interview a whole swath of people and then put together a big picture that expands the reader's knowledge. It's exciting when interviewees turn out to be more interesting, or controversial, or just nicer than you expected. This had been a good story that way.

I had my notes in front of me at the breakfast table in the Pera Palas dining room, pushing them to one side to jot a question mark from time to time. As I nibbled on fresh bread and debated whether to add cherry jam to the feta cheese I'd already spread on a browned corner, I was checking off the sides of the story we had covered: politics, economics, culture, religion. Pretty broad, as I said.

"Meez Darcy." Oh, no. Jean Le Reau was just leaving breakfast. His timing, if nothing else, was impeccable. Mine quite obviously was not.

"Hello." I kept the word businesslike.

"I am hoping we can talk," said that irrepressible soul, good cheer radiating from his pale eyes. "I am wondering, can we have dinner tonight?"

There seemed no polite way to turn down the simple request. We had seen enough of each other in passing to count as acquaintances, if not friends. We had even been through a crisis together. So I smiled. "Uh, sure, all right," I agreed. "Where shall I meet you?"

"I knock on your door as I go past," offered Le Reau.

I frowned.

"Better yet, I see you in lobby," he said. "Shall we say eight o'clock?"

Whatever Le Reau wanted, I couldn't imagine. I doubted it would be anything I would or could provide. At least he didn't suggest tomorrow, for I had arranged to see Lawrence Andover in Çengelköy after Faye and I left Leila Metin. "Stop in," he'd said cheerfully. "We'll have a quick drink and then walk over to a nice little fish restaurant for dinner." It sounded like fun.

I hadn't forgotten, or neglected, those papers of Peter's that were now stashed in a locked box at the hotel front desk. I went through them every day, especially Peter's notes, trying to decipher what I could. I was reading them with care, yet learning little. Why couldn't Peter have been more overt in his notes? I had almost no idea what story he had been chasing, other than the obvious ones of drugs, arms, and post-Soviet politics.

To give an example of how frustrating his notes were, there was one page of pictures that I spent an inordinate amount of time on. Crudely-drawn, I guess by Peter, the pictures seemed to be of animals; deer, lions, a peacock. I tried to remember all the political party mascots, and found nothing resembling those animals. I couldn't tie the pictures in with any of the underworld names I'd heard for smugglers, though that seemed the best bet to me. Silver Wolves would, of course, be animals, and come to think of it, one of the pictures looked a little like a wolf.... I couldn't think of any soccer teams, with all their attendant betting and high emotion, that could be tied in, either. I was at a loss.

The papers went back into the security box.

I was more pessimistic and optimistic than I'd been when I packed for the sad trip to Istanbul: pessimistic about the chance I was ever going to solve Peter's murder; optimistic that nothing bad was going to happen to me.

My editor Mac's cynical voice wangled its way into my mind: "What do you call 'bad?' A man's been killed in front of you. Your room's been burgled. A colleague has been hit by a car. Somebody's stalking you. What does it take to raise your alarms?"

But when I called Mac I only mentioned the innocuous things I was working on. He sounded a little bored, said "yeah, yeah," a couple of times and reminded me of the deadline for the Sunday piece. Our conversation lasted about two minutes.

33

The tumult of her mind was now painfully great.

Jane Austen, *Pride and Prejudice*

It was another tight squeeze sending material to Washington and returning to the hotel in time to meet Le Reau. The story that day was the visit of an American official who was discussing drug-trafficking intervention with Turkish counterparts. The press conference was positive toward Turkey's efforts in this line. I knew some Turks felt resentful that their government had accepted American insistence that poppy fields around Afyon (meaning 'opium' in Turkish) had to be destroyed in the interests of young Western addicts, while their destruction wiped out a lucrative crop for the Afyon farmers. It was one more case of the uneasiness with which East meets West.

I changed clothes fast, as usual, putting on my trusty woolen skirt (which I'd asked the Pera to press) with a long-sleeved off-white silk blouse (washable) and a blue wool blazer. Of course, the khaki trench coat went over the whole ensemble.

I did a quick check of my suitcase security before locking my door and putting the "Do Not Disturb" sign out. I'm sure it doesn't make any difference, but I feel better stating my preference about whether someone goes into my room or not.

Jean Le Reau was in the lobby when I came down. He was sitting on one of the overstuffed Victorian couches reading a newspaper, his raincoat beside him. When I stepped out of the elevator, he got to his feet, folded the newspaper and came over. He raised my hand to his lips. I smiled. His eyes twinkled; our handshakes must have seemed quite foreign to him.

"Good evening, Ms. Darcy. You are looking very nice this night."

"Hello, Mr. Le Reau." For the first time, I studied him in detail. He was somewhere between thirty-five and forty-two, with thinning hair that had a mind of its own. Rather attractive in a thin, intense kind of way.

It turned out Le Reau was taking me to Galata Tower, where they have a touristy restaurant with tables around the windows near the top of the pencil-shaped tower. The food would probably reflect the tourist atmosphere—i.e., be a little under usual standards. We walked from the Pera, through narrow, zigzag streets that without notice became steep stairs for a few steps before once again flattening out.

It was on-and-off cloudy and quite cold. Feeble street lights here and there gave only a hint of our surroundings. I couldn't help thinking of the intrigue and romance in *From Russia with Love*, and Sean Connery.

Jean Le Reau was solicitous at every turn, catching my elbow on the steep stairs and assisting when it was almost too dark to see the walls on either side. It was more comfortable than walking alone at night.

We were nearly there when Le Reau shoved me so hard I landed on my knees on the cobblestones. What the hell? My palms and knees ached. What did he think he was doing?

A pop sounded loud in the stillness—a gun? It came from above, on the stairs. Something pinged on a rock near my head. I ducked my head and covered it with my hands. I crawled toward the nearest wall, away from where the bullet had come. Not a good experience for my nylons or the elbows of my trenchcoat, but that wasn't foremost in my mind at the time.

In a flash, a form was upon me, pushing me even further into the worn stones of the road.

"Stay quiet!" hissed a voice.

Was this a friend or foe? I didn't have too many choices, either way. I stayed quiet. I was crushed by the body weight on me. Another pop like the one before, but much closer. From right beside me, in fact. I peered from under my arm.

Well, the guy pushing me down was Jean Le Reau, that was certain. He was firing a gun. Was he on my side? I hoped so. In the midst of the gunfire, I was a sitting duck. It seemed an interminable period. At last, Jean Le Reau touched the sleeve of my coat.

"Go stand against that wall."

I did as ordered, my heart thumping against the silk blouse. There were no more shots, but heavy footsteps ran up the stairs, away from us.

"Wait here."

Jean Le Reau took off. I stood alone against the wall.

Le Reau certainly was full of surprises. Who was this chameleon-like character? Why did he carry a gun? Who was he chasing? What did either he or his quarry want with me?

Le Reau came back, out of breath, and touched my arm. "Are you okay?"

He must be on my side.

"Yes, I'm all right. And you?"

My nylons stuck to my bloody knees and the pain throbbed. The sleeve of my trench coat was wet. In the faint streetlight, I couldn't see any blood on Jean Le Reau.

"Yes, I am fine. And now, let's have dinner, no?"

84

*...when the cars fly into the water, they
never sink like stones. For a moment
they waver, almost as if sitting on the
surface. It might be daylight, or the
only light might be coming from a
nearby meyhane [pub], but when people on the living side of the Bosphorus
look into the faces of those about to be
engulfed, they see a knowing terror.
A moment later the car sinks slowly
into the deep, dark, fast-flowing sea.*

Orhan Pamuk, *Istanbul, Memories and the City*

So our plans would continue as if nothing had happened?

"Well, I guess so. I will need to clean up, though."

"There is a ladies' room inside," said my newfound hero.

I washed up as well as I could. Nothing to be done about the nylons, so I peeled them off and threw them away. The raincoat would need dry-cleaning. I folded it and tucked it under my arm.

"I need some answers," I said, after the waiter had handed us menus and taken drink orders. I hid my messy, bloody knees under my skirt and the tablecloth, and took two ibuprofens. Fortunately, my skirt was long enough to cover my knees. Well-dressed patrons at other tables laughed and smoked. The room's aroma was a mix of perfume, alcohol, and to-bacco.

Jean Le Reau spent a long time looking out the window at the pan-oramic view of the confluence of the Bosphorus, the Golden Horn, and the Sea of Marmara. A well-lit cruise ship, tied up at the Karaköy wharf below us, looked like the Capitol Building on the Fourth of July.

"I think now is not a good time to talk," he finally said.

"But who was after us just now?" I asked, my voice rising.

From the next table the smell of eggplant and onion and delectable lamb added to the previous bar smells. Tourism had not ruined the food at Galata Tower.

The rush of adrenaline and my injuries whetted my appetite. The waiter finally brought the food we'd ordered. Mixed grill, stuffed peppers, Turkish *pastırma*, or pastrami.

After our plates were settled in front of us and the waiter left, Jean Le Reau leaned forward.

"I am not sure who was shooting. Maybe it was a rival of my company."

A rival of his company? These seemed extreme measures in a trade war.

"Just what does your company do, Mr. Le Reau?" I still vacillated between calling him "Mr." and "Jhahn." I focused on the splayed thyme-laced lamb chops on my plate, combining forkfuls of meat with butter-drenched rice *pilav*.

"We sell technology. And we assemble things in Turkey."

Sure. Didn't everybody do that these days?

"What do you make?" The ache in my knees and palms faded. Jean's face was scraped.

"Drainage pipes. Metal and cement. That manner of thing." His voice caught on the last word.

"Are you sure you're okay?"

Jean's jaw tensed. Was he in pain? I reached into my purse for ibuprofen and handed it across.

"Thanks." He took two pills and fell silent. ."Do you ever run into a man named Ahmet Aslan? He owns a big ceramics factory, and I think he does something with cement, too."

"Aslan, Aslan…the name is, how you say, familiar…but no, I do not think I know this Aslan."

How likely was that? Even with Turkey's boom, manufacturers working with cement might know each other. Maybe Le Reau was associated with a very small company. Maybe I should inquire at Istanbul police headquarters about the gunshots. Or maybe one of Haldun's friends could help.

I wasn't quite through with Jean Le Reau, however. "Why were you carrying a gun?"

"Istanbul can be a violent place."

"Does the Turkish government know you have the gun?"

Le Reau's ice-blue eyes looked away. "No. They don't." He didn't ask me to stay silent.

I raised one eyebrow. "I should inform the police. In view of what you did for me tonight, though, I don't plan to tell."

"Police? Good heavens, no. What good would they do?"

Le Reau obviously hadn't met Detective Durmaz. But if he didn't want to say anything to the police, then I would honor his wishes.

After our meal, we had the Galata Tower restaurant call a cab for the short ride back to the Pera Palas. Would I ever go for a relaxed stroll again in the back streets that held so much charm for me in this ancient, complicated city? And what about the true nature of my dinner host? A suspicious character if I ever met one.

35

She continued in very agitating reflections till the sound of Lady Catherine's carriage made her feel how unequal she was to encounter Charlotte's observation, and hurried her away to her room.

Jane Austen, *Pride and Prejudice*

I luxuriated for a few minutes in the warm shower and stepped out into the Turkish robe. My body looked like Raggedy Ann on a hard toddler day: bumps and bruises on arms, legs, knees, elbows; a scratch on my face. Tonight's adventure, together with the Haldun episode and having my room invaded gave me pause... It had been a rough few days.

Haldun wrote enough controversial columns about sensitive subjects to award him the dubious honor of becoming a target for a hit-car. Let's say Haldun was the object there in Çengelköy. But why had the same blue Murat followed me even before I met Haldun?

Something didn't make a lot of sense here. If Haldun had been hurt by someone trying to get me—for whatever reason—I had to figure out why.

The intruder in my room could have been after money and jewels. Typical burglar. Had it been the same person who hit Haldun with the car? I couldn't see the driver. But the car was the same. It had to be more than coincidence.

Maybe the person in my room was looking for something more than money. Something like papers, for example. And since the only papers I had that could be important were those of Peter's that Haldun had given me, could I be holding the solution to Peter's death there in the security box? I looked hard at the bathroom's balcony door. Insecure for a hotel room? Balconies on bathrooms, for heaven's sake! I shivered and clambered out of the warm water to dry myself and put on my nice encloaking nightgown.

About tonight's incident, I had no clue whatsoever. Was someone after me or Jean Le Reau? If me, why? If Le Reau, the same question. Who was he?

I needed answers.

36

"Forgive me for having taken up so much of your time, and accept my best wishes for your health and happiness."

Jane Austen, *Pride and Prejudice*

By morning I felt better. A little makeup helped smooth over some of the bruises. Nobody would see my knees, in any case.

"Is Istanbul always so violent?" I asked Haldun when I got to the Üsküdar Hospital.

"What do you mean?" He lifted his brows. Haldun had a sparkle in his eyes, and his voice was stronger. He was even cooperating with the doctors regarding his leg, which was still in traction but healing. "I'll take care of my leg, and you mind your own business about my smoking," I heard him tell a doctor as I entered the room.

When we were alone, I sat and let loose my pent-up emotions.

"Here you are, injured and almost killed. I call that violent! Last night I went for a quiet dinner with a Frenchman and was shot at near Galata Tower. 'No police,' he said. The night before that there was a shooting incident in Çiçek Pasajı. The police did come to that one." By now my voice had risen and I was standing.

I quickly filled Haldun in on the adventures of the two nights before, in reverse order, starting with the shooting in Çiçek Pasajı.

"So you were there."

Of course Haldun would have his sources.

"What have you heard?" I asked.

"Not very much. Someone just said there was a shooting in Çiçek Pasajı. Tell me about it. Start from the beginning."

I frowned.

"Please, *lütfen*," he added.

"Yes. Okay." We were a team, after all.

I closed my eyes. What had I seen? Aslan's possible wave to someone. Police arrival. Everyone leaving the area. The fact that nothing about the incident came across the wires.

Haldun listened intently. I had many questions, but how could I burden a sick man with them? For starters, what besides the Peter Franklin mystery was going on? I had the feeling we hadn't guessed the half of it. Who bombed the professor's car? Why was someone shooting at me, or at Le Reau, last night? Who wanted the mysterious papers in my room?

I couldn't ask Haldun to deal with all that. But I could ask him a few questions.

"How well does Lawrence Andover know Leila Metin? I saw them having lunch together. And have you heard of an American businessman called Howard Black?"

Haldun perked up. "Andover was eating with Leila?"

"Um hum. And with this American guy."

"I don't know anyone called Black," said Haldun. "Andover knows everyone. But I am interested in Leila's being there. There's been gossip about her and Andover. Not sure how close they are. It wouldn't be the usual kind of thing. Of course, I never like to gossip."

I stifled a laugh. "Of course you don't gossip, Haldun!"

He continued. "There was gossip about Leila and Peter you know."

I winced. Well, Peter did get around. He must have found lush pastures in a romantic city filled with beautiful women like Leila.

Haldun got a thoughtful look on his face and went on. "I worried what Faye Mollington would think. But she seemed to take it very well.

"You mean, Peter and Faye…" Peter had certainly cut a wide swath among hearts in Istanbul. A new perspective on his relationship with me. Obviously, I'd been right to take it casually. But I didn't want to talk about Peter and Faye.

"Never mind them," I said. "I have an appointment later with Leila. I'm going there from here, in fact. I find her an interesting character. Byzantine."

Haldun's eyelids drooped. He was tired. I stood, kissing fingertips that I touched to Haldun's brow. "Just one thing more," I said. "What's Andover's reputation?"

Haldun's brow furrowed and he hesitated. "Andover knows everybody. He's been in Istanbul ages—much longer than most Foreign Service people are allowed to stay. Everybody knows him. His Turkish is excellent, he's socially in demand, and his discretion is legendary."

"But…"

"But Andover is also known as someone who likes to succeed. And I have seen him push others to the side to do it." He plucked at the sheet. "Of course, I have seen almost every successful person do that. Lawrence Andover is an institution in Istanbul. I wouldn't worry about him, if I were you."

Haldun paused. "I mean, you don't need to worry if you aren't attracted to the man. Or if he doesn't want something from you." He tapped his chin with a finger. "I'd call him an opportunist. A sexual opportunist, maybe."

Sexual opportunist? Now there was a term I'd have to remember. "But Peter wasn't?"

"No, Peter just liked women. And it was mutual."

Even though I'd said goodbye, Haldun smiled at me. Perhaps he had the energy to tell me what everyone else seemed to know. I sat down.

"Tell me about Peter's death. I don't know the details."

Haldun nodded as if pleased. He seemed to be waking up. "Well, none of us had seen much of Peter for awhile. He had distanced himself from the usual journalist group. I thought it was because of Leila and Faye. There was a big reception at the Italian Consulate. We all were invited. Their Foreign Minister was in town. Peter told somebody—Faye Mollington, I think—he'd be there, but he didn't show up. The party was held in a Bosphorus hotel in Bebek, on the European side."

"Was that where they found Peter's body?"

"Yes. Under the veranda that goes out over the water. That night, after the party, the police called the U.S. consulate to say that a corpse with American papers on it had been found."

"So that's how Andover came to identify the body."

"Right. The Consulate handled the whole thing, including Peter's cremation, which his sister said was his wish. We held a memorial service for him in the little Protestant church on Istiklal Boulevard. Everyone felt sad. Peter was one of us."

"What was Leila Metin's reaction to Peter's death?"

"Leila has never been the same since. Believe it or not, she used to smile a lot more than she does now. Faye was very, very upset also."

Ah yes, my buddy Faye. "She doesn't seem upset now. Is that some kind of performance for me?"

Haldun sighed. "Really, how can I know? I am a mere man. I have limits. You and Faye must work out how she feels. I cannot see much interest in the subject, myself."

I stood again, and Ayla Kutlu came in. She had a basket of food for Haldun, and subtle aromas escaped from the covered dishes. Behind her, a white shadow slipped into the room and onto Haldun's bed.

"Oh, hello, Ayla *Hanım*," I said, as I petted Sultana. "Your husband looks quite good but I think you must keep him here so he doesn't run out and start working."

A rare smile lit Ayla's face, perhaps at my poor Turkish.

"Oh, yes," she said. "I will keep him away from work."

Haldun stared at the basket, stroking the purring cat. His face was paler than before.

"My dear, is that water *börek* I smell? Did you by any chance bring *çorba*? Perhaps if I have some soup I will feel better…"

You old faker. I bit back a smile. I bet you got by with this from your mother, too. Ayla pushed aside her headscarf and ministered to her man.

"*Allaha ısmarladık*," I said on my way out the door. "Goodbye and God bless."

37

*"And what has been done, what has been at-
tempted, to recover her?"*

Jane Austen, *Pride and Prejudice*

Leila was at home when I arrived at the red house overlooking the
Bosphorus. From that hill you could look straight across to the great
open fortress of Rumeli Hisar on the European side. Her house was
charming—something I had noticed in passing on my prior visit, the day
of Haldun's accident.

On entering, I soaked up an impressionistic feast of reds and blues
and golds and rustic wood polished to a sheen. The coziness of the sitting
room was enhanced by the wide view across the Bosphorus, framed by
a few evergreen branches outside the window—some of the old cypress
trees, it appeared.

Leila's face and eyes were as stony as they had been ever since I had
met her. I tried to picture her laughing, perhaps up into Peter's face. It
was hard work. On more than one count. I was learning too much about
Peter during this investigation.

"Please sit down," she offered in the most formal of terms.

"Thank you." I sat in a comfortable armchair covered in smooth Turkish wool with a fanciful design. The pattern had deer, rabbits, and wolves
running an endless chase of self-preservation and predation, surrounded
by vine tendrils. They resembled something I had seen recently. In a corner of the room was a pile of some lovely fabric pieces with half-drawn
designs on them: carnations, tulips, bluebells, and curving flame-shaped
cypress trees. Could I go over for a better look? No, I would be a polite
guest.

"I gather that my colleague, Faye Mollington, has not yet arrived. I
took the liberty of inviting her to join us."

"I know Ms. Mollington," acknowledged Leila. "I did not know of
her interest in ceramics." Was that a hint of iciness in her tone? A contrast
to what Haldun had told me.

Faye was now fifteen minutes late, and who knew how long Leila
would be willing to entertain questions?

"Actually, we are both interested in what aspect of ceramics Professor Fener was involved in just before the bombing." I would give Faye very good notes.

Silence. Leila must have been expecting this question, but she took her time answering.

"Oktay *Bey*, Professor Fener, was expert at dating pottery and ceramics found at archeological digs. It is not a very controversial subject." Leila got up to go to the kitchen door and ask someone to bring tea. I tried to make sure we didn't get off the topic.

"What aspect of Professor Fener's life was controversial, if I may ask?"

I kept waiting for the doorbell as, once again, Leila sat quietly. No ring.

Finally, an answer: "Some people thought he was leftist." The statement was in a surprisingly small voice. Was Leila embarrassed, reluctant to pass on hearsay information, or trying to protect the professor from something? I couldn't tell.

"Who would object to that, if it were true?" My tea in the delicate gold-rimmed glass was cool enough to drink, so I took a sip, lifting the glass by the rim with the hand not busy with notes. "I mean, isn't that kind of an outdated argument these days?"

Leila's tone went from chilly to ice. "Yes, I think it is old-fashioned. I really do not know who could object to something like this. And I am sorry. Your friend has not come. I must work. Please tell Ms. Mollington I am sorry to miss her."

I rose as gracefully as I could. Thank heaven I had asked a couple of questions. Didn't get that much, but at least Leila knew where my interests lay. You never know when placing a hare down a hole will bring on a predator of some sort. If Leila had something to hide, maybe she would show her hand. If she had nothing to hide, maybe someone else's hand would come into view.

As I walked down the hill where Haldun had been struck, I looked for Faye. Where was she? Faye is the type of journalist who never turns down the chance for a story. It was unlike her to miss a meeting she'd promised to attend.

ℬℬ

"...We have tried two or three subjects already without success, and what we are to talk of next I cannot imagine."

Jane Austen, *Pride and Prejudice*

Because of my precipitous dismissal by Leila, I was early for my drinks appointment at Andover's house and had a little time to myself after walking down the hill. The late afternoon sun was turning hills on both sides of the Bosphorus a chilly pink by the time I arrived at the wharf and the bustling little hub of Çengelköy village. The fishermen's catch lay out on rough wood tables for commuters to buy and take home. The fishy aroma seemed to attract the buyers. I didn't find it all that pleasant.

My feet, despite my boots, were cold and numb from the walk, so I turned into one of the waterside restaurants for a warm place to sit and have a nip of something before heading to Andover's. I knocked the mud off my boots before entering the room. A waiter was lighting candles on the tables, adding focus to the low-wattage electric lamps. You could still see across the room, but each lamp created a bright circle.

I kept my trenchcoat over my shoulders as I ordered a glass of Kavaklidere wine and a couple of *meze* items: flaky cheese-and-parsley *börek* and green beans in olive oil, tomatoes, and garlic. I would regret this once I got to Andover's well-stocked house, I knew, but it was only 4:30 and I was starved.

My table sat along the restaurant's windows, so I could see across the water to Rumeli Hisar. In the foreground a ferry came in, docked briefly, and pushed off, making a warning whoop once in each direction.

A smattering of other customers sat at tables. I stretched out my booted feet, looked out the window and sipped the Kavaklidere. Ahh. My favorite time of day in my favorite season in my favorite city. I took out my worn copy of *Strolling Through Istanbul* by Hilary Sumner-Boyd and John Freely. I'd left the other books at the hotel.

Despite massive population changes in the city since the book was first published in 1972, you can still take the historic pilgrimages suggested in the guide; nobody is going to tear down a mosque or a church or an aquaduct. My good friend, the noted Turkish writer Aziz Nesin, had said, "Istanbul must be a beautiful city. We Turks have been trying to ruin it for over a thousand years, and we still haven't managed to do it." Aziz *Bey* was a satirist, now much-lamented by his broad reading public in Turkey and neighboring countries.

Nineteen seventy-two in Istanbul. Memories were thick and, in some cases, heavy. My dad was teaching math at Boğaziçi University, which used to be Robert College. Founded by Christian missionaries, the school had then become an elite private institution and finally was taken over by the Turkish government. Boğaziçi University had the most spectacular location in Istanbul, high on the hill above the great open fort of Rumeli Hisar. I could see it from where I now sat. My childhood neighborhood, full of memories. In spring, the almond trees on the campus burst into clouds of pink, even before the leaves on the many trees had begun to show.

Those missionaries knew how to live, let me tell you. Each house had plenty of space around it, and each enjoyed a slightly different view of the shipping lanes of the Bosphorus, with the hills of Asia rising beyond. At night, you could hear the nightingales sing.

Daily living in Istanbul was addictive to my parents, though they didn't stay long. Friends were always at hand, with traditions of hospitality and long conversations over tea or *rakı*. The food was great. Leftist terrorism was a minor nuisance, although some of it was aimed directly at Americans in those days. You just had to remember to check carefully under your car before starting the engine.

Poor Oktay Fener hadn't realized that the danger from the past had lapped over to the present. A different cast of characters, with different victims in mind. Terror had done nothing more than change its spots over the years.

I peered again out the window and felt an electric shock through my body. The handsome young man who had followed me since I came to Istanbul was boarding a ferry bound for Beşiktaş and Karaköy on the European side. His slender form hunched into the wind; he threw his cigarette onto the wharf before walking up the gangplank. He was alone. My heart beat faster.

My "shadow" may have been near Leila's red house at the same time I was. I shivered. Had he followed me?

As more huddled forms with umbrellas and raincoats made their way to the ferry, I caught my breath again. There was Faye! I half-stood, ready to run outside to call out to her.

I sat down quickly. Faye looked...furtive, somehow. As if she were trying to blend in, become invisible. Faye had a scarf over her flame-red hair and a determined look on her face, as always. The ferrymen were pulling in the ropes when Faye jumped nimbly aboard. Was she following my follower?

I lost sight of her and the other passengers as they moved further into the dimly-lit cabins of the ferry. The old white vessel was released from the pier and gave a whoop as it moved away, churning the water in the rain.

Gone were my mellow memories of the past. Where had Faye been, and why had she not joined me at Leila's? Would Leila have talked more or less with Faye present? Why did Faye take that ferry? Was she in pursuit of the handsome young man?

Along with my mood, the day had changed from gold to dusk, and it was time for me to make one last visit to the ladies' room to tidy up before drinks and dinner with Lawrence Andover.

39

To walk into it is to walk into the
color and zest of the late flower-
ing of Byzantine art... The figures
seem to move, have depth, glow...

Mary Lee Settle, *Turkish Reflections*

It seemed sensible to walk the few streets to Andover's house, since it wasn't quite dark. I have always felt safe in Istanbul, but now I studied every car along the route.

I knocked on Andover's door, using the big metal knocker, and was admitted by his man.

"Hello, hello," greeted my host, as I was ushered into his elegant living room. Andover rose from the couch nearest the windows to shake my hand. Maybe the serenity of his home would help make up for my current edginess.

When my drink had been ordered (*rakı* this time), I asked if I could use the telephone.

I called Bayram, who was still at the office, of course. He assured me that no news story needed my urgent attention. As he gave me the run-down on what was what at the *Tribune* office, I enjoyed again the beautiful objects with which Andover surrounded himself. On the small, highly-polished cherry telephone desk sat a vase so perfect it made me catch my breath. The pattern of delicate red carnations and purplish-blue hyacinths twining themselves around a cypress tree on a white background. All the colors were vibrant, but most amazing was the red. It resembled the red of the special Iznik pottery of the last half of the sixteenth century. Some wonderful tiles in the Topkapı *harem* had the same red. They were genuine; this presumably was not. But what a vase. What a red...

And, oh look, there was a tile, as well. It was set deceptively to look utilitarian, like a hot plate. The tile was cobalt blue and yellow, with a stylized animal pattern—dogs, rabbits, deer—a rather unusual combination in Ottoman ceramics. Where did he shop for antiques? I had never seen such beautiful replicas of old pieces.

Back in the living room and seated comfortably, I picked up my drink.

"That vase—and the tile—on your telephone desk are exquisite!" I murmured. "Where on earth did you find them?"

Rain beat against the window where we sat. It was dark now. Lamplight reflected on the glass.

"Ah, yes. Those pieces. I have a very special antique dealer who sold me that vase. It is nice, isn't it? Not the real Iznik, of course, but about as close as an artist could come. The tile, too, is very good." He was already raising his hand in admonition. "Don't think I will tell you where I found them. I confess I would not relish having competition for what I want to buy."

"Don't worry," I said. "The price of such work would be beyond my means!"

This led to an animated discussion about ceramics and pottery, which we both loved. We talked about floral patterns on white backgrounds, especially those that boasted circlets of red carnations. Lawrence—yes, I would call him Lawrence—told me about the short-lived animal period in the Iznik patternry in the sixteenth century, when lions and snakes and wolves were depicted chasing various prey, such as deer and rabbits.

Leila must have chosen to copy those patterns on the fabrics in her house. Lawrence pointed out that a little later some Iznik potters may have copied the Yuan blue-and-white ceramics that showed peacocks, singly or in pairs, sitting in trees or the midst of burgeoning flowers. Didn't the Chinese believe that peacocks were especially sensitive to beautiful women? They would have made appropriate decorations for the Sultan's *harem*.

It was a discussion between fellow aficianados, definitely. I warmed to Lawrence and told him about the tray I had found in a Kadıköy glass and mirror shop that an art historian friend said came from fourteenth century Konya. I had presented the tray to a small museum in Ankara, where I knew the curator.

"Everybody keeps their treasures," I acknowledged ruefully. "Sometimes I wish I had kept that tray. I don't even know that the next curator will take care of it!"

Lawrence pursed his lips, though he had a twinkle in his eye. "Much better to follow the rules, my dear. I always do."

I smiled sedately as we donned our raincoats. He had a car waiting to take us to Ismet Baba's, a nearby restaurant.

Lawrence was an amusing dinner partner, lending credence to my suspicions that his earlier observations were tongue-in-cheek. He had more of a sense of humor than I'd given him credit for. Even had that not been the case, I would have enjoyed the meal.

Ismet Baba's overlooked the Bosphorus and specialized in fish, laid out on ice in a glass-fronted case. The customers seemed to be regulars, calling the waiters by name. "Hüsnü! More *meze*! Bring *imam bayıldı*!"

We, too, ate *imam bayıldı*—eggplant, tomato, and onion cooked in olive oil—so delicious a dish that apparently the *imam* fainted when he ate it, giving it its name. We also had buttery *sigara börek*, a pastry shaped like a fat cigar that enfolded bits of white cheese or meat and parsley.

For my entree, I chose panfried *barbunya*, red mullet. Lawrence ordered grilled swordfish kebab. The fish—cooked just flaky enough, not too little, not too much—came accompanied by a huge plate of the addictively-tart *roka* leaves, arugula.

The simplicity of the fresh fish, the juicy red tomato slices beside the fish, the dark green *roka*, and the perfectly-fried wedges of golden potato balanced exquisitely with the rainy night and turbulent Bosphorus outside. I relaxed and enjoyed myself. Lawrence's appreciation of beauty fanned a spark within me.

We were savoring the last of our entrees, sharing some rather malicious and unconscionable speculation on certain politicians in our own country, when a man approached and greeted Lawrence. He was hawknosed in the typical Turkish way and quite good-looking, especially when he smiled.

"Hello," he said. "I wondered if I would find you here."

90

*At dawn, the first call to prayer
came from the Blue Mosque, and
was echoed, fainter and fainter
in the distance from minarets all
over the city of mosques.*

Mary Lee Settle, *Turkish Reflections*

Aytem Fener finished her prayers for her father's soul, bending forehead down to her small prayer rug, straightening to her knees, rising and beginning over again. She and her mother were staying with relatives in Bahçelievler a few blocks from their home. The memories of that house where the fatal car blast had deprived them of father and husband were too painful. The house was being repaired, but would she ever feel comfortable there again?

Aytem would find out who had killed her beloved father. Such a gentle man! Who could have a motive?

She would need to see Professor Perihan Kıraz, her father's colleague at the university and on the Iznik dig. Maybe Perihan *Hanım* would have an idea for a lead.

And maybe they could work together to discover the truth.

91

*...The tense, expectant air in the
room brought back memories of the
séances we had witnessed as children
a quarter century ago in a house in
one of the back streets of Nisantas...*

Orhan Pamuk, *Snow*

As the man walked up to our table at Ismet Baba's, Lawrence had a
strange look on his face. Had he choked on a fish bone? He rose quickly,
dabbing at his mouth with his napkin.

"Irfan, how good to see you!" Then, with a gesture my direction,
"Elizabeth, you must meet İrfan Algar, the 'Dan Rather' of Turkey."

"Oh, yes. You're on the nightly news, aren't you? Pleased to meet
you." I held out my hand. Where had I seen İrfan before? He looked
different off-camera, but even his off-camera persona seemed familiar.

Lawrence invited İrfan to join us for coffee, and he eagerly accepted.
Conversation wasn't at all stilted, but my two companions had some
hidden agenda I couldn't understand. They compared notes on the latest
gossip in Turkish political circles; they spoke of people they both knew
and either liked or disliked.

I ate my fish in silence, soaking up political impressions from the
conversation flowing around me. From time to time I was graciously
included in the discussion, even when it fell into Turkish. Lawrence was
clearly more fluent than I.

İrfan and Lawrence knew each other very well. I was a third wheel,
even though they joked and laughed the whole time and included me
charmingly.

At one point, İrfan asked Lawrence how Haldun Kutlu was doing.

Lawrence turned to me with an eyebrow raised. "Elizabeth here has
probably seen Kutlu most recently. Any news?"

"Haldun *Bey* is recovering nicely," I said.

92

Resul Efendi closed his eyes and solemnly tore up the letter. Suddenly, like lightning, he had a vision of his resignation being accepted, of himself without a job, without a penny in the world. A wave of dizziness passed over him and a bitter emptiness froze his heart.

Yaşar Kemal, *Anatolian Tales*

After Lawrence paid for our dinner we all rose.

"You've been very kind, but I'll find my way back to the hotel. I have an early start tomorrow."

Lawrence and İrfan saw me to a taxi, carefully told the driver where I wanted to go and how (across the first bridge, not the second!) and waited on the curb as my taxi pulled away.

Glancing back at the pair, I suddenly remembered where I had seen İrfan Algar in the flesh before. He had been in the elevator that first day I had gone to the *Tribune* office and met Faye. How unprofessional of me to not even know my office neighbors yet.

The desk clerk handed me a message when I stopped to get my key. Detective Durmaz asked that I call him on an urgent matter. I raced to the old elevator and chafed at its stately pace.

It had been a long day. I slipped my shoes and clothes off, donned the robe from the back of the bathroom door and reached for a bottle of water on the coffee table. The call went through almost immediately.

"Mehmet *Bey*?"

"Ms. Darcy. I need to talk to you. Are you available now?"

How can a person be available to the police in bathrobe and wide sleepy yawns?

"Do I have a choice?" I asked.

"Not really," he said. Detective Durmaz didn't sound amused.

"Then I will get dressed. Will you come here?" I asked hopefully.

"I will send a car for you," he said, and rang off.

I reluctantly put the robe back on its hook and donned underwear, jeans, and a sweatshirt. I grabbed my trenchcoat, and returned to the lobby to meet my unwelcome escort.

93

"Your conjecture is totally wrong, I assure you..."

Jane Austen, *Pride and Prejudice*

Viewers of "Law and Order" probably think all police headquarters have white walls. Well, that may be true in some cities, but not in a lot of others. What you tend to find, as I did that night in Istanbul, is a sickly gun-metal green that is guaranteed to make suspects admit everything in five minutes, just to get out of the place. As I sat there waiting to be interviewed by Mehmet Bey, I took out the last thing I'd thrown into my purse, my solace of last resort, *Pride and Prejudice,* and began to read the part where Elizabeth and Jane are entertained at the Bingleys and Darcy begins to be enchanted by Elizabeth.

As I read the familiar and comforting words, I sneaked surreptitious glances around at the fellow suspects, or witnesses, or whoever, that shared the dingy police space. Most were male, and most were fairly young. One bearded man seemed to be studying for a university exam, his head buried in a book; another was smoking non-stop, tension in every muscle; the single other woman in the waiting room was, I guessed, a prostitute. Her unkempt hair was thick and glossy, and she looked as though she had risen from a deep sleep. She added to the smoky air with her own chain-smoking. A bit worse off than me. I, at least, had had time to take a bath.

Then Mehmet *Bey* was at his door, beckoning me to his office. His expression was grim. Gripping *Pride and Prejudice* tightly in one hand, I joined the detective and was asked to sit down.

"I would like to know your relationship with Leila Metin," said Durmaz.

Now this was totally unexpected.

"Leila Metin? I have met her twice, no, three times. I don't know her well. Why?"

"And do you know her brother, also?" Mehmet *Bey* took a deep drag of his cigarette and scowled.

"I have not met her brother. May I ask why you are asking?" Was I suspected of knowing something? Or, God forbid, of doing something?

A pause sharp enough to split Mehmet *Bey's* cigarette smoke in two.

"Erol Metin has been killed," said the policeman. "I need to know everything he has been doing, and everybody who was in recent contact with him."

My thoughts flew to a gray-eyed girl with a scarf around her hair and a determined look, getting onto the ferry just behind a handsome young man.

"May I see a picture of Erol Metin?"

He showed me a photo. I gasped. A young man looked sternly into the camera in what may have been a school picture. My "Adonis" who had been following me! Yes, now I could see a resemblance to Leila's fine bone structure and profile.

Mehmet *Bey* slowly handed me another picture, his gaze never leaving my face. A young man, clearly dead. The same person, though bereft now of spirit and life.

I sat quietly for a moment. "I doubt I have information that will help you because I haven't met the man." How could I explain that I hadn't told the police I'd been followed several times by Erol Metin, or describe my visit to Leila in trying to solve a murder case I thought the Istanbul police had bungled?

Detective Durmaz's eyes narrowed. "Ms. Darcy. We are becoming concerned about certain Western journalists operating here in Istanbul. If you know anything, we need to know."

"Journalists?" That surprised me. My voice rose. "What could you possibly mean?"

"I mean Peter Franklin, of your own newspaper. I mean Ms. Faye Mollington of the London News. I mean, perhaps, you yourself."

"What?" I was genuinely astonished. "I really have no idea what you're talking about. What could journalists have to do with someone like Erol Metin?"

"Hah! Our question exactly. What would Western press people want with a spoiled young man who just happens to belong to the Silver Wolves? You do know about that organization, don't you?"

"Well, yes, I've heard of them, but I have no idea—other than checking out possible terrorism plots, as you police do—why any of my colleagues would consort with the Silver Wolves."

Detective Durmaz's expression didn't change, but he seemed to believe me at last.

"Ms. Darcy. You are free to go. But do not leave Istanbul for any reason without checking with me. And may I suggest that you be careful with who you associate."

"Associate?" I stood, suddenly exhausted but equally on my guard.

"You have been noticed having dinner with certain people."

"Well, yes, of course I've had dinner, with *many* people! I am a free woman, you know."

Was that admiration in Mehmet *Bey's* eyes? Hard to tell, among the flecks of flint. Fury heated me.

"Yes, Ms. Darcy. You are a free woman." A female police officer with an easel and other art equipment was waiting at the door. The interview was over.

I headed for the Pera, in a taxi this time, went straight to my room, and, feeling the need after the police station, hopped into the shower for a quick wash. The warm water, scented with oil I rubbed on my body, helped me think things through.. Peter. Leila. Erol, her brother. Haldun and Faye. What connected them? What was going on? Distracted with my problems, I left the shower running longer than I usually do, especially in developing countries. Water is a scarce resource. I try not to waste it.

Suitably bathed and scented, I was ready to return to the immediate present. I phoned Faye, but her answering machine picked up.

"Hi, Faye," I recorded. "This is Elizabeth, wondering where you were today. Call me when you get a chance. 'Bye."

94

The tumult of her mind was now pain-
fully great. She knew not how to sup-
port herself, and from actual weakness
sat down and cried for half an hour.

Jane Austen, *Pride and Prejudice*

Sleep remained elusive. Detective Durmaz's news had shocked me into wakefulness.

Erol Metin, dead! Had he been the one who ran down Haldun on that Çengelköy hillside? Faye missing our appointment with Leila and apparently following Erol onto the ferry—something I knew but Durmaz didn't. What would Leila do now? Poor woman, to lose her brother this way. What would the police do about all this?

And which of my recent nights out had spawned Mehmet *Bey's* warning? I had spent time with Faye, of course, with Le Reau, with Ahmet Aslan, and with Lawrence Andover. Surely hospital visits with Haldun didn't count. Or tea with Leila Metin. If I hadn't been trying to say as little as possible, lest the truth about Faye slip out, I would have asked Detective Durmaz for particulars. As it was, anyone else's guess was as good as mine.

I turned on the light and tried again to telephone Faye, and once more got her answering machine. I didn't leave a message this time. It was two o'clock in the morning. I took a sleeping pill. Things were getting complicated.

* * * *

Before going down to breakfast, I tried Faye's number once more. Again, no answer. Again, I left no message. When Faye would return home? Until I knew more, I had nothing to say.

95

"Was not this some excuse for incivility, if I was uncivil?"

Jane Austen, *Pride and Prejudice*

When I entered the Pera's dining room for breakfast, sunbeams illuminated dust motes across the tables in the middle. Sitting at one of the tables, his thinning hair resembling a halo, was Jean Le Reau. I walked purposefully over to him.

"Is this seat taken?"

Le Reau, always the gentleman, stood quickly and indicated a chair at his table with an expansive hand. "Meez Darcy. An unexpected pleasure, I am sure. Sit down, please sit down." Was that a twinkle in his light blue eyes?

Morning is not one of my better times, especially after I have been interrogated by the police the previous evening, have not slept well—and I have had two cups of coffee. Nonetheless, I was curious about Le Reau, especially since our little adventure together. Now I was afraid he might disappear, too, like Faye.

"Yes, thank you," I muttered, signalling for the waiter and the coffee as I sank into the chair.

"Nice day, eez it not?" said Le Reau.

"Why don't you cut the polite nothings and tell me what you are really doing in Turkey?" I answered. "As someone who has shared your line of fire, I think I deserve some answers."

Le Reau stirred his coffee very, very carefully. "I am afraid I have nothing to tell you now," he said.

Was that regret in his tone?

He continued. "Perhaps soon we can, you know, talk of some things."

"Are you aware there was a murder last night? From what I've seen of you, and experienced with you, I would think that might be right down your alley." I was definitely not at my best in the morning!

"Who was killed?"

"A man named Erol Metin. The brother of a woman who works at Topkapı museum."

"Erol Metin. Hmmm. No, I believe I do not know the man. Is it your news story?"

I couldn't read the quiet, light-blue eyes.

"No, it is not 'my news story.' I was questioned by the police about it. I thought maybe you had more information than I do."

As I said the word "police," Jean Le Reau jerked almost imperceptibly. Had he something to fear from that quarter?

"I am sorry. I cannot help you. Please, to have some more olives and toast?"

There are degrees of ability to be frustrating. Jean Le Reau was quickly rising to the nth degree in my book. I felt that showing anything of the kind would be playing into his hand.

"Well, got to run. See you later," I said, finishing my last bite in haste.

This time, I left him at the table to pay the bill. Served the man right.

96

*"Young women should always
be guarded and tended, according to their situation in life."*

Jane Austen, *Pride and Prejudice*

Faye Mollington took a deep breath and tried to calm her racing heart. Three separate stories had woven themselves into one story. Following that story's fabric was her career—in at least two senses of the word.

She was not sure where she was being taken, or by whom. Judging by the smell, there was dust and mold in the vehicle. Good thing she was not the allergic type. The blindfold was uncomfortable but she couldn't remove it with her hands tied tight behind her back.

This story might just end Faye's career. In fact, it could end everything, including her life.

97

*"...Perhaps this concealment, this
disguise, was beneath me. It is done,
however, and it was done for the best."*

Jane Austen, *Pride and Prejudice*

I took a taxi down the hill from the Pera Palas and caught the ferry to Üsküdar. Haldun was out of traction and was just finishing a physical therapy session as I arrived.

"Sit down," he panted, waving his therapist off with an imperious hand.

"You wouldn't be so out of breath if you stopped smoking," I couldn't resist saying. A glare was my only answer.

I asked about the cat Sultana and Ayla *Hanım*—not in that order—and glanced into the hall. Empty. I closed the door.

"Haldun, things are happening too fast for me. Erol Metin has been killed!" The words tumbled out. Damn. I had resolved to go easy on Haldun. He was now settling himself back into the hospital bed.

"Hmmm. Yes. Someone called and told me that, actually. What do you think happened?"

"I have no idea. But listen, Haldun. Faye Mollington was with Metin last night, or right behind him. I didn't tell that to the police. I didn't know it was Erol until the police showed me pictures. And now they seem to be suspicious of me."

"Are we talking about Mehmet Durmaz here? Homicide division?"

"Yes, that's right. Detective Inspector Mehmet Durmaz himself. He told me not to leave Istanbul."

Haldun was smoking away like a chimney, of course, polluting what would otherwise have been a nice clean room.

"Durmaz is a good man," he said.

Heat crept over my face. "Oh, I see. You agree with him, then, that some of us Western journalists are involved in things we should have left alone."

Very childish. Old habits are hard to break. Haldun looked amused.

"What journalist isn't?" he asked. "You can't blame the police for wondering."

I found myself grinning through my irritation. "You can't completely blame them," I acknowledged. "Is there anything about Peter and, say, Faye, that I should be aware of?"

What was that sound? I walked toward the closed door as I spoke. I jerked it open.

98

She could not yet recover from the
surprise of what had happened; it was
impossible to think of anything else...

Jane Austen, *Pride and Prejudice*

A nurse stood there. I hadn't seen her before. She may have had business near the door; she may not. I would take the low view and assume no innocence.

"*Efendim?*" I asked coldly. I stared at the attractive young woman with all the authority I could summon. *Efendim* can mean lots of things, including "my good man" or "my good woman" when said in the correct tone of voice.

The nurse had the grace to blush and look quickly down at her feet. "*Bir şey yok,*" she muttered. "Nothing. Just checking on the patient."

I didn't believe her for a minute. The only question was, was she just a snoop or working for someone? If so, who? On the face of things, it would be someone official, who could get her into a position like this, at a hospital. But Istanbul is a tricky place. Someone could have contacted a person already in Üsküdar Hospital, and offered some incentives for surveillance.

Or, of course, she was just curious. Haldun had a reputation in Istanbul and many eminent people had come to see him.

I'd keep an eye on this particular nurse, and suggested that Haldun do so, too. Going back into the room, I glanced back. The nurse walked down the corridor. I closed the door with a definitive click.

Then and only then did Haldun and I talk.

99

Eat and drink with your friends, but
don't do business with them.

Turkish proverb

Howard Black stretched long legs in his suite at the Çirağan Palace along the Bosphorus. The ice in his glass clinked satisfyingly on Black Label Scotch.

He liked these trips to Istanbul. What a change from Houston! Well, Houston was okay in its way, and it was home. But the view from the Çirağan was incomparable: great cargo ships carrying oil (being Texan, he loved oil); ferries carrying passengers; a few fancy speedboats. And on the other side, in Asia, pine and cypress trees lined the tops of the hills while old wooden yalis made a line of tempting residences along the water. In between the tops of the hills and the Bosphorus, some modern houses, built at enormous cost both to their owners and to the beauty of the city, tried to mar the view.

Black just hoped his business deal would go through. He really didn't care whether it looked attractive to outsiders or not.

He was from Texas.

100

But self, though it would intrude, could not engross her.

Jane Austen, *Pride and Prejudice*

It was downright frustrating. There had been a murder. I knew who the victim was and who might have been close to him at the time of death, but until an announcement was made of Metin's demise, I couldn't even write a news story, to say nothing of asking people questions. Why didn't the police make an announcement? My position with them was so tenuous it was best not to break what Detective Durmaz might consider the confidences of the night before.

I wanted to question Leila Metin, but even I didn't have the unmitigated gall to ask for an interview at a time like this. The woman seemed unhappy enough to start with; losing her only brother would be a devastating blow.

There was one thing in my favor. While I suspected that Leila and Erol Metin were not very religious people, they were, by their names, Moslem. Moslem ritual calls for burial within twenty-four hours of death. The body is usually taken to the noon prayers at the nearest mosque and then interred in a simple box, with none of the fanfare and expense of Western funerals. To me, it had always seemed an unusually benign and natural way to deal with death—so unlike our Western system, where every death is considered a failure of science and a major disaster. And a lucrative opportunity for the undertakers.

Part of the Moslem ritual is to welcome to the funeral anyone who wishes to say goodbye to the departed. It might not work, but I'd go to the mosque nearest Leila's house in Çengelköy for noon prayers. Wait. Women usually pay their respects at the home, rather than at the mosque. So I popped into a shop near the Üsküdar hospital to buy a large, modest scarf, and headed for Leila's red house in Çengelköy.

101

"...Dear Lizzy, only consider what he must have suffered. Such a disappointment! And...having to relate such a thing of his sister! It is really too distressing. I am sure you must feel it so."

Jane Austen, *Pride and Prejudice*

I took a taxi from the hospital to Çengelköy.

The car rounded the last curve before the top of Leila's little overlook, and the house seemed quiet, although there were a few cars parked parallel along the narrow street. The air of desolation was more poignant than crowds of weeping mourners. Nonetheless, a number of neighbors stood outside their houses in small groups. From what I knew of Leila, she probably had not welcomed their participation in something so private as her last farewell to her brother.

I asked the driver to wait, then went to the door and knocked. A long silence, and I was about to turn away when a soft voice—Leila's maid—asked who was there.

"Elizabeth Darcy," I answered.

The door slowly opened. The maid bit her lip and ducked her head. I asked her gently if Leila *Hanım* were within.

"*Evet. Burada.* She's here," said the girl.

"May I see her?" I asked.

The girl led me through the hallway into the elegant, cozy sitting room. Today, the room was cold because the beautifully-tiled coal stove had not been lit. A number of well-dressed women sat around in uncomfortable silence. To one side, a small group of girls in jeans huddled together miserably—perhaps the only real mourners except for Leila, as they shared Erol's age.

The simple coffin containing Erol's body was set in the middle of the room. The wooden coffin was closed, the body had already received its ritual washing. Leila was not to be seen.

I went around the room shaking hands in the polite, noncommittal Turkish way, indicating to one and all that I was there as a friend. The young girls cried, genuinely upset. School friends of the young man? Or perhaps female members of the semi-illicit group he had joined? Unlike the middle-class neighbors outside, the other guests seemed uncomfortable with the rituals; they shifted in their seats, wrinkling their silks and checking their wristwatches, desperate to leave. That couldn't happen, of course, until the chief mourner had put in her appearance.

We did not wait long. Leila Metin walked in, a haggard shadow of her usual self. She moved like an old woman as she entered the roomful of colleagues and women of influence who, unlike the neighbors, could not be turned away. Mechanically, she made the rounds to hear the beautiful words of ritualized comfort and receive a gentle kiss on the cheek.

"May Allah give him eternal life. May Allah give you peace."

When Leila reached me, she stiffened. She put out her hand and I shook it carefully and said the same words that had made their way around the room: "*Başını sağ olsun. Allah rahatlık versin.*" She nodded, no expression on her face.

The only man in the room had been the *imam* who was leading Arabic prayers that few repeated after him. The old man in the worn suit seemed as out of place in this group as I was; clearly, the Metins and their friends were far from devout.

As soon as Leila had made the rounds, it was time to go to the mosque. Husbands had gathered in another room, but they came out now to carry the coffin to the little mosque that sat under the leafless plane trees near the central square.

There were tears from most of the women—though not the stony-faced Leila—as the procession of men carrying the coffin left the red house. These were Turks, after all, and Turks express their emotions overtly. How many of those in the little party really knew Erol, or cared about him? Some of the younger men seemed to be the most affected; four of them insisted on being the ones to carry his coffin. Their eyes were dark, grief etched in lines on their faces; youth acknowledging that life is not unending, even for someone their own age.

I stood with the women on the veranda of Leila's house. Below us, two members of the male entourage seemed out of character. Both wore trench-coats, but that was not what set them apart. One look at their impassive faces and watchful eyes revealed them: cops.

However tragic this young man's death—and given what was rumored about him, that statement could be challenged—my own situation was becoming more and more perilous. A report had probably already gone to Mehmet *Bey* that one of the suspicious players in the drama had attended Erol Metin's funeral. I was willing to bet I would be asked to explain my presence here today, and I wasn't at all sure what I would answer if asked: "Just felt like making the gesture." "It seemed the place to be." Actually, I felt my reasons might be more complex than merely "getting the story" would dictate.

As I climbed into my taxi, I took off the scarf. All the way to the ferry landing and on the little trip across the Bosphorus I thought about the mysterious Erol Metin, about Leila and her grief, and about one person I would very much like to run into now: Faye Mollington.

I glanced over my shoulder as I was about to get off the ferry. A man with an impassive expression and a nondescript raincoat stood behind me. Like Erol Metin, I had become an object of interest to the police. What an honor.

102

Surprise was the least of her feelings on this development.

Jane Austen, *Pride and Prejudice*

By the time I reached the *Tribune* office, the official reports of the Metin death were on the news wires. They quoted the police spokesman as saying only that investigations were ongoing. No reference was made to the young man's alleged terrorist connections. Leila Metin, "a prominent curator from the Topkapı Museum," was listed as the only survivor. Bayram and I put together a brief account for the paper and sent it to Washington.

When we finished, I turned to Bayram.

"I haven't heard from Faye Mollington for a day or two. How is her office handling her absence? Do they know where she is?"

Bayram dug into his worn briefcase.

"I believe, Ms. Darcy, yes, I believe I have key to Ms. Mollington's office. Yes, here it is. Do you want I should go look?"

I was up in a flash, hitting my thigh on the edge of the desk. "That's okay, Bayram. Give me the key and I'll look."

Limping slightly, I made my way as fast as possible down the hall, Bayram right behind me. Okay, fair enough. He, after all, had had the key. Why did he have the key? And why didn't he tell me earlier?

At office number 64, we stopped and unlocked the door. Lights were on. Had someone been there? Faye didn't have an assistant, but perhaps she had left them on when she went out yesterday. It seemed years since I'd seen her boarding that ferry behind Erol Metin. In fact it was less than twenty-four hours.

"Check the wire copy machine," I ordered Bayram. "We need to know when stories were last pulled." Faye and Faye alone would have pulled copy; it might give us a hint as to when she had left the office—or whether she'd been back. While Bayram searched for the elusive end to the roll of wire copy lying in graceful mounds on the floor, I glanced at things on Faye's desk. They were pretty standard for a relatively sloppy journalist, which most of us are: notebooks everywhere, computer printouts of unfinished reports, a blinking answering machine. Maybe this could tell us when Faye was last in her office.

The tape whirred back when I touched "play." The first message was from a man speaking Turkish. "This is İrfan Algar. The interview you requested now appears to be impossible. I will contact you if that changes." No number given. He obviously thought Faye knew it. The time of the message was 4:30 pm the day before.

The second message was from Faye's head office in London and had come in soon after the other. "Alastair here," said the clipped voice. "Ring me when you get in. Want more details on the ceramics story. 'Bye."

The third and fourth messages were also from Alastair in London, about half an hour apart and each sounding more frustrated than the last. "Deadline approaching," said the fourth. "If we don't hear from you, we kill the story." I guess that's what they decided to do, because there were no messages from London after 7:45 pm.

There was an 11:18 pm message that I replayed several times. The voice was whispery but familiar somehow. I couldn't place it. Static crackled on the line. It was hard to distinguish words. It sounded like "peacock head down, peacock head down" over and over. I jotted the words down on a piece of paper from Faye's desk and put it in my pocket.

A couple of calls had come in during the morning, including a curt request from the News headquarters in London for Faye to reestablish contact. Headquarters seemed to be getting worried.

Bayram, meanwhile, had found where copy had last been ripped from the wire machine. It was about 3:30 pm the day before. That plus the telephone messages confirmed that Faye had disappeared at about the time she should have left for our appointment with Leila Metin.

I shivered. Out of character for her. Yet I had seen the glint of reddish hair peeping out from under the scarf as Faye boarded the ferry after Erol.

103

*What could be the meaning of it? It
was impossible to imagine; it was
impossible not to long to know.*

Jane Austen, *Pride and Prejudice*

As Bayram left Faye's office, I took a final glance around. The only thing out of place for a newsroom was a glossy book open to pictures of Turkish antiquities. The photos displayed a range of objects, from ancient Greek and Roman statues found at Turkish archaeological sites to the delicate ceramic plates and vases of Konya, Kutahya, and especially, Iznik.

The glowing pomegranate-red of the late 16th-century Iznik potter dominated the open page. That vase—I'd seen it before. At least, I had been exposed to an excellent copy; the one resting on Lawrence's elegant telephone desk in Çengelköy. It looked exactly like the one in the book: red carnations, blue hyacinths, a cypress tree.

I picked up the book.

We locked Faye's office, leaving the lights on. Were those footfalls fading in the distance as we walked back to our own office?

Ghost footsteps.

10⍭

*"There are few people whom I really love,
and still fewer of whom I think well."*

Jane Austen, *Pride and Prejudice*

What with middle-of-the-night police interrogations, an emotionally-taxing funeral scene, and the discovery of yet-undigested mysteries in the *London News* office, I was exhausted. I went back to the Pera early for a nap.

There was a message at the desk that Lawrence Andover had called. I was too tired to reply. He could wait.

In my room, I pulled the drapes almost closed, so that the fading autumn sunlight was held at bay but not obliterated. Then I disrobed and fell onto the bed, tossing the ceramics book onto the dresser before pulling the bedspread over me. After that, I slept.

At 6:15 the phone rang. Streetlights through the windows striped the walls. I grabbed the receiver.

"Yes?"

"Ms. Darcy? Jean Le Reau. Can we have a drink downstairs?"

"Uh, sure. That is, give me time to grab a shower. Half an hour, in the lobby bar?"

Warm water and olive oil soap soothed my tired body and brought me gradually to alertness. A drink with someone who'd been a pest since my arrival? Why did that sound inviting? Maybe because he had saved my life that night on the cobblestones near Galata Tower. Anyhow, my excuse was that I needed to learn more about him. I had no idea who Le Reau was, but I suspected he knew much more about what was going on around me than he would admit to.

Caressed by the water, I quickly went over the events since my arrival. Less than two weeks! The intruder in my room. The blatant attack on Haldun—or was it aimed at me? The bomb that killed Professor Fener. The whatever-it-was that killed Erol Metin. The shooting and police chase while I was having dinner with Ahmet Aslan in Çiçek Pasajı, and the pursuit of Le Reau and me in Pera streets by shadowy figures shooting at us. The disappearance of Faye Mollington...

And oh, yes, the event that, for me at least, had started the whole strange saga: Peter Franklin's death. If anything, I was more confused now about what had happened than I was when my plane landed two weeks ago.

Drying myself vigorously with the thick white hotel towel (Turkish towel, of course!), I tried to wipe away some of the gloom that had settled over me. And as I threw on brown corduroy pants and a red sweater, I glanced at the book from Faye's office.

On the cover was a picture of an Iznik plate with a pattern of gracefully-entwined flowers. The petals of the flowers, red as only that one special sixteenth-century potter could make it, leapt off the shiny paper. Sending me a message. I shook my wet and unruly hair to clear my brain—an exercise of limited efficacy—and gave it a few strokes with a hairbrush.

I closed the book, set it on the bottom shelf of the bedside table and headed down to meet Jean Le Reau.

105

"To oblige you, I would try to believe
almost anything, but no one else could
be benefited by such a belief as this..."

Jane Austen, *Pride and Prejudice*

Jean Le Reau, too, was wearing a sweater and corduroy pants. He seemed taller as he rose from his chair to greet me. He nodded in a businesslike way and guided me through the ornate lobby with its small conversational groupings toward the darker corner of the lobby bar. We sat on two small sofas placed at right angles to each other and facing the high windows that now reflected small lamps around the room.

We were not alone. At a coffee table near the secondary entrance to the little room, legs crossed and newspaper in front of him, sat a person whose profession I could tell at a glance. What is it about cops? I can nearly always tell when I am encountering one. Was I still under suspicion related to Erol Metin's death? I leaned close to Le Reau, and spoke softly.

"Tell me what you are doing in Turkey," I demanded, before the waiter arrived with drink orders.

Le Reau crossed one leg over the other and then recrossed them the opposite way.

"It is not time," he murmured. "Please trust me." A crease between his brows, above his blue-gray eyes. Combined with thinning blond hair, he had an innocent, almost vulnerable look. I wasn't about to be taken in.

The waiter came then and we ordered. A glass of red wine for me. A whisky and soda for Le Reau. The waiter left. The man with the newspaper near the door re-crossed his legs.

"I asked you for a drink to see if you would like to visit an archeological dig with me," said Le Reau, his previously overdone French accent missing. "Archeological" had the accent in the right place, at any rate.

What? My voice rose. "A dig? But why? What dig?"

Le Reau didn't smile. He had not smiled since the last time I'd seen him. I missed the rows of white teeth, so annoying at first.

"I am going to Iznik," he said, after a pause.

"The old Bythnian capital." And home of priceless ceramics.

"I am going tomorrow," he said.

Leila knew about Iznik ceramics. The Topkapı with its beautiful tiles swam before my eyes. Lawrence Andover's collection had fascinated me from the first.

"I am going, too," I said impulsively. All my lines of information seemed to have dried up in Istanbul, and anyway, the closest thing I had as a clue to what had happened to Faye dealt with ceramics in general, and Iznik in particular.

Jean Le Reau bowed his head in acquiescence to my going with him. At least, I'm sure that's what he meant.

I excused myself and telephoned Detective Durmaz from the front desk. Would there be a problem about my going to Iznik for the week-end? He asked for the names of those who would be accompanying me, and then he indicated grudgingly that I had permission to wander that far.

"But be back in Istanbul on Monday," he admonished. I said I would, and hung up.

The drinks arrived, but neither Jean Le Reau nor I drank much. Both of us were quiet. Perhaps I was still exhausted. For some reason I respected Jean Le Reau's reluctance to level with me at the moment. I would pump him when we were travelling together to Iznik. When my glass of wine was half-finished, I stood. Le Reau rose, too.

"What time?" I asked.

"Seven. Better be prepared for staying overnight."

As I left, I walked past the plainclothes cop in the corner. He, of course, was reading his newspaper. My attention was on him, so I almost bumped into two men entering the lobby bar. One was the photogenic television anchor I'd met with Lawrence; the other was the three-piece-suited companion of Lawrence and Leila Metin at the Topkapı restaurant. Howard Black, I thought I remembered. Deep in conversation, neither of them looked up, so I didn't make a point of greeting them. Threads were appearing, but for the life of me, I couldn't see a discernible pattern.

When I reached my room, I ordered room service and packed for the next day's mini-trip. I checked the road map I'd brought; Iznik wasn't far from Istanbul, but to get there by road involved the unpleasant drive along the heavily industrialized northeastern coast of the Sea of Marmara. But from the uninspired city of Izmit, according to the map, the road turned blessedly upwards into the olive groves and vineyards of ancient Bythnia.

Bythnia! Even the name was romantic.

106

*"Do not consider me now as an
elegant female intending to plague
you, but as a rational creature speaking the truth from her heart."*

Jane Austen, *Pride and Prejudice*

I made a quick telephone call to Haldun before going to bed. The patient was beginning to improve in spirits as well as body. It wouldn't be long now before he was out of hospital.

"Who is Jean Le Reau?" was his very sensible response to learning about the trip.

"Your guess is as good as mine," I growled. "Maybe I'll know more by the time I get back."

"By the way, did you hear any more details about the subject we were talking of last time? That he was shot and thrown into the Bosphorus?"

Erol Metin. One of Haldun's media colleagues had undoubtedly shared with him underground gossip that we foreigners would be the last to know. It was frustrating not to be able to talk freely on the telephone.

"Elizabeth, I want you to take care," said Haldun.

"Oh, don't worry about me," I answered. "You need to concentrate on getting well. Tell Ayla *Hanım* hello for me. And pet that beautiful cat, if she comes."

I had neither energy nor inclination to return Lawrence's call after talking to Haldun.

10?

*I found almost at once that I had been
as naïve as the pasha. I had forgotten,
except intellectually, that shadowed
behind it all [Istanbul], like a huge
broken monument of memory, was
Constantinople, the Byzantine Empire
of Constantine the Great, Justinian
and Theodora, Julian and Apostate.*

Mary Lee Settle, *Turkish Reflections*

Early the next morning, I was relieved to learn that Le Reau had arranged for us to take the big ferry from Eminönü direct to Yalova on the southern Marmara coast rather than going all the way by road, along the crowded highway. From Yalova we would take a taxi to the old capital. I breathed a sigh of relief.

After we boarded, the Yalova ferry gave an anticipatory wail and slid from its moorings, past Topkapı Palace on the right and Galata Tower on the left. Instead of veering left to head up the Bosphorus, we rounded what Turks call Saray Burnu, the Nose of the Palace, to the right and set course for the opposite shore of Marmara Denizi, the Sea of Marmara.

It was freezing cold and overcast that October morning. Le Reau and I spent two minutes out on the foredeck before taking shelter on the pew-like wooden benches inside. As we sipped the ever-ready glasses of hot, sweet tea and nibbled *simit*s (only good when they are fresh), the ferry glided past the five little Princes islands that face the Asian side of Istanbul.

Tea is not as effective for me as coffee in the morning. I was groggy even after two glasses of the strong stuff. Thankfully, Le Reau didn't seem inclined to talk much. I was anxious about Faye and her possible role in the Metin murder. Perhaps that colored my mood—the sense of overall threat that pervaded my search for Peter Franklin's killer. Had Le Reau played a role in Peter's death? God, I hoped not.

Huddled in my corner of the "pew," gazing out the window to gray skies, gunmetal water, and now the industrial mess that sits on Istanbul's outskirts on the Ankara road, I struggled to control my rising panic. How could I be a danger to anyone? Still, I had no idea who had killed Peter, the man by the Pera, and Erol Metin. Would they kill again? Maybe Peter's death was not the first in a line of successful homicides. And where was Faye Mollington? She must be more than tangentially involved in recent events.

The ferry headed south, across the narrow finger of the Marmara that separates Istanbul from Yalova and from Mount Olympus (one of a dozen of that name in the ancient world) looming over the city of Bursa. The opposite shore came into view almost as soon as we turned. With the trick of lighting common to Istanbul when the wind is blowing and the skies are overcast, the distant shore appeared far more clearly than on a sunlit day. Yes, there was the snow-covered peak of Olympus, Uludag, as the Turks call it.

Le Reau roused himself.

"This dig in Iznik…" he began. He said "deeg" and "Eeznik."

"Oh, cut the accent. Please cut the accent," I begged. "You aren't French, and I know it." I'd been even more suspicious of the accent since it seemed to come and go at will.

For a moment, Le Reau glared. Then he glanced around, and murmured, "I would appreciate you not advertising your suspicions. It's fine to be annoyed, and even to look annoyed. Just keep your voice down."

Great, more intrigue! I glanced around the cabin. Who could Le Reau suspect was listening to our conversation? It was Saturday, earlier than schools let out for the half-day, so our fellow passengers were mostly husbands and wives, some accompanied by small children, who were probably returning to their villages for the weekend. A very middle-class bunch.

Ah, yes, there he was. I should have known. Sitting a few rows behind us, an ostentatious newspaper held up. Really, couldn't the police find a better disguise? What would happen if I walked up to the snoop and said a loud "*gün aydın*, good morning."

And yet… And yet… I was vexed by the presence of the law, but it was also comforting. Since I knew I was innocent, in a sense I had acquired my own personal bodyguard. Under the circumstances, it didn't matter that my guard very possibly suspected me of a crime.

108

A few minutes later, headed for the inevitable ladies room stop, I casually glanced into the rear section of the ferry. A man sat on the third bench, and he wasn't reading the newspaper. He was looking out the window. That profile was familiar—on the ferry and in the car that had followed me on my arrival; perhaps in the car that had hit Haldun on that rainy hillside. A dangerous man, one who more than likely had known and worked with Erol Metin.

The hair on the nape of my neck stood up. What evil had this man engaged in? Erol, a young man with a promising future, was dead. Had this mustachioed man led him astray? Maybe even killed Erol, for some reason of his own?

I finished my business in the rather shaky washroom and slipped back to my seat beside Le Reau. How much should I tell him?

I had to risk making a mistake. I rummaged in my purse for a pen and piece of paper. "Man in second compartment may have been driver of car that hit Haldun," I wrote, and gave it to Le Reau.

Le Reau's expression didn't change by so much as a hair. He handed me back the paper. "Draw diagram," he said, as though discussing the gray, cold weather outside.

I drew a little map on the other side. Le Reau excused himself politely and headed toward the back. I glanced over my shoulder; Le Reau checked his watch ostentatiously near the undercover cop, then moved on into the second compartment.

Soon he returned, sitting beside me with an air of nonchalance and holding an English-language newspaper. He must have stopped at the shipboard kiosk. He handed me a newspaper, too—my old friend, *Cümhüriyet*—but I didn't even bother to unfold it. The non-incident had awakened me as even coffee couldn't do. Fortunately, we were getting ready to land in Yalova, so I didn't have long to sit and chew my nails.

In better weather, Yalova would have been a great place to spend a day or two. An ancient spa on the unpopulated shore of the Sea of Marmara, the mountains of Anatolia forming a backdrop. On this clear-but-overcast day, you could actually see the skyline of Istanbul across the water, just as we had been able to see Mount Olympus near Bursa on our way over. Domed mosques with graceful minarets gave the distant city an ethereal air it doesn't have close-up.

Like other passengers, I had automatically prepared to stand, to file down to the gangplank when the ferry started docking, but Le Reau stopped me with a slight pressure on my arm. When the compartment was less crowded, we stood and walked toward the exit. I didn't see the policeman—he must have disembarked earlier. I didn't see the macho Murat driver, either.

We crossed the gangplank without incident and immediately began bargaining with a taxi driver. I did most of the talking because Jean insisted my Turkish was better. We managed to hire a guy with a reasonably well-kept old green Chevy. Because our destination was some distance, we agreed on a price for the whole day. Even in this off-season we could get another taxi the next day if we ended up staying in Iznik overnight.

The road to Iznik from Yalova is winding but full of charm. On this autumn day, the orchards, of course, were leafless, but spiky evergreen cypress trees and silver-leaved olive groves provided dramatic emphasis to the dormant countryside. The smell of cut wheat infused the air. No wonder one of Alexander's generals (Antigonus the One-Eyed) decided to establish his capital in this part of Bythnia in 316 B.A.D. Even seen with one eye, in the off-season, the view would be worth founding a city on: silver lake, silver olives, and bare silver birches; mountains in the background, black with forests.

Emerging from trees at the end of the lake was Iznik—and the Middle Ages: ramparts built originally in Hellenistic times and rebuilt and repaired by Byzantines and then Ottomans, with massive turrets and great gates through which once walked five Emperors, Roman or Byzantine, all of them residents of what was then called Nicaea.

I caught my breath. "No wonder they made such lovely ceramics!"

The pottery-making came later, in the heyday of the Ottoman Empire, and lasted for two hundred years. Once that age ended, Iznik became a small, sleepy town. The terrible battle between Turks and Greeks in 1922 had unfortunately ruined much of what had withstood even Tamerlane and the Goths.

To my surprise, Le Reau had a detailed map of the Iznik area. It even showed which little road to take toward the mountains for two kilometers to the dig supervised by Istanbul University experts. Our taxi driver wanted to stop in the town first, so we parked on Main Street (that is to say, Atatürk Boulevard, as it is in all Turkish cities). While the driver was buying his breakfast at a coffee house, Le Reau and I took a short walk, my companion walking just slightly behind me. Was this his way of being protective? Was his gun available? My personal protection, Jane Austen, was in the carrier bag containing my overnight things.

That bag, of course, was back at the taxi.

109

*"He can be a conversable compan-
ion if he thinks it worth his while."*

Jane Austen, *Pride and Prejudice*

We were approaching the Nilüfer Hatun Imareti, or Soup Kitchen,
dating to 1388 and now the Cultural Museum of Iznik. Le Reau caught
his breath.

I glanced to the left as a familiar figure strode toward us. The handsome features and immaculate London Fog raincoat made him an ano-
moly in the old ruined town. His chiseled lips were curled into a smile.
Le Reau's body language, taut and tense, said, in that Neanderthal male
way, "threat." Aslan's eyes narrowed. Their metaphorical ruffs bristled.

"Ms. Darcy!" Aslan's smile broadened.

"Ahmet *Bey*." I extended my hand. He took it, giving me a meaningful look from dark, almond-shaped eyes. Le Reau stepped ever so
slightly between us to hold out his hand in an alpha dog greeting.

Suddenly, even before I could introduce the two men, I started laughing. A reaction to all the tension, no doubt. My uncontrolled giggles
put them both off their stride. Wonderful! Two pairs of bewildered eyes
stared at me, no longer would-be opponents, but men wondering what in
the world a woman was thinking.

"Jean Le Reau, meet Ahmet Aslan," I managed to say.

Aslan now took Le Reau's hand, and both men nodded. You couldn't
call the meeting friendly, but it fell within the minimal bounds of civility.

"What are you doing here?" I asked Aslan.

"My factory is near here," was the reply. "I thought you knew that."

"No, I had no idea where it was," I said. Then I turned to Le Reau:
"Ahmet Aslan owns TürkKeramik. You've probably seen items with that
name."

Le Reau's mouth was a thin line which he managed to tilt into a smile.
"Ah, yes. I have heard of that company."

"We came to sightsee in Iznik and to visit the dig outside town."
Maybe I explained too much. All three of us were more nervous than
called for.

Ahmet Aslan unbent. "I am not sure anyone is at the dig in October. There is not much to see, but I hope you enjoy your day. By the way, please come to my factory for tea this afternoon."

I turned to Le Reau. "After completing our business, do you think we could make it?"

Le Reau, too, relaxed. Perhaps he had not expected me to include him in the invitation—Aslan certainly hadn't.

"We can try," he said.

"Count on us," I assured Aslan. "Would three-thirty be okay?"

"Three-thirty will be fine. The guards will be expecting you and will bring you to my office."

Aslan turned abruptly on his heel and headed down the street. A bright red car was parked amid the old clunkers of the taxi drivers and the modest Murats of the middle class.

Le Reau and I were silent for a minute or two after Aslan left.

"Is that the industrialist you told me about?" asked Le Reau, forgetting his accent completely.

"Yes. I'm still surprised you don't know him."

"Well, I do now," said Le Reau.

I might have missed something.

110

*The driver was a slim and wiry
man with thick backbrows. He wore
black shalvar-trousers and a shirt
of artificial yellow silk. His cap was
new and set at a rakish angle.*

Yaşar Kemal, *Anatolian Tales*

In the courtyard of the soup-kitchen-cum-museum, we admired marble statuary and pieces of columns from the Greek era. I have seen so many similar artifacts, especially along Turkey's Aegean coast, but I never get tired of them. Every bit of Anatolian clay or sand you walk on has the imprint of centuries on it. It is humbling.

Entering the cool, high-ceilinged hall where shabbily-robed beggars used to huddle to be fed, the wonderful tiles of Iznik were lined up for approval. A favorite motif in the tiles is flowers—delicate tracery images of real flowers, like carnations and primroses, mixed with geometric, impressionistic blooms. Another motif, rarer than the flowers, depicted animals. There were a few mostly-broken examples of the animal motif here: deer and rabbits chased by dog-like wolves or lions, the odd snake curling up a branch toward a bird.

I was becoming familiar with these classical beasts, and was, in fact, beginning to empathize with them, particularly with the animals of prey! I felt a hunger to possess some of these bits of history.

Past the tiles were samples of Ottoman weapons, and pieces of statuary from Roman times. It was a pleasant moment in what had been several days filled with tension. A ray of sunlight from one of the high windows glanced off an Ottoman shield and became a glowing focal point to the room. Breath-taking.

The little old man who was in charge of the museum told us about the various exhibits in educated but quavery Turkish. Instinctively, I addressed him as "*Amca*," Uncle. Le Reau wandered around the room during the speech, probably because his Turkish wasn't very good. I felt such kinship with the dignified old guide I impulsively asked if we could visit the Byzantine catacombs outside town. (You must have a special key and escort to get into the underground tomb.) Probably because I had assigned myself the role of "niece" to the old man, he agreed to take me.

Le Reau frowned when I mentioned the plan. "Surely we haven't time," he said. Then he switched gears. "I must do something before we go to the dig. Perhaps there is time for you and the gentleman to go to the catacombs."

I was being foisted off, no question about it, although Le Reau probably had not figured out how he was going to do that until the catacomb project appeared. He said he wouldn't need the car for his errand, so the old caretaker and I set off for the outskirts of town in the green Chevy with its taciturn driver. Did Le Reau hand something to the driver before we started? Tipping him in advance? For taking care of the woman? I said a cold goodbye to Le Reau.

We headed out of town through the ancient gate in the city walls known as Istanbul Kapısı, retracing for a little the way we had come from Yalova. The countryside in autumn sun with the lake as backdrop was so lovely, and the town of Iznik so typical of small Turkish towns—especially western Anatolian towns—that I shed my worries, as I had in the museum, about who was following me, and why.

The old man told me how Yerebatan Mezar, or the Byzantine catacomb we were about to visit, was discovered in 1967, in a remarkable state of preservation.

"It is from the fifth century," he murmured.

We arrived at the small hillside tomb, and after unlocking the door, my guide and I went inside. The driver stayed with the car. I was eager to see what the 5th-century artists had left.

The elderly guard's flashlight caught the glowing murals on the ceiling first. Peacocks sitting in trees, flowers; whoever rested in this tomb had had a garden buried with him or her. What was the meaning of peacocks? Oh, yes. It might be the resting place of a woman, or of a man who liked women.

I leaned back to see more of the ceiling when the doorway into the cave-like tomb darkened.

My first thought on realizing someone else had joined us in that underground cavern was, "Here we go again." My second thought was "hell." My pulse quickened. This was clearly danger.

My third thought was, protect the old man, my honorary "amca."

Using instinct instead of sense, I struck at the flashlight in the guide's unsteady hand and the unwieldy thing fell, illuminating the age-worn stone at the bottom of the wall of murals. I pushed the old man rather unceremoniously to the ground, much as Le Reau had pushed me in the dark Istanbul streets. Then I moved in front of his recumbent form protectively, ready to handle anything short of a gun.

The form at the door moved closer, still without a voice. Clearly, a threat. I kicked out and hit something yielding—a groin? A gasp sounded loud in the confined space, and I reached out and grasped a head of abundant hair. I had two fistfuls of hair and was holding on for dear life.

My would-be assailant—or victim?—was wriggling and squirming, but so far not lashing out. I could see nothing, save what was illuminated by light from the doorway.

Then, "*Hanım, hanım*, lady, lady," came a plaintive, familiar voice.

I released the hair. Our driver. The man who, though he didn't talk much, had exchanged pleasantries with all of us.

"What are you doing here?" I demanded, in Turkish. I bent down to retrieve the flashlight. The driver staggered out the doorway. I could see his silhouette as at the end of a tunnel, doubled over and groaning pitifully.

"*Afedersiniz!* Please forgive me!" I shouted. Then I turned to the old guard, and gently helped him regain his feet. As we all gathered outside the tomb in the October sun, I felt my face glow like the murals inside.

"Please forgive me," I said again to both of my shaken companions. Then, looking at the driver, "I thought you were someone else."

"*Hanım*, I just wanted to see the tomb," muttered the driver, who could now at least stand upright. "And anyway, the man back there told me to watch out for you."

"You mean the man I was with in the museum? The man who came from Yalova with me?"

The driver nodded. He could now stand.

Wait until I told Le Reau where his excess of protectiveness had led.

The old guard was still in a state of shock, but he managed to gasp, "So you were saving me? That is why you pushed me down?"

"Yes, *amca*. But I was wrong to assume the worst. I have had some bad experiences lately." I held out a tentative hand to each man in turn, who with the hospitable instincts of Turks, took the hand and shook it. The driver was a little less cordial than the guard. That didn't surprise me.

His story would make the rounds of the coffee houses of Iznik. I guessed I'd be a new-born legend, and not in a good sense.

111

*"Dede Korkut" is a collection of the
earliest Turkish legends, from the
heroic age of the Turks when they
first came to Anatolia. There are the
black forests, the women warriors,
the nomadic pride and riches.*

Mary Lee Settle, *Turkish Reflections*

We returned to the taxi and drove, very deliberately, back into Iznik through the majestic Istanbul Gate. I glanced back several times. Yes, we were being followed. The car behind us, a black Murat, had stayed there despite our slow speed, while other cars passed us. Nonetheless, without incident, we pulled up in front of the museum and the old guard got out. I gave him a handsome remuneration for his traumatic adventure and apologized once more.

Le Reau appeared as from nowhere, a worried furrow on his brow.

"Hi," I said from the Chevy window. "Shall we go straight to the dig or have lunch first?"

"I have picked up lunch for us to take," was the rather surprising answer. I never expect men to take a domestic initiative like that—though I've encountered enough rule-breakers to give me pause.

The driver gave Le Reau a pitiful look as he got in. Only my unwelcome presence kept the Chevy owner from telling this foreigner that no tip is big enough to cover tangling with an unpredictable wildcat of the opposite sex, respectable though she may have appeared at the start. There was a sullen silence in the car as we headed out of town through the Lefke Gate in the ancient walls, on the road that leads first to the mountains and eventually to Ankara.

Le Reau had little to say on the short trip. What was he thinking? I would have given more than a penny to know. Once I glanced out the rear window and caught sight of a black Murat. I nudged Le Reau and pointed. He nodded without much interest. I had a nasty suspicion he wasn't surprised to learn we were being followed.

You had to know where the dig was to find it. We turned off the Ankara road a few scenic kilometers out of Iznik, and bumped along for fifteen minutes on a road that didn't deserve the name. The Chevy's shock absorbers weren't up to the challenge, but its motor appeared to be. I didn't complain. Neither did Le Reau, but then this particular excursion had been his idea. I glanced back to see if our black Murat was still with us. It was. What did they want? By now I was so used to being tailed it occasioned no special alarm.

To a novice, the dig wasn't more than a few stones disarranged in a haphazard way. There was another car parked near where a small basic shelter had been erected—apparently for archeologists to spread out their treasures protected from sun or rain. The car was tan and middle-aged. Walking toward it were two women, one statuesque and determined, the other slender and uncertain.

112

*"Ask me what happened. Ask me
what I feel. Let them talk. You
ask my heart. It's burning inside
me like a live coal. How can I
stop grieving for Zala, ever?"*

Yaşar Kemal, *Anatolian Tales*

As I got out of our taxi, I peered at the women. The older one was
Perihan Kıraz, the archeologist. I didn't know her companion. Perihan
changed course and moved toward us.

I waved and called, *"Merhaba!"*

"Hello!" she replied, in one of those socially balanced situations
where people use each other's language. The girl with Perihan, I saw
now, was scarcely more than eighteen. She didn't look happy, but how
many teenagers do these days?

"How do you do?" I asked, stretching out a hand, first to Perihan, then
the girl. At the same time, I muttered Le Reau's name as a sort of fuzzy
introduction. He, too, shook hands all around.

"This is Aytem Fener," said the archeologist. Perihan's eyes were
dark with pain, as they had been earlier. "Her father worked at several
digs in this area, including this one, and she wanted to come visit, so I
brought her."

Fener. My mind immediately pulled up "bomb blast." This must be
the daughter of the professor who had been killed by the car bomb. No
wonder she didn't look happy! How could she be?

"I am so sorry about your father," I said, resting my hand on the girl's
arm. My words were inadequate.

Aytem nodded.

I turned to Le Reau. "Aytem's father was killed recently," I said.

"Yes, I know."

113

The tumult of her mind was now pain-
fully great. She knew not how to sup-
port herself, and from actual weakness
sat down and cried for half an hour.

Jane Austen, *Pride and Prejudice*

Le Reau asked no questions, but murmured condolences of his own. It was an uncomfortable moment, but death should not be treated as though it were unmentionable. Let the bereaved hear the words often enough so they can accept what their hearts may be trying to fool their minds about; the loved one is gone, and is not, in any recognizable way, going to return.

Aytem's eyes filled with tears.

"My father love this place, especially," she said in faltering English. "This where he always happy."

The two women gestured to us to sit with them in the little open-sided shelter, and I gladly followed. Le Reau said he would join us shortly, and headed off toward the edge of the dig near some cypress trees. Maybe he was heeding a call of nature.

As we three sat together on the coarse wooden bench, Perihan did most of the talking.

"We wanted to come here for two reasons," she said, after she had asked me how Haldun was doing. Trust the gossip mills to leave no stone unturned!

I assured her Haldun was doing as well as could be expected. My close friendship with Haldun seemed to give me an entry ticket into the cliqueish Istanbul intellectual elite.

"The first reason we came," Perihan continued, "is purely sentimen-tal. Aytem wanted to come. Her mother wasn't up to bringing her. I was." She smiled at the girl.

I sensed an old family friendship. Given the comparison with Ay-tem's mother, Perihan might have had a competitive edge where Profes-sor Oktay was concerned, but her concern for the girl appeared genuine.

My earlier impression that something had existed between Professors Perihan and Oktay appeared to be correct.

"And what about your second reason for coming? Did that have something to do with the dig itself?"

Perihan's face hardened. "The second reason," she said sharply, "is that Aytem and I would like to know who killed her father. I hoped the dig might yield some clues."

"The dig? How so?" Wait. Oktay Fener had been shot on the dig. The car bomb had not been the first attack on that gentle man. I was still in the dark about the forces that had brought death to one friend, injury to another, disappearance to yet a third, and violent deaths to two people I didn't know well. For once, I kept my mouth shut.

"I wanted to look at the place where the team was working last summer," said Perihan. "I was here only for a few days, because my mother was ill. But I recall some artifacts were missing from the list that I saw later."

That was a tack I hadn't thought of. Aytem's father had been the director of the dig. "So you think the attacks might have had something to do with thefts of antiquities? Did you ever talk with Oktay *Bey* about that?"

An expression of regret in her eyes—I suspected she never got a chance to tell Aytem's father many things. I pulled myself up to fill in the blanks. Perihan *Hanım* did not answer. She stood like a statue as Aytem stared off across the broken stones of the dig.

"Who besides Professor Fener was working this site last season?" I asked.

"Several of his students and some of mine were acting as researchers…assisted by laborers from the village over there past the cypress trees." Perihan's eyes grew even harder, if that was possible. "And Leila Metin, from Topkapı Museum, was also working here," she said.

"What is her specialty?" I asked.

"Leila knows the business," was the cryptic response. "She is a design expert. She was in charge of restoring and displaying artifacts to go into Topkapı."

"And have some of the things from here gone to Topkapı?" I asked. "Where are they being stored right now?"

"Yes, they're at Topkapı," growled Perihan. "When she gets over her brother's death, I plan to ask her to show them to me. But in the meantime, I am keeping my eyes open…" And here Perihan stopped. Le Reau was approaching again.

Damn the man. He was the master of inopportune appearances.

11 ♀

*"I certainly have not the talent
which some people possess" said
Darcy, "of conversing easily with
those I have never seen before."*

Jane Austen, *Pride and Prejudice*

The moment was irretrievable. Gone. Perihan and Aytem pulled their coats around them as the sunny day headed toward a chilly evening.

We all said goodbye, and I took the chance to say to Perihan, "I'll telephone you in Istanbul next week, all right?"

Her assent was rather grim as she led Aytem to the tan car, opened the passenger door, got in, and started the engine. Le Reau and I stood and watched as the car drove off with loud wheezes and jolts.

"I can't tell whether that's the driver or the car," muttered my companion.

"Are you ready to go?" I asked. "It's nearly time for our tea engagement."

"Uhhhh. Right. To the tea party," said Jean Le Reau. He was an unenthusiastic participant.

We headed for Ahmet Aslan's factory on the Istanbul side of Iznik. We would be late and were not very presentable, but I would not miss the opportunity to see the factory and talk with one more suspicious character in this unfolding drama. I glanced at Le Reau. Was he really a friend?

And what about the black car following us? Jean didn't seem concerned about it.

* * * *

My face grew warm and I tried to ignore my muddy hiking boots as we sat in Ahmet Aslan's lavish office-cum-apartment at the factory between Iznik and Izmit. My preoccupation with the latent violence surrounding me led me to forget the most basic duty of a guest in a Turkish home: taking off one's shoes at the door. The fine Caucasian carpet with its characteristic motif of blue flowers and birds would regain its full glory only with considerable attention and the cold water one is supposed to use on handmade rugs.

Le Reau's boots were as bad as mine, but he didn't seem embarrassed. He sat beside me in an elegant paisley-patterned, silk-covered chair that accentuated his worn jeans and the faded denim shirt peeking out at the collar from a tan sweater that had seen better days. The brown plaid woolen jacket he still wore might have been bought at the Salvation Army, although in its day it had been a quality garment. Le Reau's thinning blond hair could have used a trim. His blue-gray eyes were as expressionless as always.

Aslan was the opposite of Le Reau, and yet not quite. Where Le Reau's style of dress could be called oblivious, Aslan's was perfectly coordinated: dark brown corduroy pants worn just enough to have acquired a patina; a white shirt that no doubt had a signature Polo rider on it, now covered by a knitted vest in one of those off-beat red-orange colors you have to pay about three hundred dollars to get, topped by a sports jacket that mixed browns and tans with exquisite balance. Aslan's thick black hair did not need a trim; it was impeccable. His dark eyes, though, were almost as expressionless as Le Reau's, except when he looked at me. Then they gleamed in a disconcerting way.

A battle of wills was taking place that could only be described as "a male thing." Instead of feeling complimented, I felt outnumbered.

But I did notice similarities in the two men with whom I sat. They could be boiled down to a couple of words: Ego. Will power.

Aslan and I were drinking tea. Le Reau had asked for, and received, a large glass of beer.

Aslan was his usual, suave self. "What did you find at the dig? I haven't been there recently." His servant, a young man dressed in white, handed around shortbread cookies as we talked.

"We saw Perihan Kıraz and Professor Fener's daughter there," I said. "They weren't working on the dig so much as looking for clues to Fener's death."

Aslan's face went blank. "Clues? Here?" He looked confused. "The bomb was in Istanbul."

"Yes, but before that Oktay Fener was shot at here in Iznik," I reminded him. With his strong connections here, he should have remembered that on his own.

"Yes." An ambiguous answer. I was about to follow up when Aslan said, "Do you have any interest in seeing my factory? I can arrange a special tour."

I thought it might be getting too late, but Le Reau jumped right up and said he would be delighted.

"Sure," I said, rising. "That would be interesting."

115

*When an artist showed Atatürk a
'heroic' painting of the Battle of the
Sakarya, he said, "That picture should
never be exhibited. All those who took
part in the battle know very well that
our horses were skin and bone, and
we were hardly any better ourselves.
Skeletons all of us. In painting those
fine warriors and sleek horses, you
dishonor Sakarya, my friend."*

Mary Lee Settle, *Turkish Reflections*

The factory was large, well-lit, and modern. Two hundred or so workers—about three-quarters men and the rest women—refilled containers
on a conveyer belt that deposited just the right amount of white sandy
clay in the one-piece molds. The molds were then shunted off to a waiting area for the mixture to harden.

In the next procedure, the excess clay was emptied out of the molds,
and another drying period began. Further along, people applied a white
creamy slip as background layer and the objects were again left to dry.

Then, in a process used only with fritware (Islamic stone paste) like
this, containing glass with lead, it was time for stenciled patterns to be
applied to the vessels. The stencils were dusted with charcoal so that
artists could see where to draw the lines. Some of the designs were geometric, some floral, and others could best be described as "art deco." The
colors ranged from mauve to turquoise to gold. Sometimes patterns were
outlined in black. They were as well-coordinated as Aslan's clothes.

Again, after waiting for the paint to dry, the carefully-prepared lead-
based glaze was poured over the now-colorful vases and plates and
bowls. There would be another wait overnight.

We watched as the next-to-last conveyer belt moved semi-finished
products from yesterday in a sedate parade to the great shelved kiln that
burned brightly but safely in an ell off the main room. Tomorrow, those
would be ready for a showroom. The whole procedure was like a grand

and stately dance that took about a week to finish. I was impressed, and glad we'd taken the tour.

Aslan told us more than a third of what his factory produced was sent out of the country. "The pieces that don't contain lead," he added, with a laugh. "We are growing in the export area, though, from this and our factory in Beykoz, near the Black Sea end of the Bosphorus."

Then Aslan took us to a walled-off corner of the factory, where a few men were working with their hands, feet, and potting wheels, shaping vases and plates and bowls. A smaller kiln was used for these pieces.

"We do a little custom work," said Aslan rather proudly. "These are expert potters, some of whom are descended from the Iznik artists of the Ottoman times."

His eyes gleamed as he looked at the beautiful hand-painted objects. I recognized the gleam. What did I have in common with this unusual art form? I am not fishing for a compliment when I state that I am not beautiful. It is a plain fact: I am not. What could be going on in Ahmet Aslan's mind? Whatever it was, it wouldn't detract from my pleasure in the unexpected tour.

This smaller room was less bright than the mass-production room, and the equipment seemed handmade. Each man sat on his own low wooden chair with the white paste twirling in front of him on a wheel that he kept going by energetic kicks. They gracefully pulled and shaped it, and I wanted to join them, to sink my hands into the tactile mixture that was turning under our very eyes into lovely shapes. What a satisfying outlet for creativity! But no. Even in Girl Scouts I was inept at anything dealing with arts and crafts. I sighed.

Le Reau seemed quite interested in the artisans' work. He walked over and examined the bins of clay, and watched closely as each handful was pulled forcibly into shape. He found the process as mesmerizing as I did.

"Isn't it nice?" I asked.

"Nice? Yes, it is nice."

Le Reau was still reserved, as he had been on this whole little sidetrip from Istanbul. Odd, he had once been such a chatterbox.

The tour was short, and when it finished, we took our leave. Aslan said he was staying the night, as he had a few things to check on the next day. He issued an invitation for us to stay in his living quarters, but I quickly declined. It would not be relaxing to sit for a whole evening between two men who obviously didn't trust each other.

"Thank you very much, Ahmet, but I need to get back to Istanbul," I said, for both Le Reau and me.

"Actually, I do, too," said my companion, cooperating for the first time.

Aslan relaxed a little, and showed us to the old Chevy with scarcely a curl of his well-shaped lip. For Le Reau, he had a cold impassive handshake. For me, a gallant kiss on my hand and a rather meaningful, "See you in Istanbul."

We took off in silence once more, although having tea with a rich man like Ahmet Aslan had enhanced our standing with the much-abused taxi driver. His expression was less sullen all the way back to Yalova. And, yes. A black car trailed us again.

116

*"It seems to me to show an
abominable sort of conceited
independence, a most country
town indifference to decorum."*

Jane Austen, *Pride and Prejudice*

Le Reau and I rode back to Yalova without much conversation. He seemed preoccupied. The driver kept his eyes on the road. I was trying to think things out. Professor Fener: were the roots of his demise in Iznik rather than Istanbul? If so, did that say anything about Ahmet Aslan? Should I re-examine him as a suspect? Leila and her brother still hovered around the edges of all the stories. How well had Peter known all these people?

Peter. I hadn't thought of him at center stage for a few days. Does death erase our immediacy so fast? In worrying about Haldun and Oktay Fener and the missing Faye, my primary purpose in Turkey had been pushed aside. I wondered how many of the untoward events of the past week related to the mysteries surrounding Peter.

The Istanbul ferry had left Yalova when we got there. Ah, well. Lights along the shore twinkled invitingly. "We have to stay," said Le Reau.

"Yes. How about that hotel over there?" I thought the place calling itself Marmara Evi looked small and cozy, unlike the neon-lighted one that probably boasted first place on the tourist lists for Yalova.

We paid the driver, took charge of our cases and walked to the Marmara Evi. Yes, they had two rooms. We gave the man our passports, asked for them back right away, and threw our belongings into the rooms.

The sun was setting into the Marmara as we sat down at a corner table overlooking the sea. I felt relaxation sink into my bones as we drank our glasses of Yenişehir white wine. I stretched out my legs and smiled at Le Reau. He dropped the preoccupied air that had engulfed him on the ride from Iznik. "Yes, let's talk," he said.

Talk became even easier over baked *kağitta levrek*—sea bass and vegetables in paper, aromatic bay-leaved steam rising from each wrapped packet. We squeezed pieces of lemon over the fish and dug in eagerly.

"Where did you grow up?" Le Reau asked. From there we launched into personal reminiscences of my early days in Colorado and his in, of all places, France. We had mountains in common.

"Is that why you use a French accent?" I asked, rather amused.

Jean grinned.

Wait a minute. When had I started thinking of him as Jean rather than Le Reau?

* * * *

In the upstairs hall, as we were unlocking our doors, Jean made a gesture as though he wanted to say something. He paused, took a breath, and started to speak. I looked up expectantly, but he wiped the grin off his face, scowled a little, opened his door, and said a curt "good night."

So be it. I closed my door and stood there a moment. Desire surged through me, catching me by surprise. Damn. It's so unpredictable. This was not a good time, place or person. I would be firm with it.

I took off my travel-worn clothes, brushed my teeth, splashed cold water over my aching feet, pulled on the trusty white nightgown with long sleeves, and sank gratefully into a bed that was at least partially horizontal, if rather banana-shaped. Though *Pride and Prejudice* was within comfortable reach, I was too tired to read for even five minutes.

About midnight, I woke to voices. Intense, low-pitched. Furtive. They woke me out of a deep sleep. The voices came from Jean's room next door.

I pulled the curtains back to check my bearings by the dim, yellowish, twinkling street lights. There were a few cars parked along the curb. Rubbing sleep out of my eyes, I noticed one car that looked familiar: a black car just like the one that had followed us during the day.

I suddenly understood.

I saw red. "Jean," indeed. That guy was Le Reau in my book.

11?

"I have every reason in the world to think ill of you."

Jane Austen, *Pride and Prejudice*

As I pulled on jeans and shirt and sweatshirt, adrenaline born of anger erased all trace of sleep—and I don't usually wake up easily. Grabbing my own key, I crept into the hall, even more dimly-lit than the street outside, and knocked quietly but purposefully on the door next to mine. Tap, tap, tap—tap. The voices inside stopped. I knocked again, using the time-honored rhythm: shave-and-a-haircut, two bits.

A lock clicked. The door opened slightly. Le Reau's eye was visible at the crack, and I pushed the door toward it.

"May I come in?" I demanded in a whisper, falling into the room as I spoke.

As the door closed behind me, I glanced around. Two other men were in Le Reau's room. One was a stranger, or at least we'd never been introduced. I'd seen him sitting near me with a newspaper held up in front of his face. The other was Detective Inspector Mehmet Durmaz from the Istanbul police.

I paused for a moment. "*Merhaba,*" I said, smiling at their collective dismay. The two Turks had instinctively stood up at the presence of a woman.

I sat on Le Reau's bed and the others regained their places.

"Okay," I said. "Time for me to become part of the team."

It was gratifying to see three pairs of eyes—two dark and one gray—looking at me. No one said a word. They must have thought I would sleep through their sneaky discussion.

"What exactly is going on?" I asked.

Le Reau was the first to open his mouth. Turning to Mehmet *Bey* he said, "Perhaps it would be best. She knows too much already."

A knot formed in the pit of my stomach. Had I made a fatal error? Was Le Reau some sort of criminal, and the two policemen what are so often called "bad cops?" I stood and took a step toward the door. I wouldn't stand a chance with these three, but maybe I could scream...

"Yes," sighed Mehmet *Bey*. "I agree. Sit down, Ms. Darcy."

He appeared more frustrated and exhausted than evil. I sat.

"You're a policeman, aren't you?" I asked Le Reau coldly.

"Of a sort, yes," he admitted. "The D.E.A. kind. Drug Enforcement Agency. Home base is New York."

The Turkish policemen looked at their feet.

"And you and Mehmet *Bey* and his friend here are looking for something. What?"

"Probably many of the same things you are," said Le Reau, with no trace of a French accent. "Murderers." He paused. "And Faye Mollington."

Oh, no. Was Faye was being implicated in at least one of the murders?

"I don't think you should make hasty judgments," I said.

They all looked confused. "It is not a hasty judgment to search for someone whose office in London has called us in," said Mehmet Durmaz.

"You mean something has happened to Faye?" Relief and worry weakened my knees, and I slumped back. She wasn't a murderer. And yet… "You are looking for Faye?" I shook my head. Stupid question.

"We are looking for Ms. Mollington, yes," said Mehmet *Bey.* "Can you help us in any way, I wonder?"

Decision time. Could I trust this trio or should I hold them, as I'd been doing, at arm's length? I hadn't been much help to Faye so far, trying to operate on my own, with a little advice from hospital-ridden Haldun. If something had happened to Faye, it was time to call in the big guns. I'd badly miscalculated in not doing so earlier.

"I can tell you where I last saw her," I ventured.

118

Astonishment, apprehension, and even horror, oppressed her.

Jane Austen, *Pride and Prejudice*

I outlined what had transpired at my appointment with Leila Metin and the fact that Faye had missed it. I spoke about seeing Faye board the ferry after Erol Metin—though I hadn't known it was he until Mehmet *Bey* showed me a picture of his body.

"And then you visited her newspaper office," prompted Le Reau.

Ah. That explained the furtive footsteps in the hall. Even then I was being followed.

"Yes. I read a few things on her desk, listened to her telephone messages, and took one book," I admitted. "I was worried about where she was."

I thought for a minute. "I'm even more worried now," I said. "Presumably you have reason to think she did not kill Erol Metin, which was what I believed all along. I thought you suspected her. That's why I didn't come to you. What can you tell me about the circumstances of Metin's death?" I curled up comfortably on Le Reau's bed, and he sat gingerly on an opposite corner.

"Metin was shot through the heart. He probably never knew what hit him," said Le Reau. "Someone called in an anonymous message to the police, which is why they found the body so quickly. The message came from a woman."

"Faye?" What could have happened between Metin, Faye, and a killer as yet unknown?

"Probably Faye Mollington," said Le Reau. "We found something at the wharf where the call originated to indicate it was Faye."

"What did you find?"

Le Reau almost grinned. "A picture of a peacock. Faye worked with us on occasion, and when she did, 'Peacock' was her alias."

A light flashed into my brain. "And you had tried to warn her in that silly coded message I found on her answering machine? Something about peacock…yes, 'peacock head down,' or some such."

"That doesn't matter now. What we must do is find her. Fast," said Le Reau, with grim determination.

119

How little we really know about brave
and unknown people in the brute face
of silence, the manipulation of facts,
the terrible comfort of old hatreds.

Mary Lee Settle, *Turkish Reflections*

Ahmet Aslan called three of his supervisors to his office.

"Has anyone visited this plant when I was not around?" he asked.

The men shuffled their feet and kept their gaze on the floor. It was never good to have to answer to the Big Boss. He was a good employer and they were grateful for the jobs. He was also known to have a hot temper and a short fuse. His lips were tight, a muscle twitched in his cheek.

Mustafa, the night manager, spoke first. "No one came in on my shift. I am sure of that."

Veli, who worked the graveyard shift usually, said the same. Both would check with their workers. They were practically bowing in abject apology.

Cemal, who managed things during the day, said no strangers had come. "Only the lady you work with sometimes," he said. "The lady in beautiful clothes." It would have been impolite to call a woman unrelated to him beautiful.

Ahmet Aslan met each manager's eyes and frowned. They were all telling the truth.

The twitch in his cheek got more pronounced.

He had a big decision to make.

120

*"Really, I know not what to say. Per-
haps I am not doing her justice. But
she is very young; she has never been
taught to think on serious subjects..."*

Jane Austen, *Pride and Prejudice*

The hotel room was full of smoke. I'd even grabbed a cigarette from Le Reau's pack, though it made me choke. Anything to be one of "the boys."

"But why is the D.E.A. looking for Faye? Wouldn't this be in Mehmet *bey's* territory, the Turkish police?" I waited, cigarette in hand, looking expectant while the men got their stories together.

"We are looking for Faye Mollington because she is missing," explained Le Reau. Yes. That would be a man's answer. I must have looked a little impatient.

Mehmet *Bey* took up the thread. "There are some questions about what Erol Metin was involved in. We are looking for someone who hired him on a regular basis. It may be there is a U.S. connection. And we think if we find that it could lead to, um, other activities we are interested in."

Le Reau was rubbing his hands through his hair as Mehmet *Bey* talked. Was he frustrated at having all this explained to an outsider?

"What are we talking about here?" I demanded of them all. "Drugs? Arms? Terrorism? What?"

"We are talking about all of the above. And possibly there is one other element, too. We are getting hints that antiquities from Turkey are being stolen, probably by international underworld organizations. Antiquities, you know, are the second most lucrative smuggled item, after drugs." Mehmet *Bey's* voice held a bitter note.

"Really? I didn't know that. I would have thought arms would come next. But continue. Do you have leads on any of these activities? And what about Professor Fener and Haldun *Bey*? Is Istanbul usually this violent?"

"It has its moments," admitted Mehmet *Bey*. "Not like Washington or Detroit..." Now, there was a dig.

They probably had a whole stableful of suspects, informers, and double agents. I would cut to the chase.

"Where are you looking for Faye? How can I help?"

Le Reau and Mehmet *Bey* shared a glance, Le Reau's face darkened. With embarrassment? Was it because they didn't want my help? Or maybe they did, and weren't happy about it?

"We are afraid Faye is being held somewhere. Either that, or ...but we hope not," began Le Reau. "I have to admit that we came to Iznik hoping to learn something. Durmaz here has had us followed, in case we needed backup."

I nodded graciously to the handsome detective sitting modestly in the little hard-backed chair near the window.

Le Reau narrowed his eyes. "Entering Aslan's factory was one of the goals. We think drugs are sent from around here, and there are indications that they're being put into pottery for shipment out. It helped that you knew him."

Okay. So I was, in a way, a part of the team. But since they hadn't let me in on the plan, I felt used.

"But why would a big industrialist like Aslan want to take a risk like that? It doesn't make sense, does it?" Weren't men supposed to be the logical ones? I didn't say that.

"We don't necessarily suspect Aslan himself. However, it is unlikely anything goes on in his factory without his knowledge. Aslan, or someone who works for him, certainly knows about the drugs. It's possible the drugs are leading to murders." Mehmet *Bey* shrugged.

So he wasn't convinced of that. Interesting.

Le Reau nodded. "There's been so much trouble between Kurds and the Turkish army, Aslan could have some motive we don't yet understand. He's Kurdish, you know."

The atmosphere in the hotel room was a mix of cigarette smoke, toothpaste, and cheap hotel soap, overlaid with tension.

"Before anything else, we need to find Ms. Mollington," said Le Reau, slowly. "From what you say, she may have seen who murdered Erol Metin. If that is true, she may have been captured, or even killed— as a result."

My blood ran cold. I didn't want to think about either option..

I sat up and pulled myself together. "Just fill me in on one thing. Do your investigations point to anyone who had a motive for killing Erol Metin?"

So much work had yet to be done. My investigation of Peter's death had been paltry in comparison. And maybe Peter had played into the entire tapestry; I had had no idea of patterns when I began.

This time Mehmet *Bey* answered. "Metin's fingerprints were found at the scene of the bomb blast that killed Professor Fener. We think he did it, but we suspect he was hired by someone. The motive would depend on who hired Metin, and why."

There was a bleak look in the policeman's eyes. This was not an easy case for anyone. The three men looked worn-out and worn thin. The light from the bare buib hanging from the ceiling did not help.

Mehmet *Bey* and his colleague got up. "We'll catch some sleep now. See you at half-past six?" He gestured tiredly toward Le Reau.

"Yup."

Mehmet *Bey* and his colleague left.

"Since they had another room, why did you three talk in here? You must have known it could wake me up?" I asked. How strange that Le Reau would no longer plague me with his fake accent.

Silence for a while. Then, "Because we didn't want to leave your room uncovered. You may not have noticed, but someone seems interested in stopping your snooping."

Le Reau reached across the bed and grasped my hand before stretching his lanky frame out flat, with his head on the pillow. As though it would be the last thing he did before drowsiness overtook him, he raised my hand to his lips, very deliberately. His eyes were half-closed, but I detected a gleam that surprised me. Gently, tiredly, he pulled me toward him.

Equally gently, I removed my hand from his and slid off the bed.

"I'll sleep in my own room," I said. "You lock your door, I'll lock mine. And don't worry, if anything happens, I'll knock on the wall."

"Okay, angel," came the reply. "I'm too tired to argue with you, and there isn't any argument on an issue like this. Go now, though, so I can lock up."

Le Reau grunted as he rose and followed me to the door. Just as I grabbed the doorknob, he took my chin in his hand and kissed me, hard, on the lips.

Angel? It took me a little while to get to sleep.

121

*"You must, therefore, pardon the
freedom with which I demand your
attention; your feelings, I know,
will bestow it unwillingly, but I
demand it of your justice."*

Jane Austen, *Pride and Prejudice*

When I finally fell asleep, my dreams were multicolored and upsetting, all about foxes and rabbits and other prey that are chased into holes. Elements of the Iznik designs, I thought... If just once I could be the chaser, not the scared one running away. Thank goodness it was just a dream. In real life I'm braver. I think.

Before the sun came up, in a chilly bullet-gray dawn, the four of us gathered in the unpretentious little hotel lobby to drive the few blocks to the ferry landing. All three policemen looked slightly better than they had last night; well, two did. The one I would always think of as the "newspaper snoop" never seemed to change; he had appeared fine last night, when the rest of us were dropping in our tracks. I suppose sitting around reading all the time is a pretty energy-conserving occupation.

I had foregone my usual morning shower, daunted by the prospect of ice-cold head-to-foot drenching. How did Le Reau—no, Jean—feel this morning, after surprising me with The Kiss? I had to admit I had enjoyed his little overture. Annoying, however, that I liked it. At any rate, it was a good thing that I hadn't taken advantage of the man's fatigue last night. He needed all the strength he could muster for the complex search we were all engaged in.

We sat once again in the spacious front cabin of the Yalova-Istanbul ferry. A man in an old navy-blue jacket and pants sashayed down the wide aisles. He held a gracefully swooping tray of hot, sweet tea in glasses set on little tin saucers, and did a brisk trade with our bedraggled little group. Fortunately, *simit*s, too, were available. We sat bleary-eyed on the plastic-covered long seats, chewing the sesame-covered circles while we drank glass after glass of tea.

It was strange to be consorting openly with the guy who had been spying on us on the trip over. Just for the fun of it, I tried to engage him in conversation a couple of times, but he was apparently a man of few words. Probably he turns in written, not oral, reports on the subjects he surveils.

It was foggy, with some rain, as we landed at the Eminönü wharf at the foot of Palace Point, where the cupolas and towers of Topkapı loomed like a fairy-tale city wrapped in gauze. Mehmet *Bey's* black car had traveled on the lower deck of the ferry, and he offered Jean and me a ride to the Pera.

My least-favorite clerk at the front desk was obviously surprised to see Jean and me come in together. He handed us our keys with a raised brow and curled lip, all the while making the required obsequious noises. He also handed me a stack of messages that had come while I was gone.

We rode together in the open ironwork elevator, where I got off on the third floor and he continued. He touched my arm as I exited, saying "Call me when you're ready for a proper breakfast."

I was ready only for the haven my room promised.

122

*"I told him we should not be able to keep
our engagement. That is all settled."*

Jane Austen, *Pride and Prejudice*

What was that "Do Not Disturb" sign doing on the door? I didn't
put it there. Twisting the key, I finally got the door open. Then I gasped,
entered, and shut the door shakily behind me.

I'd had a visitor, or maybe the plural of that. Everything in my room
had been taken apart and thrown helter-skelter. The mattress was half off
the bed, as though someone had checked under it. Drawers were pulled
out. A few hangers dangled crookedly in the closet, my clothes lay in
a heap on the floor. That made me maddest. I had paid good money to
have that green silk dress pressed the other day! My woolen skirts and
sweaters were so crumpled they might need steam pressing. The whole
place was a mess, not the haven I'd looked forward to.

The first thing I did was to prowl the room. I kept my knees bent in
the stance taught me by the Washington cop squad, at the time Peter and
I were being threatened by drug lords over our investigative reporting. If
anybody was still here, they might be fooled into thinking I was a cop.

No one had remained at the scene of the disorder, so after I had
checked all the corners, including the bathroom, I threw my overnight
bag down behind the door—the only clear space on the floor—and
stuffed the telephone messages into my purse. Then I made my way
to the old-fashioned bathroom, where, in a dignified and mature way, I
vomited up the tea and *simits* from the ferry.

I wasn't quite ready to face anyone else yet. I went back into my
room. Surely I had some clean underwear... Ah, there on the dresser. I
glanced in the mirror and made a face at the white visage reflected back
at me, and then nabbed a clean but rumpled pair of jeans. The sweatshirt
I was wearing in Iznik would have to do. It was too much trouble to find
another.

I re-checked the lock on the bathroom balcony before turning on the
blessed hot water. Today it had the duty of washing off the contamination
from the intrusion into my room. Like others who have been burgled, I

felt dirty and violated. Standing in the tob with the shower on,, I closed my eyes. Was the balcony door locked when I checked it before leaving? I was sure it was.

I took my time in the tub, scrubbing every part of my body twice and thrice over to wipe cobwebs and nausea away. It worked, sort of, and when I emerged dressed I had the strength to deal with the mess. The first thing I did was to call Jean's room. It was time to swallow feminine pride.

"Uh, hi," I said, when he answered in the false French accent. "Could you come to Room 307, please?"

"Is this a trick question?" His voice, back to normal, was amused and maybe a little something more.

"Not a trick. Just come. Please."

123

*"...It is really too great a viola-
tion of decency, honor and interest, for him to be guilty of it."*

Jane Austen, *Pride and Prejudice*

My voice broke on the last word.

Jean said "Right," and hung up.

I was standing by the door and flung it open when the quick tap-tap came a minute later. He entered the room slowly, glancing around before touching anything.

"How are you?" was his first question, as he touched my shoulder. "What have you moved?" was his testy second.

"I got some clean clothes from that pile over there," I answered briskly. In response to his look, I went on, "I needed a shower to deal with this. Other than that, everything is the way it was when I came in."

Jean went into action so smoothly I was surprised that I had ever found him clumsy. That early klutziness was all part of an act, no doubt. He bent over and checked each pile of things pulled from drawers, still without touching. Then he went to the phone, pulled out a handkerchief to pick it up, and dialed.

"Yes. Inspector Durmaz, please. Yes, all right. But tell him it's an emergency. Le Reau is my name." He spelled it and looked at me expressionlessly as he waited.

"Durmaz? Developments. At the Pera. Uh huh. In her room. Great. See you in a few minutes. Bring your fingerprinters, okay?" Jean hung up.

I hadn't said a word. As he spoke to Mehmet *Bey*, fury had washed over me, all these intrusions, this violation... I could hardly differentiate between harmful and helpful.

Without batting an eyelash, he stepped over to me. His eyes didn't change much, but his arms enfolded me and he pulled me to his chest. I trembled, and it felt wonderful to be held. I clung to him and sobbed.

"Easy, easy," said Jean's low voice into my hair. "The worst is over. This is relief."

124

*Around them, spreading as far as the
eye could see, the flat boundless ex-
panse of brown ploughed land, green
fields and yellow crops shimmered
under the impact of the sun, and before
them the lonely, dusty road uncoiled
across the plain like a white ribbon.*

Yaşar Kemal, *Anatolian Tales*

After a few more tears, I wiped my eyes and tried to pull away. I must
regain my dignity. Instead, I was held more tightly, and my companion
turned my face up toward his. I wanted to crawl into a clam shell, not be
kissed, but it was the latter that happened. After a moment, I responded
in a way that surprised even me. Good thing there was no bed ready
to fall onto—at least, no bed that could afford to have anything moved
before the crime team got there.

We indulged ourselves for a bit, holding and clinging and pressing
and kissing, kissing, while, on my part at least, warmth spread through
semi-paralyzed limbs and I came out of my nauseated lethargy. When
we finally separated, keeping hold of hands, I wasn't the only shaky one.

"Well!" I was no longer crying. "I needed that. Should I thank you?"

"Thanking me would be weird." A wry, mischievous smile lit up his
usually expressionless face. "I suggest we take a rain check on the pos-
sibilities. Hmm-mm?"

"Maybe," I said.

* * * *

Mehmet *Bey* and his group arrived within fifteen minutes, which is
pretty good considering Istanbul traffic. They fingerprinted everything,
including me, when I told them I had made one call on the telephone
after entering the room.

I was happy to see that one member of the crime scene team, the collector of bits of evidence, was a woman. Stocky and unflattered by her
army-green uniform, she looked every bit as tough as her male co-horts.

She placed various bits of lint from the dresser and dust from a partial footprint in the bathroom into her array of little bottles. As soon as the group had gone through things on the flimsy armchair, I asked if I could move them and sit down.

All the time, I answered questions. Yes, that shirt was mine. No, I didn't see any differences in it, other than wrinkles. Yes, the bathroom balcony door was locked when I came in. No, I hadn't left anything valuable in the room.

"I did leave some papers with hotel security before I left," I said. "I assume they still have them."

"Let's go see," said Mehmet *Bey*.

Jean stayed in the room.

125

"That she could be in danger from
the deception never entered my head.
That such a consequence as this
should ensue, you may easily believe
was far enough from my thoughts."

Jane Austen, *Pride and Prejudice*

The clerk with the leering eyes was on duty, as he always seemed to be when I needed him least. The eyes this morning were bright with curiosity—he had received no complaints before the police arrived.

Alas, the manager was out for awhile. Could he help us? He straightened up and tried to look as alert as possible when Mehmet *Bey* asked him questions. If the *hanım* had the coordinating key to the safekeeping box, he would be happy to help open the box so she could check on whatever she had left there.

"Your help won't be necessary," said Mehmet *Bey*, taking the master key from the hapless fingers. "We will call you when we have finished."

The papers were there. Peter's handwriting, Haldun's scribbled notes, even my question marks were intact. I breathed a sigh of relief as I held them. I was no longer solely responsible for them.

"Shall we look at them together?" I asked.

"Yes. And then, would you like me to put them in my office safe?"

I hesitated, then nodded. "But I would like to copy them first," I said.

As we left the safety box closet, Mehmet *Bey* turned once more to the clerk. "Call your manager."

When the dapper suited man arrived, the detective began his questions. "Who has cleaned Madame's room? And has anyone else been granted admittance?"

The manager signalled for us to wait a moment while he made a telephone call. We could hear his end of the conversation.

"So who took her place yesterday?" And then, "Send him down."

When he had hung up when he arrived. I knew right away he would have no good information the phone, the clerk turned back to us. "There was a substitute room cleaner yesterday. His name is İhsan, and he will come."

Ihsan was not a prepossessing sort. He groveled before the manager and the policeman. "Madame's room I cleaned. I did not see anything." The man had a pitiful look. I believed him. I guess the others did, too. Ihsan was dismissed.

The manager turned again to Mehmet *Bey* and included the clerk with his eyes.. "And your other question? Oh, yes, did anyone else enter Madame's room. No one, sir. No one at all. Except, of course, the person from her office who stopped by."

"Office?" Mehmet *Bey* and I spoke together and shared a startled glance.

"The one that Madame asked us to let in," went on the clerk. "In the telephone call."

"Telephone call?" My voice cracked. "You believe I made a telephone call to you?"

"Oh, yes. It was after you and Mr. Le Reau left yesterday. Madame telephoned from a distance, I think from a ferry landing, and told us to let her assistant into her room. I myself was on duty."

It was a pleasure to see confusion in his eyes. No doubt he realized he had been duped into doing something the senior policeman was going to be angry about.

"Is there something wrong?" His tone was satisfyingly plaintive.

"There is something wrong. I did not make a telephone call, and your clerk here has been on duty long enough that you should have known it was not me. Can you describe my assistant?" I continued. Mehmet *Bey* had his notebook out.

The clerk glanced from me to the detective and then to his manager.. "The man had dark hair and dark eyes."

Right. Just like ninety-odd percent of the Turkish population.

"Anything else that you can, with your good memory, recall?" My voice dripped with sarcasm.

"He is high, like this." He gestured above his head to indicate tallness. "And he has big mustache. He carry notebook, like all journalists."

Well, Bayram wasn't very tall and didn't have a mustache, so we were apparently dealing with someone else. Or, of course, with a Bayram in disguise, being described by a man who tended not to notice things.

"I will send a police artist to draw the man you remember," said Mehmet *Bey*. "You will please tell her everything you can remember."

"Yes, yes, sir. I will tell her."

Except that in Turkish, there is one pronoun for he, she, and it, so the poor clerk had no idea that he would be forced to deal with a police

officer who wasn't a man. I only knew because I had seen her in conference with Mehmet *Bey* at the police station the night I almost got
arrested. I bit back a smile.

"One more thing," I said, as we turned to go back upstairs. "I would
like a really good cleaner from housekeeping in about an hour."

I raised an interrogative eyebrow at Mehmet *Bey* as I set the time, and
he nodded.

"Yes, of course," said the desk clerk. "And, madame, recently there is
telephone call for you. A Mr. Andover. He say it is urgent."

126

"Oh! You are a great deal too
apt you know, to like people in
general. You never see a fault in
anybody. All the world are good
and agreeable in your eyes..."

Jane Austen, *Pride and Prejudice*

I took the telephone message from the clerk. Since the police were still busy in my room, I handed them the papers we assumed had caused such a fuss and asked Jean if I could use his room for a phone call or two. He gave me the key.

The key was marked 411, a fact I'd not noticed when asking for his room in Turkish. He was one floor up, then, in the room where Agatha Christie wrote *Murder on the Orient Express*.

I was instantly jealous. Why hadn't I been smart enough to ask for that room myself? It turned out to be smaller than my room, and like mine, it overlooked the busy main road before catching glimpses of the Golden Horn. The bed was the same size as mine, full, meaning pretty small. I imagined that he would have to sleep diagonally to stretch out.

Enough distractions. I turned to the phone and began making calls. First, of course, I called Bayram.

"Ms. Darcy! I am glad you called. I did not know where you were. You did not come in this morning."

"I have recently come from Yalova," I said, truthfully. "Did you by any chance send anyone to get things from my room while I was gone?" The question was bald. I needed to know.

"You mean things from the Pera Palas?" If Bayram was shamming, he was good. His trustworthy voice sounded bewildered, rather the way a Labrador retriever looks when it is asked who has just eaten the snacks on the coffee table.

"Yes, things from my room at the Pera." I deliberately kept my voice calm and non-accusatory.

"No, I know nothing of this. Who do you say came to your room?" Bayram's voice rose, and his English deteriorated. He must realize I was talking about something very specific.

"A man asked for the key to my room and was given it. He messed up the place looking for something." I realized I was just spitting it out. Sometimes it's best. In my heart of hearts I didn't suspect Bayram. He was so sweet, so innocent. And since the office had been used as a decoy, it was unlikely he would have wanted to draw attention to himself if he had been involved.

"But, Ms. Darcy, is terrible! Can I help? What do you want from me?"

"Just tell me what is happening on the news front. Do I need to come in this morning, or will this afternoon be all right?"

"No, no. Nothing big. I have sent news notes. You can come later."

Bless the man and his conscientious attitude! How could I have suspected him for even a minute?

127

She could see him instantly before her, in every charm of air and address; but she could remember no more substantial good than the general approbation of the neighbourhood, and the regard which his social powers had gained him...

Jane Austen, *Pride and Prejudice*

My next call was far overdue, returning Lawrence's message from the Friday night before I left for Iznik. There were two more from him in the pile I'd picked up at the desk. As I dialed the American Consulate, I glanced out the window and was comforted by its staid, stone presence just down the street. Why on earth had I not called him earlier, to talk over the question of Faye, if nothing else?

Soon his secretary was on the line, and saying he would be with me in a second.

"Hello, Elizabeth. Andover here." The voice was as well-modulated and smooth and upper-class American as I had remembered. It gave the impression its owner could handle anything. Does the State Department train them to sound like this, or does it choose people who already have an authoritative manner? It was comforting, at any rate.

"I'm sorry I haven't had the chance to call you back," I said.

"I quite understand," said Lawrence. "I trust that things are going well?"

"No, not too well," I admitted. "Could I drop by your office later today, say in about two hours?"

"Come now, if you like."

I was surprised, as I always am in the circumstances, that a busy man could make time more or less on demand.

He continued. "I will tell security to expect you, and when you get here, your pass will be ready. My secretary or I will escort you up."

"Right. I know. See you in a few minutes, Lawrence." Well, that felt good. I was moving right along.

The next call, to Üsküdar Hospital, was a real challenge to manage on an insecure telephone line.

"Haldun? How are you? I'm back from Iznik."

"I'm glad you're back. When the hell are you coming over here? Today, I trust."

I covered my nervousness with a laugh. "I'll make it this afternoon for sure. I can't promise exactly what time. Do you need anything? When are you going home?"

"Who knows when I'm going home? The doctors around here are right out of Nazi concentration camps. And they don't tell you anything."

One of the alleged medical criminals was probably within earshot.

"Okay, Haldun. See you soon. Give my love to Ayla *Hanım*."

"Come as early as you can."

"I will."

The other receiver was slammed down.

Sounded as if Haldun needed to see me. Fine. I needed to see him, too.

Back in Room 307, the painstaking collection of evidence continued, although three of the officers had left. Jean and Mehmet *Bey* seemed to be working closely together; watching their single-minded attention to detail. I would not have wished to have them allied against me.

"I'm going out for half an hour," I announced. "Will you still be here when I get back?" It was a general question, which Jean answered.

"I'll be in my room," he said. "That is, if you would be so kind as to return my key?"

A bit red-faced, I dug it out of my bag and handed it over. I hoped he didn't think I kept it on purpose.

Turning to Mehmet *Bey*, I asked about the files we'd retrieved from the hotel's safekeeping.

"I will have copies made," he said.

"If you don't mind, I will have copies made," I returned. "I need those papers today. And I have an appointment right now, so I could do it on my way."

"Perhaps we should go together now across the street to the copy shop," said Mehmet *Bey*. "I, too, would like to look at these papers that have not been shown to me so far."

Well, touché and all that.

I didn't even have time to comb my hair before being escorted past a now-respectful desk clerk out to the street and across it. He got his copies; I got mine, which went into my briefcase. Then Mehmet *Bey* returned to the Pera, while I stepped over to the American Consulate.

128

She was now struck with the impropriety of such communications to a stranger, and wondered it had escaped her before.

Jane Austen, *Pride and Prejudice*

I walked through the metal detector and into a waiting area. Lawrence's secretary ushered me to his office, where he sat at a large, nearly-bare desk that showed off its fine wood grain. Behind his leather-upholstered swivel chair was a window with a view. Today, the main feature of the panorama was a large leafless tree stretching bare branches toward a gray sky.

The office itself was all I would have expected of Lawrence. Rows of books on built-in shelves were perfectly aligned and dusted. Flamboyant pictures by two of Turkey's best-known impressionist artists contrasted with white walls. They also gave me an insight into how complicated a person Lawrence was. Like a fine diamond, he had many facets. This was nothing at all like his classic-themed home.

Two photographs stood on the immaculate desk: one of him smiling and leaning in the doorway of his Bosphorus *yali*, the other of an aristocratic-looking older woman with white hair in front of what appeared to be a large New England mansion. Mom? Like mother, like son. Fantastic houses must be in the genes.

More comfortable, leather-covered chairs were grouped around a coffee table, with a spectacular Diyarbakır kilim creating an orange-and-black focus underfoot. Lawrence stood and gestured toward the chairs, and I sat. Lamps that didn't appear to be government-issue accentuated the warmth and security of the room, while making the gray day outside seem grayer.

"You look worn-out," said my host. "What's been going on?" His voice held concern. His sympathy was disarming.

"Well, now, that is quite a long story," I began. It had been awhile since we had talked. "I suppose you know about Erol Metin."

"Certainly. His death was in the newspapers. What does that have to do with you?"

"I visited his sister the day he died. And somehow…" I struggled to say the words. "I lost Faye Mollington in the process." My hands clenched.

A crease appeared between Lawrence's patrician brows. "What do you mean, you lost her? Faye is missing? I hadn't heard about that."

So I told him about seeing Faye board the ferry after Erol. I also told him my room had been ransacked while I'd been away for the weekend.

He frowned and the crease between his brows deepened. "What were they after, do you suppose? And no word from Faye, you say? Have you reported this to the authorities? While Ms. Mollington is not an American citizen, I feel we here at the Consulate should do anything we can to help locate her."

What? Why would he lie to me? The U.S. and British Consulates must keep in constant contact with one another. Surely Faye's diplomats contacted the Turkish police—and probably the U.S. Consulate, as well. Why wouldn't he know that? He must know. Why was he feeding me pure diplomatic b.s.?

"You seem a bit out of the information loop, if I may say so," I ventured. "Perhaps I should go to the Consul General, who will no doubt be briefed on this matter. Can you arrange that or shall I?"

A look of mock horror—or was it real?—marred the chiseled features for a moment. Then the usual bonhomie was back.

"Calling my bluff, aren't you? Well, you can't blame us poor bureaucrats for trying to get more information than we give. Here, let me order some tea, and I'll tell you a few things."

129

*His countenance, voice, and man-
ner, had established him at once in
the possession of every virtue.*

Jane Austen, *Pride and Prejudice*

The tea in Lawrence's office was of the finest export quality from Rize, on the eastern Black Sea coast. Lawrence, unlike most diplomats, used a china set and his secretary was trained to brew the expensive leaves exactly the right length of time, to a color of rich mahogany, with the flavor of the green mountains themselves. The minute the tea was poured, the secretary left, quietly pulling the heavy door shut.

He hesitated as he shared the American government's concern over some of Leila Metin's activities.

"We fear she may have been involved with a terrorist group, the Silver Wolves. Her brother was in that group. Also, some drug-smuggling allegations have come up. So far, she has managed to keep her respectable job at Topkapı, but we expect any day that she will be taken into police custody."

I was surprised to hear that much candor. "What about Faye Mollington? Do you have any inside word on where she might be? I'm quite concerned about her."

"We think it is possible Ms. Mollington is not precisely what she pretends to be. It is—you will forgive my saying this—within the realm of possibility that she killed Metin for some purpose of her own. No, no, do not become angry. I am merely sharing with you what we here at the consulate are considering."

I had started to rise, but then settled back.

"Thank you. I appreciate any information I can get. But...could all this have anything to do with Peter Franklin? I still maintain he was killed, and not by his own hand. Seems to me too many journalists, foreign and Turkish, are being killed, injured, or abducted in this country."

Lawrence tapped a long finger against his chin; perhaps he was considering how much he should tell me. I had assumed for some time that he was one of those diplomats with double duties, overt and covert. The man just knew too much. And he had been in Turkey for such a long time. Silence on my part might encourage him to part with more information.

"Tell you what," he said at last. "I need to check with some people before we talk further. I assume you're going to the Independence Day cocktail party tomorrow, at the Consul-General's house in Emirgan? Afterward, plan on joining me for dinner. I know just the place, not too far from that part of the Bosphorus. I am inclined to think that it is time we brought you in on some things, but I must consult first, as I said."

Cats can be enticed into water by the lure of fish. Flies happily enter spiders' webs. I had the feeling something of the sort was going on here. Did the U.S. government really think it could subvert an honest journalist into its nefarious subterranean purposes? Well, we'd see about that.

130

*"...there are such people, but I hope
I am not one of them. I hope I never
ridicule what is wise or good."*

Jane Austen, *Pride and Prejudice*

I clutched my briefcase, took my leave, and headed for Üsküdar Hospital. It was time to see Haldun, without a doubt.

I almost lost the briefcase enroute to Üsküdar. I was sitting on the ferry—still the fastest way to get from where I was to the other side—gazing out at Leander's Tower just off the Asian coast. I was musing about philosophical paradoxes surrounding the little lighthouse, since despite the name, Leander had not lost his life swimming across this narrow strait at the mouth of the Bosphorus to his love, Hero. That ill-fated mythical journey in the mist happened at the Hellespont, between the Sea of Marmara and the Aegean, a couple of hundred kilometers away. Some ill-informed European had dubbed the lighthouse Leander's Tower, and the name had stuck, inaccurate as it was. How much of history was skewed in this manner?

The ferry toot as it was about to land at Üsküdar wharf woke me from my reverie, and I reached down to pick up the briefcase at my feet. It wasn't there; must have slipped back. I jumped up to look more closely, and saw a man walking toward the gangplank, which would be available in a minute or two. An oblong-shaped bulge distorted his jacket. I moved.

Most passengers were just rising from their seats, and I reached the blue-coated man, insinuated my hand up under the jacket, and gave a sudden strong tug.

My briefcase fell. The man hid his face and ran, making a flying leap across nearly ten feet of churning water.

On the wet and slimy surface of the wharf's edge, his feet slipped. Would we have one more casualty in the long line of incidents following Peter's death? The passengers near the gangplank gasped. At the last moment, he regained his balance and dashed past the official at the gate, melting quickly into the crowd at the wharf.

At least three men stepped forward to ask, with concern, "*Yardım lazımmı?* Do you need help?"

I shook my head. "*Hayır, teşekkür ederim*. No, thank you very much. *Lazım değil*. Not needed."

As I'd been a number of times on this trip, I was wrong.

131

*"Let me recommend you, however,
as a friend, not to give implicit confidence to all his assertions..."*

Jane Austen, *Pride and Prejudice*

The papers were still with me and anyhow, the police had the originals. I breathed deeply and nabbed a taxi to the hospital, driving past the big mosque overlooking the wharf area market.

Haldun was not amused at the story of the attempted theft. "Now, I wonder who else is in on this game?" he muttered.

As I filled him in on the eventful weekend, though, he looked thoughtful.

"So, you are consorting with the D.E.A.," he said. "That is probably good. And the D.E.A. must be in contact with the American consulate, so we can assume that backing. But the D.E.A. must have contacts here who are Turks, as well, and I would guess they aren't all police. Let's think through who might be secretly on the side of the law, and who might be their prey."

Haldun looked so much better. He was an investigative journalist, even from his hospital bed.

"I wonder if this was what Peter was up to," I murmured. If anyone was listening at the door, they wouldn't hear much. Then I held up a finger: "Leila Metin is clearly a woman of mystery. She could be on anybody's side, though I would opt for an illicit one." Another finger. "Ahmet Aslan is a natural suspect, and I have heard the international police are interested in him regarding drug smuggling." A third. "Perihan Kıraz seems like a straight arrow; I'm going to leave her out, I think. We can safely omit all of Professor Fener's family, too, unless something was going on there that we don't know about. Though I suppose if we include Leila, who lost a brother, we should include Aytem Fener, who lost a father." I lowered my hand.

"Don't forget that Erol Metin could have been a double agent, as well," said Haldun. "And how much do you know about your assistant at the *Trib*...what's his name, Bayram?"

"I've thought of Bayram and rejected him as a spy, but you can keep him on your list, if you want. Now, Erol, hmm. I suppose he could have been fooling everyone. But who killed him, if he wasn't involved?" I warmed to the topic. "And, of course, the people around who are not Turks, and who could, I suppose, have connections. Look at Faye, for example. If she was…is…just a journalist, why is she missing?"

At the words, my heart contracted. And what of Peter? He may have been involved in more than gathering news, though in a rather hypocritical way, I hated to think it. Spying and information-gathering for readers have a lot in common. You just report the results differently.

Peter. My spirits sank. Peter, the first victim. That victim, my friend. That victim, who might once have been my lover…whose death was my reason for being in Turkey.

Haldun scratched a healing incision on his leg. "How much do you really know about this Le Reau fellow?" he asked. "If some of these others are in law enforcement, we have to think about the possibility of a crooked cop. He and Durmaz could be working together, I suppose, though I don't like to think it of Durmaz. Or Le Reau could be playing Durmaz for a fool." He looked at me as he continued: "Like some others I know."

I ignored Haldun's scrutiny. "By all means, put Jean Le Reau on your list," I said. "We have to consider everybody. Unfortunately, I've got to run now. Told Bayram I'd be in. I'm leaving these papers with you, and you'd better have a solution for me soon."

I kissed Haldun on the top of his bristly head as his wife came in, carrying a basket on her arm. Food would be in the basket. Ayla *Hanım* would never trust hospital food for her husband. The food had a companion in another section of the basket—the white Van cat, Sultana.

Haldun broke into a big smile as the graceful feline jumped from the basket to the bed and reached her nose to the patient for petting.

"Now, *kedi*, what have we here?" he murmured. "Did you come to see an old man?"

Sultana nuzzled him as she would a kitten. This cat had clear views on ownership. Who owned whom was less clear. She did her duty checking the room, sniffing corners and opening the door of the little cabinet beside the bed. I'd never seen a more enchanting cat.

When I left, Ayla *Hanım* took my face between her hands and kissed me on both cheeks. Her head-scarf brushed my cheek. How did the old married couple get along so well, considering their differences? Haldun called himself an atheist, or at least a non-practicing Moslem. Ayla *Hanım* was clearly devout. Opposites attract, I suppose.

I chuckled to myself. Yes, I know for a fact that opposites attract. Look at virtually all my relationships!

Or, at the moment, at me and Jean. If you call that a relationship.

* * * *

I hailed a taxi to take me to the wharf, and transferred to the ferry back to Eminönü. As the ferry rounded the point of land that held Galata Tower, with Topkapı on the left, I frowned. Haldun had said that the D.E.A. would certainly be in touch with the consulate.

Of course it would. But neither my D.E.A. contact nor my consular protector had mentioned anything of the sort. Was I being strung along by everyone?

By the time my taxi on the European side had snaked up to the *Trib*'s building in Cağaloğlu, I was grumpy and ready to pick a fight.

132

...it was impossible not to feel
that there was gross duplicity on
one side or the other; and, for a
few moments, she flattered herself
that her wishes did not err.

Jane Austen, *Pride and Prejudice*

Work was finished, thank goodness. We'd done a few small stories—paragraphs, really—but my mind had strayed back to the session with Haldun and the many unanswered questions. I was ready to call it a day. Bidding Bayram a brusque goodnight, I fled to the Pera.

Why wasn't I surprised to find a message that Mr. Le Reau in room 411 had asked that I call him when I returned?

Before making the call, I ordered from room service—plain rice *pilav*. The dish isn't plain at all, steamed to fluff each kernel up to wheat-size, dripping with butter, with a flavoring I couldn't identify but which might have been cinnamon. I had them add an order of white beans cooked with onions and garlic in olive oil. Of course, yogurt, creamy as only buffalo milk can be, accompanied the beans. And a small Turkish salad of sliced tomatoes, cucumbers, and onions with little, tangy black olives. "Oh, and please send two beers to go with that." But I didn't intend to drink two beers alone.

I picked up the telephone. "Jean? Elizabeth. I am finally back. What's been going on?"

"Glad you called. I mean, really glad. May I come down?"

His voice was rich with promise. Jean and I had the same thing in mind.

"Yes, why don't you do that."

The rest of the evening was, shall we say, an interesting interlude that left two beers unfinished on the big Victorian dresser. I forgot I was tired; felt invigorated, in fact.

The man was a gentleman. He had no hormonal deficiencies. It was satisfactory, to the point of comparing favorably with a whole pan of crisp, flaky, buttery *baklava* oozing pistachios and honey. That earlier flash of desire had not been a false indicator. That's an understatement, of course, but details are nobody's business but our own.

On the politically-correct question of safe sex, I would simply say that neither of us was born yesterday. Beyond that, a lady doesn't talk. (Nor do I, for that matter.)

I woke up feeling refreshed.

Jean had not stayed through the night, fearing correctly that my reputation would be compromised. As he left, he'd asked if I would be free the following evening for dinner.

"Sorry. I have a boring diplomatic party to attend and then might have dinner with someone from the consulate."

"Who?"

"Lawrence Andover."

A long silence ensued. "At least I needn't be jealous," was the reply, at last. "Have a good time. And call me if you are so inclined when you get in."

"Maybe I will," I said, pulling the covers up to my chin and peeking out like a small child. "By the way, Jean..."

"Yes?"

"Are you married?"

Another long pause. "Yes, I am, actually." His face darkened.

"I kind of hoped that's what you would say," I said, and smiled. "Friends, okay?"

My answer seemed to take him aback. "Okay" he said, and stopped by the bed for a last gentle kiss on his way out.

It's necessary to put idealism aside at times. Live for the moment and all that. Still, I would not stick around to hear Jean Le Reau tell me what a bad marriage he had or that his wife didn't understand him.

133

Worldly love is merely
A deadly kind of food,
When we see the end with wisdom,
We turn down that poisonous food.

Yunus Emre, 15th Century Turkish poet

Roses were delivered to my room the next morning. No message came with them.

I stretched and opened my heavy velvet curtains.

The gray semi-rain of the past few days showed signs of breaking; a stretch of blue sky greeted me. I felt refreshed in body and mind, ready to celebrate Turkish Independence Day.

I hoped that Faye still had some independence. It seemed a very long time since I had seen her.

Bayram and I had put the finishing touches on an Independence Day feature the day before, and sent it. In it, I had tried to capture the competing forces in Turkey that make it a society held together by centrifugal force: Islam and secularism; Europe and Asia; ornate civilization and nomadic horsemen; fierce warriors and hospitable hosts; Turks and the minorities in the country: Kurds, a few Armenians and Jews and Caucasians; traditions of female subservience and a woman Prime Minister.

I had interviewed old people who still remembered the great upheaval at the end of World War I, when French, Italian, and Greek armies were poised to slice up the remains of the bedraggled Ottoman Empire. They found themselves facing off against an impetuous young *pasha* named Mustafa Kemal, who pulled the Turks together to protect Anatolia in Asia and a small piece of European Thrace. A new, modern nation was born, and its first leader was, who else, Mustafa Kemal Atatürk, one of the most remarkable men of the 20th century.

The history was not all admirable—nobody's independence struggle is, after all—but it made a colorful and intricate, though violent, panorama. Each time I came to Turkey, I experienced it again, glowing like one of the intricate carpets hanging from shops in the Covered Market.

After breakfast, I lay on my bed reading the notes that I'd given Haldun copies of. Someone had wanted badly to get hold of these notes, hard as they were to decipher. It did look as though Peter had suspected Ahmet Aslan of something, but the notes in the Drugs file were inconclusive: "Aslan/Beykoz. Visit cer. fac.? Ask L. Check w/con." So Peter had been at least thinking about Ahmet Aslan and his ceramics. Perhaps I should visit the Beykoz factory as well as the one in Iznik…. Did "con." mean the U.S. consulate? And did L. stand for Leila?

Someone reliable—Haldun?—had intimated there might have been something between Leila and Peter. It was possible, of course, that Lawrence was the undercover drugs person at the consulate. So Peter would presumably have interviewed him. I made a note to ask Lawrence at the party, if I got a chance, whether Peter had talked with him about the story, or whether the event of his death had stepped in to make news-gathering intentions moot. Of course, in government circles there is always the "need to know" restriction. I wasn't sure either party would feel free to tell me anything.

In another file, Peter had written Lawrence's name. "Andover/ Çengelköy" was there, with three question marks. Peter had doodled on the page, scribbles that looked like Ottoman designs.

Once again, reference perhaps to the woman who had allegedly been his lover: "L./Top." Topkapı, maybe. The doodle here was of a vase like that inhabited by Barbara Eden in the old television series, "I Dream of Jeanie." Well, given Leila's figure, and her work with pottery, that wasn't a surprising connection. At the bottom of the page, Peter had written: "Hrm. d.r. Bot. row." Right. I knew what I would do with my day, provided that no major news story erupted on the horizon. Bayram was getting paid to keep an eye on things at the office. I'd make the trek to Topkapı on foot, since today was a holiday and taxis would be hard to come by. I wore my hiking boots, both for uneven cobblestones and for warmth. My jeans were back from the laundry so I put them on, with my now-nicely-laundered sweatshirt. My lightweight, hooded GorTex jacket allowed for the chance of rain.

There weren't many people on Galata Bridge, and only about half the little bridge restaurants were open today. I strode along the level below where cars were driving. I couldn't help slowing my pace walking past the restaurants, though the smell of fresh fish from the markets got a little overwhelming. The breeze was crisp and my nose chilled.

A couple of times, I wondered what Jean was up to today. Why hadn't he contacted me, other than with the roses? Maybe a touch of remorse? Maybe he called his wife this morning, and that caused regrets.

13⅔

*"Vanity, not love, has been my folly...
I have courted prepossession and
ignorance, and driven reason away,
where either were concerned..."*

Jane Austen, *Pride and Prejudice*

It was a weekday and a holiday, so Topkapı was unusually empty. Pulling my jacket around me, I walked up the cobblestone road on which Sultans' chariots used to drive. The big, white-barked plane trees had dropped the last of their broad leaves long ago, and urban-immigrant sweepers from Anatolian villages had gathered them with their coarse brooms. Blue sky peeked through the branches of the trees on both sides of the old chariotway.

At the top of the hill, I stood in the old Court of the Janissaries, with the ancient Church of the Divine Peace, St. Irene or *Aya* Irini, on my right. Today, musicians carried their cellos, violins and wind instruments in for tonight's Independence Day concert. I wished I could attend to hear the classical music amplified by *Aya* Irini's classic bricked interior.

All the walls, presumably once plastered and painted, had been ruined by years of the Janissaries' storing weapons in *Aya* Irini. The Turkish army continued to do that after Independence, until the country decided to restore the sixth-century building.

Out in the center of the square, the Janissaries, who came from European children recruited as slaves and security guards by the Sultan, occasionally overturned the great vats of rice *pilav* provided them. Terrifying the residents all around, the soldiers would pound on the vats like drums. When that ominous drumming happened, the Sultan himself was likely to be overturned, as well, raising the question, who, in fact, was slave to whom? So often the question. . .

I bought my ticket to Topkapı at the Middle Door to the palace complex—the door where heads of out-of-favor noblemen were displayed on pikes in times past. In summer, rows of tourist buses from five-star hotels and cruise liners lined the street outside the Middle Door. Today, only a few tourists, most Turkish, entered the grounds with me.

I walked past the old sprawling kitchens on the right, where I had first met Leila Metin. On the left lay the cupola-covered Imperial Council Chamber, where once the Grand Vizier met with council members to discuss matters of state. Today's wind and lack of visitors made the Kubbealtı seem bleak and isolated—as indeed it must have been during certain Ottoman reigns, under cruel and devious Grand Viziers.

The entrance to the *harem* is just past the Kubbealtı, where the Black Eunuchs stood guard. There, I showed my all-inclusive ticket and slipped into the cold and forbidding hall, where tradesmen used to deliver goods for inspection and distribution by the Black Eunuchs. These men ruled the realm of the *harem*—often with complicity from one of the chief wives. The chief Black Eunuch was, in fact, the third most powerful official at the Ottoman court, after the Grand Vizier and the Supreme Islamic Judge. Keep those women under control, at all costs, I thought uncharitably.

The multitude of rooms in the *harem* have been under renovation for years. Four main Sultanic wives, or *Kadins*, had their own private quarters. The concubines, who could number in the hundreds, slept in small, cell-like rooms, awaiting the eye—and bed—of the Lord and Master. With great good luck, one would bear the Sultan a son and acquire a position within the Palace. The whole place, quite naturally, was a beehive of intrigue and jealousy, lending a very special meaning to the term, "sexual politics."

The second room I came to, before the monk-like sleeping quarters of the Eunuchs, seemed to be undergoing some work, as the wall on one side was covered with scaffolding and canvas. I supposed the museum authorities were taking advantage of the lull in tourists to spiff up the place. But no, it looked on closer observation as though part of the wall had started to crumble; they seemed to be in the process of repairing sections of the wall in small pieces and re-cementing the tiles to the new wall.

The tiles...

I stood there for a full minute, in shock.

135

*...it may be easily believed that
the happy spirits which had sel-
dom been depressed before, were
now so much affected as to make
it almost impossible for her to
appear tolerably cheerful.*

Jane Austen, *Pride and Prejudice*

This room between hallways, in the tradesman part of the Eunuch quarters, is home to some of Turkey's best tiles, all from Iznik. The most famous Iznik color is red, like the reproduction vase I had seen in Lawrence's house. However, those sixteenth-century pottery masters had used other colors, as well.

In spite of the scaffolding and canvas, I admired the greens and yellows of the wall tiles. Now, where had I seen something similar to this? I looked more closely at the pattern. Of course. There were animals on these tiles, like those on the tile at Lawrence's house. Deer. Dogs or wolves. Lions. And a peacock in a pear tree, sang my irrelevant inner voice.

I stared at a covered stack of something on the floor, behind the canvas-covered scaffolding. I glanced around; I was alone. Probably the whole museum was operating with fewer guards than usual, letting employees take a longer Independence Holiday.

I pulled aside the bricks that held down the plastic cover over the pile. Yes, it was tiles waiting to be placed back on the walls. I couldn't move many, for obvious reasons, but I saw what I had expected to see.

I slipped one tile out of the bunch and into my purse, praying the guards would not check my bag on the way out. Just as the tile disappeared under a ball of purse-bunched Kleenex, a lone Turkish tourist entered and began studying the intricate tiles on the walls. I wandered through the stone door into the Eunuch's sleeping quarters.

The tourist stayed behind.

136

*Reflection must be reserved for
solitary hours; whenever she was
alone, she gave way to it as the
the greatest relief; and not a day
went by without a solitary walk, in
which she might indulge in all the
delight of unpleasant recollections.*

Jane Austen, *Pride and Prejudice*

For two reasons, I headed on through other rooms in the *harem*. The first, of course, was not to have my thievery detected. The second was to visit once more the dining room, where all the central tiles boast bowls of appetizing fruit. Near the top and bottom of the room are tiles reflecting the color motifs of the fruit: reds and oranges and yellows.

An elderly American couple poked around the room. "Oh, sweetie, don't you just love all this fruit? I mean, it would look great in our kitchen in the lake cabin, don't you think?"

"Hmmmph." The usual male response to such a question. Then the couple moved on into other chambers used by the Sultan and his wives and concubines. That was the direction of my favorite room, where a strategic fountain masks conversations—a crucial element in a place like the *harem*, where secrets were the grist of every lazy, luxurious, danger-filled day.

Today, I didn't have time for the fountain room, though. When the other people had left, and I couldn't see anyone around, I leaned down and checked the tiles on the second row from the bottom. There had been some restoration done here, too. Some of the tiles had a different hue from the others. They looked a bit newer and cheaper. I snatched my tiny Olympus from my bag, being careful not to jostle the purloined tile, and snapped several pictures of the dining room walls, concentrating on the lower rows.

Very interesting, in light of Peter's notes.

As I was leaving the room, I heard footsteps, and the lone Turkish tourist entered. I nodded to him politely, and to the guard who was on his heels, and then I walked as nonchalantly as I could toward the back door of the *harem*, leading out into the Third Court, which is where the Sultan himself used to be ensconced.

I love that Third Court, with its garden center surrounded by all the main Ottoman treasures, including jewels beyond price in the Treasury and holy relics of the Prophet Mohammad, peace be upon him, such as his cloak, a hair from his beard, and a letter in his own handwriting in the suite of rooms known as the *Hirka-I Saalt*.

There was no time for dawdling today, though. I pulled my hood up and clutched my bag to my side as I walked back through the Third Door, into the Middle Square, where the kitchens are. Striding ahead, bent against the chill wind, I wasn't even planning to look toward the kitchens, with their ceramic treasures and the tragic, arrogant woman who was their principal caretaker.

"*Merhaba!*" The voice that accosted me held urgency.

I looked up to see Leila herself. Dressed in a fur coat, she nonetheless had retained the years she'd put on since her brother's death. She was now a middle-aged woman in a fur coat, not an expensively-clad beauty who would not have been out of place in the best days of the *harem*.

"Hello, Leila *Hanım*," I said, finding unconscious sympathy in the tone. "How are you?"

Grief is a dreadful thing to deal with alone, especially when you suspect the person who died brought it on him or herself. All that anger at the other person, and the guilt of what we, ourselves, did or failed to do.

Speaking of guilt, I hoped my cheeks didn't look redder than could be accounted for by the wind. I was, after all, carrying on a conversation with the very person in charge of the tile I had so sneakily swiped in the *harem*. I hoped it wouldn't start to glow or anything.

"May I speak with you?" It was the first time Leila had initiated any discussion between us.

"Certainly," I said. And we headed toward her office in the kitchens.

The office would have been as cold as the rest of the museum, except for a small fire in the coal stove. The stove reminded me of the great iron monstrosities in classrooms when I'd first taught in the Anatolian hinterlands. There had to be a disruptive rotation of pupils at least once during each class period, so the ones who had been roasted for twenty minutes could go freeze for the other half of the period, and vice versa. The teacher (I) kept moving around the classroom in a futile attempt to thaw out various appendages so as to gesture grandly in explaining the Simple Present Tense.

There were only the two of us in the office now. I set my bag down beside my chair very carefully, so the tile would not make a sound, or even worse, break against the stone floor. These colors—greens, blues, yellows—were low-fired, thanks to the Islamic stone paste spread over them. Breaking was a real possibility.

"I want to thank you for attending my brother's prayer service." Leila's voice had a leaden quality.

"I'm really very sorry he passed away."

"I think your friend, Ms. Mollington, is missing," said Leila, abruptly changing the subject. "Perhaps I know where she is."

I tried not to show my eagerness at information, any information, regarding Faye. I instinctively reached a hand toward Leila. "Where do you think she is?"

Leila shivered in her fur coat, and edged closer to the semi-lit stove. "I would rather not say, but perhaps we could go together," she said. "Are you free tonight?"

"I have some things scheduled for tonight, but finding Faye comes before either of them," I said crisply. "What time do you want to leave? Where do you want me to meet you?"

"Come to my house in Çengelköy," said Leila. Her voice was clipped, brusque. Was she angry at me? No, I didn't think so. She was controlling anger at what could not be controlled. "Come at nine o'clock."

I nodded. Was I making a big mistake in accepting Leila's invitation? I hoped not.

"I will be there," I promised.

137

Count the French and English words
on billboards and posters, in shop
signs, magazines, and businesses;
this is indeed a city moving westward,
but it's still not changing as fast as it
talks. Neither can the city honor the
traditions implied by its mosques,
its minarets, its calls to prayer, its
history. Everything is half formed,
shoddy, and soiled... But as my reason
reasserts itself, I remember that I
love this city not for any purity but
precisely for the lamentable want of it.

Orhan Pamuk, *Istanbul, Memories and the City*

I exited the Topkapı grounds through the First Door, near the corner of Saint Sophia cathedral-cum-mosque-cum museum. A taxi cruised around the Fountain of Ahmet III. I signalled to it and got in as quickly as I could. One other person was flagging down the taxi, too. It was the lone Turkish tourist I had seen twice in the *harem*.

"*Yok, yok*," I said sternly to the driver. "I don't have time for you to pick anyone else up." A European fare over to Pera was worth listening to, obviously. The driver drove past the man, who was left standing with a palace gate behind him, and a spectacular fountain and a holy building a millenium and a half old before him. It made him look so insignificant. Was he another of Mehmet *Bey's* omnipresent police? Just in case, I gave him a decorous wave.

When I got to the Pera, I called Room 411—just wait til Jean heard about my acquisition of the tile. There was no answer, and I hung up before the clerk picked up and asked whether there would be a message. Where was my ardent companion of the night before?

There was just time for a rinse-off and a little primping before the cocktail party in Emirgan. I donned my green silk dress, which had come back from the cleaners during the day. Should I take a taxi all the way up the Bosphorus to Emirgan, past Rumeli Hisar, or once more resort to my favorite method of travel, the ferry system?

This time I chose the taxi. I had to carry my big bag, party or no, since my cashmere shawl and the tile would not fit in my small handbag. Maybe when I got to the party, I could set the bag down behind a chair or something.

Would the event allow for privacy? Most big diplomatic bashes do. All those people, all thinking of how they look, with so little real interest in each other. You could walk through lugging a steamer trunk, and if you asked each person some interesting question about herself or himself, they would look at you, not the trunk.

"Just a minute," you could say, "I'll hear the rest when I get back from depositing this." And the idle chatter would go on.

At least that's the way I hoped it would be.

* * * *

Before going in, I got the taxi driver's name and asked him to wait. It would cost. Never mind.

The venue of the party was a large old wooden mansion on the European side, set in a big garden that stretched down to the lapping edge of the Bosphorus. The scale of this party was clearly intended as a tribute by the Americans, who had their own Revolutionary War, to the independence struggle of the Turks: the place was lit with hundreds of tiny lights, lending a fairy tale aspect to what would have been a romantic setting in any case. The red and white Turkish flag, with its Islamic half moon and star, flew in tandem with the stars and stripes. The governor of the province and the mayor of Istanbul were two of the guests of honor. Tomorrow, of course, they would be hosting parties of their own. Many of the guests here would be invited to those.

My taxi slid to a stop under the portico where several cars with CD license plates, indicating members of the diplomatic corps, were letting out passengers. It was a chill night, and there were many furs in evidence. International social events like this were some of the last places, perhaps, where a woman could safely wear the skins of animals without protesters ruining her coat and her evening. I actually had mixed feelings about that. It seemed a little hypocritical to eat meat but throw red paint on fur coats. On the other hand, I can't bring myself to wear fur, luscious and cozy as the feeling is. I like my cuddly fur animals alive, thank you very much.

The consular staff and servants were out in force to greet people, making it hard for me to conceal my large bag with its geometric ethnic fabric motif. Fortunately, the color scheme fitted more or less with my green silk dress and navy blue raw silk jacket. Those could be glimpsed through the open front of my trenchcoat, which was the only outerwear I'd brought to Turkey, except for my GorTex jacket, which really would have been out of place. My shoes were sturdy and comfortable black Italian mid-heels—ready for anything, even a party like this. I could only hope they would work as well for who-knew-what adventures later with Leila.

The big entry hall was buzzing with conversation as I arrived. I shook hands with the Consul-General and his wife, and with the Turkish guests of honor, and then looked for an unobtrusive corner where I could park my bag. Ladies' coats were being eased from their shoulders by black-uniformed servants and checked in one of the side rooms downstairs. They must be relying on visual security, as there was no metal detector in sight. Whew. That would have been fine for my trenchcoat, but not for my bag. I was not in a position to withstand even a cursory security check, much less a knowing—or lucky—thief.

Just then, I heard my name being called.

"Elizabeth! Glad you could make it! Did you get a drink? How are things?" And Lawrence was kissing both cheeks, Turkish-style.

"Fine, Lawrence. Fine. Nice party, I must say."

It was good to see my perfectly-groomed companion of the morning in a crowd of unfamiliar faces. He wore the blackest of evening suits, just short of a tux, with a silk tie I bet had cost hundreds. His hair, as always, was cut stylishly and was not a centimeter too long or short. His blue eyes were cool and, well, diplomatic. Like the State Department spokesman, they didn't tell much.

What role does he play in the covert areas of my country's overseas operations? Does he know Jean Le Reau? And this time I wondered whether this tall, elegant man standing with me so politely perhaps even knew what I had been asking myself all day, the whereabouts of my midnight lover. I certainly wasn't about to ask!

Across the room, Perihan Kıraz caught my eye, and signalled for us to meet by one wall.

"Excuse me, Lawrence. There is someone who wants to talk to me. By the way, I'm afraid I won't be able to make the dinner we were talking about later. I have an unexpected appointment."

Lawrence smiled benevolently. "Oh, that's all right. You'll be missing a good dinner, though. I called the chef at the restaurant and asked him to do something special." He waved his long fingers dismissively. "Not a problem. I'll find one or two others to enjoy the food."

Glancing around, I saw the handsome television anchor I had met, or almost met, on a couple of other occasions. Oh, right. İrfan Algar.

I gave him a little wave as I moved toward Perihan, who was slowly making her way through the crowd, stopping to chat with various people. She looked better today than she had at the dig. Her face smiled, though her eyes didn't join in.

The hand on my shoulder surprised me.

"Hello! You are Ms. Darcy, aren't you? Remember me, Howard Black?" It was the three-piece suit who had been with Leila and Lawrence at the Topkapı restaurant.

It seemed ages since the incident. Ages which were actually only a few days ago, when Faye and I were looking into more-or-less-ordinary crimes, like drugs and murder. I smiled, though he hadn't impressed me favorably at the lunch.

"Hello, Mr. Black. How long are you staying in Turkey?" I shifted the bag to my other shoulder.

"Can I help you with that? Looks pretty heavy," said Black.

"Oh, no, no. It's not quite the bag I'd have chosen for an event like this, but you know what it's like travelling."

"Certainly. You're a journalist, aren't you?" Black was sipping his Scotch and nibbling on delicious little rolled *börek* pastries filled with cheese and spinach or minced lamb. His hands were full. Did he have an extra one to help me with my bag?

"That's right," I acknowledged. "With the *Washington Tribune*. I'm afraid I can't remember what you said you do…"

"Import-export. I'm in and out of Turkey often. We do quite a bit with ceramic tiles."

"So you must know Ahmet Aslan," I said. "Isn't that him right over there?"

Black turned toward where I was gesturing, where an unusually handsome profile was placed in relief against the french windows leading out to the terrace. Really, I knew quite a few more people at this party than I had first thought.

A surge of the crowd separated us. Perihan and I finally met, and gave each other warm pecks on the cheeks. Perhaps she'd felt the same glimmering of sisterhood I had when we had met and talked at the Iznik dig.

"I was going to call you," said Perihan. "I thought maybe we could talk."

"Well, yes. Of course. How is your young friend, Aytem? Is she coping with the tragedy?"

The shadow in Perihan's eyes deepened. "Aytem is quite strong. Her mother is in worse shape." Perihan's voice dropped to a whisper. "I am getting seriously concerned about ceramics. . . . Are you free after this?"

"I have to be on the other side of the Bosphorus by nine. But I could meet tomorrow." My curiosity was thoroughly piqued.

"Come to my office, then, at ten am," whispered Perihan. "I'll be expecting you."

* * * *

Back near the entrance hall, a waiter presented a piece of paper to Lawrence. He looked around, caught my eye, and beckoned me.

"You have a phone call," he said, when I got within earshot.

"Oh, thanks very much," I said. "Where shall I take it?"

"The man will lead the way," he said.

So I followed the man into one of the anterooms off the entrance hall. He indicated where the telephone was, and then took himself off, closing the door softly behind him.

"Yes? Elizabeth Darcy here," I said. The line crackled.

Just as if another extension was off the hook.

138

*Elizabeth, as she affectionately
embraced her, whilst tears filled
the eyes of both, lost not a moment in asking whether anything
had been heard of the fugitives.*

*"Not yet," replied Jane. "But
now that my dear uncle is come, I
hope everything will be well."*

Jane Austen, *Pride and Prejudice*

It was Haldun on the phone, speaking so low I could hardly make out the words.

"Antiquities," he rasped.

"What do you mean, antiquities?" I demanded, keeping my own voice low.

"Franklin was killed because of antiquities," whispered Haldun. "Vases. Tiles. Faye maybe knew. There's a note here... Not drugs. Antiquities...undercover..." His voice got louder as he turned away from the receiver. "*Evet, evet.* Yes, I know it's time for my injection. No, I'm not ready for my injection. Now, go away... Elizabeth?" The last was again whispered.

"Yes?" I asked.

"Vases are the clue. I hope you are understanding me. But don't go alone." And the phone clicked off.

I stood for a few minutes and looked at the instrument. Maybe I understood. Maybe I didn't.

Under the circumstances, I had to guess where Haldun was sending me. Who could I trust to go with me, with layers of mystery and suspicion lying heavy over everyone I know? I might have been willing to trust Jean LeReau. Would have been ready, in fact. But he had pulled a disappearing act, and I could only hope it had something to do with the D.E.A. I wished very much he were here.

For just a moment, I considered pulling Perihan aside and begging her to accompany me. Picturing the matronly figure sneaking through potentially dangerous areas brought me to my senses.

No. I would go alone. Afterwards I would meet Leila, who could very well be planning to lead me astray. I wanted to give Faye any chance she had.

I went to the ladies room on the second floor, waited in line in a cloud of perfumed, coiffed and beautifully-made-up women, and finished my business. Then, trying to be as inconspicuous as possible, I presented my check stub to the servants who had taken my coat, and waited in the hallway for them to bring it.

"Aha, there you are!"

The smooth, rich voice swirled around me. And I was trying to escape notice.

"I saw you but we have not yet talked, eh?" It was the handsomest guy in any room, anytime, Ahmet Aslan.

My heart pounded in my chest. Not now. I rubbed my sweaty palms on my dress. He strode toward me, interest alive in his dark, almond-shaped eyes.

"Ahmet *Bey*! How nice to see you," I lied.

"What is this? You are going so soon? You must at least come and have some of the seafood *meze*. Really, I insist. Don't you agree, Ando-ver?" he asked, as Lawrence sauntered in our direction.

Lawrence glanced at the trenchcoat being held by a servant.

"She is surely welcome to whatever we have," he said. "However, it looks as though Elizabeth is on her way out."

Thank Heaven for diplomatic interventions! I smiled into the cool blue eyes, as I awkwardly slipped my coat over my bulky bag.

"Thank you so much for a lovely time, Lawrence," I said warmly. "I'm sorry I have to run, but that phone call was from my office, and I need to be going."

Aslan, of course, never missed a beat. "Do you need a ride anywhere? Anywhere at all?" he asked. "I am nearly ready to leave myself, and I would be happy to drop you wherever required."

A plethora of male attendants. How gratifying. Where were they when I was sixteen and insecure?

"You are much too kind, Ahmet," I said. "I asked my taxi to wait, so I don't need a ride. But I do appreciate the offer." I shook Aslan's well-shaped hand, and Lawrence's slim one. Then I found the Consul-General near the edge of the crowd and shook his hand, too.

Niceties must be observed, no matter how dangerous the crisis.

139

As a child I counted these ships
heedless of the disquiet, agitation,
and mounting panic they induced
in me. By counting I felt as if I
was giving order to my life.

Orhan Pamuk, *Istanbul, Memories and the City*

When I emerged into the brisk night air, I breathed in several lungfuls thankfully. I needed all the oxygen I could inhale.

The staff offered to call my taxi to the big doorway under the portico, but I thought it would be less conspicuous to find him myself. I tried to walk as nonchalantly as possible, making the bulky bag look a part of my outfit. Happily, I didn't turn an ankle on the uneven cobblestone driveway.

My driver was half asleep, but he stirred when I knocked on the window, and let me in. I settled into the back seat gratefully, kicking off my shoes and curling my feet under me for warmth.

"What time is the next ferry to Çengelköy?" I asked as we drove out to the main Bosphorus road.

"*Bilmem,* I don't know," was the rather surly answer.

I could practically hear the guy's mind working: The woman has me endure a long, cold wait and then she ditches me.

"Of course, I would pay for your time, including the trip back into Istanbul," I said. The offer was far too generous at this early evening hour, when he could easily pick up a fare back.

"We will ask," was the less-unpleasant reply.

We drove into the Emirgan ferry landing. I slipped on my shoes and got out to check the departure board. I kept my bag under my arm. I was in luck. A south-bound ferry was due at 7:57, just ten minutes from now. It would be much faster, to say nothing of pleasanter, to take the boat. I paid my driver an extravagant amount, and went in to wait in the little passenger holding area.

* * * *

I huddled in a corner of the waiting room. Only as the mournful whoop of the ferry announced it was about to arrive did I look around. One of the people in the waiting room with me was not a total stranger. He was bundled up and had a scarf wrapped around the bottom part of his face, but the hinted-at profile seemed familiar. He must have come in while I was lost in reverie. He was reading a newspaper, but he wasn't a cop.

I would be riding with the infamous mustachioed driver of the blue Murat.

What could I do? I could go to the official in charge of the one-way turnstile to the waiting room and tell him I had changed my mind. But the other guy would probably wriggle out of taking the ferry, too, and I'd still have him on my tail. No. I would stay with other people on the short trip across the Bosphorus, and during the twenty-minute trip I'd devise a plan.

Unfortunately, there were few passengers on this particular trip. I stood beside the shipboard kiosk, where a man in a worn jacket was making tea that would be delivered by a colleague in a grubby, ill-fitting suit.

I leaned against the wall across from the kiosk and avoided meeting either tea-man's eye, which is a shrouding tactic I've learned over the years in the Middle East. Rarely will you be threatened by a man you don't know in cultures like these; eye contact, though, unless it involves something like a legitimate business transaction, can be construed as willingness to know a man and can lead to unpleasant effects.

I'd lost my pursuer. Where was he? With one hand in my bag, where I could feel the precious purloined tile, I plotted how to shake the fellow in Çengelköy.

140

"I wish this may be more intelligible,
but though not confined for time, my
head is so bewildered that I can-
not answer for being coherent."

Jane Austen, *Pride and Prejudice*

The plan was less than full-blown when the ferry whooped and slowed, bumping gently and grinding its protective tires against the wooden wharf. Nonetheless, I followed my instincts and jumped off guickly, before the men had laid the gangplanks across the roiling water. Then I walked decisively, hand still on the tile inside my bag, past the offical collecting used tickets.

At the edge of the landing building, I ducked left and around the corner and into a ladies room. No one there. I had to trust that no Turkish man would take a chance on entering the precincts of women, at least where anyone could see him. My pursuer would be waiting outside, probably leaning against a wall as I had during the trip.

Let's see. There were officials around. Not many and not high-level, but uniformed, at any rate. What could I tell them that would protect me, without jeopardizing my mission? Of course! I collected myself. I just had to make a quick dart out of the toilet to the ticket booth just twelve feet away.

I reached the booth.

"*Efendim*? Sir? Sir? Excuse me, but I feel faint. Do you have a cup of tea I could have? Ooh, my head, my head...."

It was a performance guaranteed to have men getting rid of me as quickly as possible, short of sending me out into the night alone, which would be a breach of Turkish hospitality. With luck, they would take me to a woman, any woman, where I might have a chance of getting myself out of this bear trap. Maybe I could nudge them that direction....

"Oh, sir, I am sitting on this bench, but I still feel faint. Is there a place I can lie down somewhere?"

The two officials shared a dismayed look, which boded well for my plans. I groaned a few times to keep them uncomfortable, and they spoke to each other in low tones.

Finally, one came over to me and said, "*Hanım*, my house is just over there. I will take you there, and my wife can help you. *Buyrun*, please come. Let me take your arm."

As we stumbled over the cobblestones to the house near the village square, the back of a young, agile man with a scarf around his face headed away from the square. Hah. Foiled you this time.

The official's modest house was warm and inviting, and Sevim *Hanım*, his wife, equally so. Her grizzled husband was as relieved as I when she said, "*Ben bakaram*, I'll take care of her."

When my official host had taken himself back to the ferry landing, where he was on duty, I could speak. I would throw myself on the mercy of the kind woman who was dabbing lemon cologne on my temples and easing me to a recumbent position. For her sake, it was best to mix lies with the truth.

I sat up straight and looked her in the eye. "*Afedersiniz*, Sevim *Hanım*," I said. "I am not ill. I am afraid. Perhaps you can help me."

Sevim hid her surprise, and came gallantly to mother lioness mode. "*Evet*, of course. What can I do to help?"

The lemon cologne, a fixture in every Turkish home and used for everything from washing guest's hands to disinfecting cuts, stayed open in her hand, letting its clean, pungent smell permeate the closed-up room.

"It is my husband," I said. "He sometimes gets very rough when he has been drinking, and then he chases me. We were at a party just now, and he followed me on the ferry and I am afraid he will find me. I, of course, did not want to say this to your husband and the other officials."

I used the word for officers rather than for officials, since that would subtly confer a higher rank on her husband than he probably had. A harmless form of flattery. And she deserved every bit of it.

"So you need to get away from here without your husband knowing," she muttered. "Yes, yes, I see. What can we do?" Already, she was digging about in a trunk she had pulled from under the bed. During the day it was made up like a sofa.

Sevim, obviously enjoying the unexpected chance for a little drama, took a Turkish village outfit from the trunk. There were aubergine-colored baggy pants of coarse cotton, with a long wrinkled shirt in an off-white, non-processed color, and a subdued silk vest with a geometric pattern.

I pulled off my dress and started putting the things on, while she went through some long dark scarves with equally subdued patterns, checking each before throwing it to one side. Finally, she found one that met her approval, and stepped over to me to wrap it around my head, leaving a length to pull over my face at will.

I looked in the cracked old mirror and my eyes widened in surprise. I was unrecognizable, even to myself.

But what about my trenchcoat and my ethnic handbag? Sevim handed me a rough, handwoven, woolen stole, and a smaller bag, again of coarse wool. I switched the papers and the tile.

Sevim smiled at me as she started packing up all my clothes, except for the Italian shoes, which I was going to have to wear. Her feet were short and wide, mine long and narrow, and a trade simply wasn't possible.

Sevim had been so kind. I would ask her one enormous favor more.

"Could you put this somewhere, with my clothes?" I handed her the ethnic bag. After a moment's thought, I added the tile I had stolen from Topkapı. Without that tile, my case against a cold-blooded criminal would be weaker. If possible, I wanted to keep it safe for the police.

"*Hay, hay*, certainly," was the answer, as I knew it would be.

When it comes to taking care of guests, Turks are unparalleled. That fact isn't as widely known in the West as it should be. I was going to owe Sevim *Hanım* something major, when I found Faye and got myself out of this.

"When," not "if." The half-hour of genuine caring had nurtured my hope, as the previous sense of threat had diminished it. Amazing what a little kindness can do.

1ଫ1

Not Lydia only, but all were con-
cerned in it; and after the first
exclamations of surprise and hor-
ror, Mr. Gardiner readily promised
every assistance in his power.

Jane Austen, *Pride and Prejudice*

Since my would-be pursuer knew which house I had been taken to, it seemed wise for Sevim to walk with me sedately across the square, past the wharf, veering left down the small street leading along the coast, with walled *yali*s along the Bosphorus side blocking a water view. If we were dressed the same, like two matrons from the village, perhaps no one would question our identities.

I chuckled to myself as Sevim *Hanım* put on make-up and fluffed up her hair before enveloping herself in the anonymous shawls and scarves.

"Are you expecting to see your husband on the way back?" I teased.

"Maybe not my husband," she laughed. "I think it is best that my husband not know you are going dressed like this. Men, they do not understand. Often, they do not understand."

Well, that was indubitably true. No time to discuss our shared feminine insights, though. It was getting on for 8:45, and I had plenty of things to do before climbing the hill to Leila's house at 9:00. Already, I was going to be late.

We wrapped our bodies and our faces in the natural woolens and stepped out into the cobblestone square. Another ferry was preparing to land, its flurry of activity occupying all the officials at the wharf, including Sevim's husband. My mustachioed predator was probably in the shadows somewhere near, and I hoped his feet were freezing.

Sevim and I had decided to speak (in Turkish, of course) in low voices, to look as normal as possible. We even waved goodbye ostentatiously to the empty entryway, calling *"Allaha ısmarladık*, we leave you in God's hands."

There were still a number of people hurrying from the little shops around the square to their homes, and a few heading toward the wharf to catch the next ferry. We passed the wharf and were well into the darkness of the little street. Had I put Sevim in danger? What if my attacker thought I was still in the house? Alone, perhaps? Sevim must go back, but she must be seen to not go alone.

I pulled her into a niche in the wall, from where we could see whoever else came into the street.

"You must go home," I whispered. "But I want you to stop and ask your husband to go with you. Think of some excuse. Do not go into your house alone, without someone, do you understand?"

At this point, it was a Catch-22 for me, since taking her with me would almost certainly be dangerous, while leaving her could present other threats. Sevim looked at me with a little fear and a lot of courage in her eyes.

"You think your, uh, husband may look for you at my house?"

"I just want to be sure that's not a possibility. If you are put under any pressure, though, give my clothes and other things to whoever wants them. Promise me, Sevim *Hanım*!"

Nothing, not even evidence that could help convict Peter Franklin's killer, was worth putting Sevim at risk. She didn't know anything, but would those on my track realize that?

"I will not go back to my house right now," said Sevim, with decision. I think she suspected now that I was involved in something more frightening than a drunkard of a husband, though plenty of women in the world have had reason to fear that savage beast.

"Here is where I will be, if you need me," said Sevim, handing me a sheet of paper from her pocket. "It is a house near mine. Now, go. And godspeed. *Güle güle*, go laughingly."

She gave my hand a quick squeeze and then she was gone, to all intents and purposes a lady who has been to visit a close neighbor in the early evening.

I watched her a moment, and then continued down the street to the house that was my target. If two and two still made four, I had at least the possibility of finding Faye, if I acted intelligently. That was more important than being on time to Leila's.

When I saw the impressive gateway to Lawrence's *yali* up ahead, I slipped down an alley that led to the Bosphorus. It may once have been used by boatmen for the rich owners of the wooden mansions along here. Now, it appeared to be the only way a car could drive into the Andover estate.

The high wall to my left must separate the alleyway from Lawrence's garden. Bare branches of trees silhouetted against the neon-tinted urban clouds, and dry clumps of summer vines had crawled to the top of the wall before they lost their greenery. The garden was probably lighted, although it didn't appear from here to be bathed in floodlights.

In the distance came the muted roar of vehicles crossing the second Bosphorus bridge. The swinging bridge lights outlined the ship-like profile of the cables. I wished I were in one of the cars, driving, driving anywhere. Driving somewhere safe.

More practically, I wished for soft-soled tennis shoes instead of little heels that went click, click, click on the cobblestone path. I walked on my toes to make minimal noise. A tiny verge of winter-drying grass helped.

Once, I heard footsteps. I stopped, flattening myself against the wall, and pulled the dark scarf over the lower half of my face. With my back to the wall, I glanced toward the entrance of the alley.

Someone walked by, all right. Did the figure pause for a moment? My heart stuttered, afraid to beat for fear of making noise. The figure walked on, and I slumped, relieved and shaking. I could have sworn my stiff backbone turned to liquid and flowed down the wall.

Enough. Time to pull myself together for the rest of what must be done.

1ꝗ2

Suddenly, the world was huge and
desolate and he was sinking into a
horrible darkness. He felt a tangible
loneliness, sharp as a knife, piercing
him to the very marrow of his bones.

Yaşar Kemal, *Anatolian Tales*

At the end of the wall, near where it met the gently-lapping Bosphorus, I found a gate. It was high, but it had the advantage of potential footholds in its fretted iron surface. Glancing once more back up the dark alley, I grasped a piece of the ironwork on the gate and pulled myself up. As I climbed, laboriously searching for purchase, I found the baggy outfit unsuited for this sort of activity. A couple of times it snagged on sharp points in the gate. The scarf and shawl kept sliding off; I feared one of them catching on the gate and either leaving me suspended or dumping me unceremoniously onto the cobblestones below.

The distraction helped me make that last supreme effort to get my first foot up and over, and then its mate. There was no time to waste, so I hung for a minute and then dropped as silently as I could to the other side.

My instincts said "hide," so I rolled from my landing position on the driveway directly under a bush, which gave me some sort of vantage point, at least. The driveway turned right, into a garage that backed on the Bosphorus. The garage doors were shut. A path led from here toward the house, and there was a fork that allowed one to head directly to the boat-dock to the right, or turn left along some landscaping in the garden to the main-entrance street side of the *yali* where I had first entered with Lawrence.

The garden was, as I had feared, lit, though dimly. Deep patches of shadow remained outside the perimeters of yellow lantern light scattered among laurel trees and rose bushes. I didn't see anyone in the garden. Two of the rooms in the lower part of the house were lighted, but drapes were drawn. The large sitting room overlooking the Bosphorus seemed to be dark, but that didn't mean someone wasn't sitting there gazing pensively out toward where I lurked.

My first need was to check out the garden. This would, of course, be my only escape route, if all went well. You generally leave a party in the vehicle in which you came—shanks mare, in this case. Thinking of escape—possibly not alone, if I were really lucky and found Faye—I decided to investigate one other option, since I was on this side of the house. Clinging to the generous clumps of shadow made by bushes, I made my way toward the area directly under the sitting room window.

When I'd looked at Lawrence's *yali* from the ferry, there was a boat-dock under the house about here; not very high, but spacious enough to park a couple of small craft. Perhaps I could row away, if all went well.

The rocks at the corner of the house were slippery with algae from the Bosphorus, washed by gentle waves that at times became more turbulent in the wake of a fast boat skimming by close to shore. The water was dark here, as the Bosphorus is always dark. Easing around the corner of the house to the side of the little boat port, I stopped after each step to listen for any telltale sounds that could indicate I was not alone.

Swish, swish. Was that the noise of oars being drawn through the water, or just a large fish breaking the water's surface? I paused, one foot in the air and one precariously balanced on the mossy rock. My foot slipped and my right leg hit the icy water, causing an involuntary screech to escape my lips.

143

*He closed his eyes and counted
his beads. "Allah protect
us, Allah protect us!"*

Yaşar Kemal, *Anatolian Tales*

That splash and my outcry must have been all they were waiting for. In a moment, the night was alive with murmured voices and the sound of bodies converging on where I stood. My leg quivered in the cold water.

Almost before I had pulled my leg from the water, my arm was grasped roughly by someone in the garden. Sevim's thick woolen shawl was pulled across my face. I couldn't breathe in the darkness. That wasn't helped by the tight grip around my waist of whoever had grabbed me.

Naturally, I kicked as hard as I could, but it didn't seem to be doing any good. Even worse, in the commotion, my bag slipped from my shoulder and made a genteel little splash.

A quiet conference took place around me, all in Turkish. It would be better to stop struggling and try to figure out what was going on.

"What shall we do with her?" said a voice I didn't recognize.

"Put her with the other," came the gruff reply. "The master will be here soon; let him decide, for once."

The shawl was held tightly in place over my head as I walked between two men. I was disappointed not to see the garden as we walked through it. All I could tell is we were walking on a gravel path. If my sense of direction didn't fail me, we were heading toward the entrance side of the house, away from the Bosphorus. Once, I bumped against a barrier—stairs? Were we were walking up and across it? This could be where the main door stairs went up from the gate at the street.

If only I could scream. Someone might be outside that gate. When I yelled, muffled as I was under the shawl, someone struck the side of my head. Not a good idea to scream. Whoever these toughs were, they apparently weren't in the mood for fooling around.

The tromp around the garden didn't last long. We paused, and then a muffled clank and a creak—a door? Someone pushed me, and I stumbled forward, falling on my face onto a concrete floor. At that moment, I was glad my captors had thoughtfully wrapped my head so it would be cushioned a little. Even so, the jolt hurt—a lot—and I cried out in pain.

"You will stay here and you will stay quiet, or we will make you quiet."

The long Turkish word-sentences, made by adding suffix after suffix to a root verb, had never sounded threatening before, but now the overwhelming impression was of a snake whispering curses. I would stay quiet, at least for the time being.

My wrists were roughly tied behind me, and then the shawl that was over my face was removed. A flashlight beam bobbed around a small shed. I lifted my head, which was a mistake. The man standing behind me quickly pushed a gag between my teeth and tied it behind my head.

"There," he said. "Now you will be quiet."

And the door closed, with another metallic clank. A padlock being attached and locked, I guessed. Multiple footsteps walked away. As the human noise receded, waves sounded against rocks. I found them comforting.

1ФФ

"Would to heaven that anything could be either said or done on my part, that might offer consolation to such distress. But I will not torment you with vain wishes…"

Jane Austen, *Pride and Prejudice*

My first instinct was to move to a more comfortable position, so I rolled over onto my back. As I did, my hand touched flesh and I almost levitated from where I lay.

"Aaah!" I believe is what I actually said.

Had they put me in here with a dead body? Whose? Sheer, unmitigated electric fear coursed through my veins. With the surge came a slight loosening of the rope around my wrists. I sat up abruptly.

Yes, there was another body, but I could now, with my senses sharpened, detect breathing from the still form. I also smelled something sweetish. Chloroform? Or, more probably, an up-to-date version of the same.

Wriggling around, the inside was partially visible from a little light seeping through cracks in the door. I leaned forward to get a better view of my companion.

Thank God! Faye Mollington was lying here near me. A cold, hard lump gripped my gut. Who knew what shape she was in? How long had she been drugged, and had she been fed since I'd seen her?

Let's see, it seemed like ages, but it was actually only four days. Faye had disappeared Thursday night; now it was Monday. They must have been feeding her and keeping her at least minimally warm, or she wouldn't still be breathing.

That was the good side. The bad side was, now they had both of us, and how were we going to get out of here? It seemed hours since Haldun's telephone call had confirmed the identity of our adversary.

There would be no mercy. He had too much to lose. The best thing I could do right now was to get my hands, and possibly my mouth, free as soon as possible.

Standing up with difficulty, my head reeling from the blow, I took a moment to balance firmly in my Italian shoes and to check out the shed as well as I could. Only the faintest light came in through the cracks, but some objects hung on the wall nearest me. If things were hanging, they must be hanging on something. Something sharp? I backed to the wall and began carefully rubbing my bound wrists against whatever they encountered. I was spurred on in the endeavor by the tightness of the ropes, which I was afraid could cut off circulation in my numbing fingers.

I also wanted that gag out of my mouth pronto. It is a fearsome thing to be gagged. You feel as though you can't get enough air. Your saliva can't lubricate your throat.

Aha, there was something. A nail, maybe. I stood as firmly as possible and rubbed the ropes. It was slow going, but some of the hemp gave way. In only a week or two I should make real progress. My heart sank.

Rustling sounded on the other side of the shed. An animal. Mouse, rat, whatever it was, the thought of its running around on Faye's sleeping face spurred me on.

I stepped across the shed to protect her. Could our rodent gnaw the ropes that bound me? Oh, for pity's sake. That was the most idiotic idea ever. I came to my senses quickly. Oh, right, Elizabeth. When in doubt, call a mouse.

I sank back down on the cold cement floor in a sodden depression. It had taken only twenty minutes of captivity for my mind to snap. At least Faye had remained unconscious through my silly fever. No doubt she would have blamed the aging process somehow. Faye didn't realize I had had these aberrations since I was a child. My family called it imagination.

The leg that had gone into the Bosphorus had completely frozen and turned to ice. At least, that's what it felt like. Chafing my leg from the side as well as I could with bound hands, I heard sudden footsteps outside the shed. Light steps, coming our way. I lay down quickly. I would play dead. That probably wouldn't be too far off the mark, the way things were going.

145

"Assistance is impossible; condolence,
insufferable. Let them triumph over
us at a distance, and be satisfied."

Jane Austen, *Pride and Prejudice*

Someone jerked on the locked padlock. Perhaps our captors kept the key somewhere near. Scraping sounds, and then a click. I held my breath and closed my eyes. The door opened quietly, then closed again behind the intruder. I knew by the perfume who now shared our shed.

Oh, well. I had had an appointment with her, anyhow.

Even my closed eyes could see the glow from a flashlight, as we were checked over. When the light wasn't on my face, I opened my eyes a slit. Leila Metin held her flashlight in one hand, a knife in the other. So our villain had an accomplice, and one who felt no investment in life right now because of her grief.

I closed my eyes again, thinking one last time of my loved ones, my colleagues. At least Leila would be efficient about her task; maybe we wouldn't feel a thing. There was a tug at the gag around my mouth, the touch remarkably gentle. What was she doing?

I opened my eyes. She worked at the gag intently, the light from her flashlight half-obscured by my scarf.

Leila's eyes met mine, and she gestured silence. Not a murderer's actions. I took a breath. Maybe I was wrong.

146

"The horror of what might possibly happen, almost took from me my faculties."

Jane Austen, *Pride and Prejudice*

Even with Leila's knife, it took awhile to cut my bonds and untie the gag. I tried to moisten my tongue and coughed; my tongue was covered with woolies. I'd worry about that later, along with the cuts at the corners of my mouth from the gag. I managed a tremulous smile at Leila, and grasped her hand for a moment. My fingers were still numb. We both turned to see about Faye.

The red hair looked wilder than ever, this time not with any trendiness. Faye was very pale and her skin felt cold, so I quickly tucked my shawl around her. Faye's breathing sped up and grew more regular.

Could we do something to help her wake up? It probably wouldn't be long before someone came to check on us. We needed to get out of here.

Leila must have had the same idea. She reached into a bag she had at her side and opened, bless her practical sense, a thermos of hot, sweet tea. She set it on the floor beside her. The burnt, leafy smell gave a whole new dimension to the little potting shed, which Leila's subdued light revealed to be our current residence. Red clay garden pots in various stages of breakage stood around the edges, except for the wall where I had tried to cut my ropes on the nail.

Leila took another small bottle from her pocket and opened it, then lifted Faye's head and held the bottle under her nose. The ubiquitous tangy-odored lemon cologne! If this worked, I would like that comforting smell even more than I already did. Leila picked up the thermos when Faye's eyes flickered, then opened to show us a bewildered gray-irised gaze.

"Shhhh," I said.

Leila poured tea into the thermos lid and held it to Faye's lips. She took a drink, then another. Her movements grew a tiny bit stronger.

"We must go," said Leila quietly, capping the thermos. "I have a boat nearby."

We lifted Faye between us, supporting her on both sides. Her legs were weak; I presumed they hadn't had much exercise in the past few days, and if she had been drugged most of that time, it would take awhile for the drugs to leave her system. She was coming more awake after the tea.

The door creaked loudly as we opened it far enough to get Faye out. I was sure we would be detected.

"Take Faye and run over there," I said, pointing at some thick bushes near the garden wall, maybe twenty feet away.

Leila took charge of the wobbly Faye. I put the padlock back in place and locked it, slipping the key in my own pocket to give us maximum getaway time, should we be granted any.

As I ran across the little patch of grass to the shadows at the edge of the garden, I glanced toward the house. Had pursuit begun?

I didn't see anyone actually in the garden, so I hoped for the best, put my head down, and moved as fast as I could with a half-frozen foot in an Italian shoe and bruises developing from the rough treatment. If anyone besides our captors had seen me, they would have assumed a witch was loose, I'm sure, with flowing homespun garments, hair in total disarray and a gait reminiscent of the Ancient Mariner.

As I reached the bushes behind which Leila stood and Faye sat, the door of the *yali* opened and a man headed toward the shed. My mustachioed nemesis. The ubiquitous follower. The man from the ferry on my first day. He turned to speak to the man behind him, I recognized his voice. He was one of the two men who had dragged me to the shed, the one with the serpent voice. So that's what his speaking voice sounded like! It felt like we already had a long relationship, of sorts, but never until tonight had I heard him utter a word.

He was someone who did not improve upon further acquaintance. Much as I disliked Macho Man, I had felt no thrill of fear in his presence. Could that be because I had outwitted him a few times?

But the person following him toward the shed? A chill ran up my spine, and my gut twisted. He was an evil force to fear and grudgingly respect.

He was someone I had never managed to outwit.

1Կଣ

*His behavior to herself could now
have had no tolerable motive;
. . .every lingering struggle in his
favour grew fainter and fainter. . .*

Jane Austen, *Pride and Prejudice*

It was, of course, Lawrence Andover. Lawrence the Smooth, the complicated lord of an empire I could only guess the dimensions of.

For just a moment, my knees sagged. How would I have felt, lying bound and gagged on the cement floor of the potting shed while he looked me over? Our current vantage point was far from safe, but at least we weren't bound like lambs for the slaughter.

Faye was awake now, lying quietly where Leila had pushed her.

The two men stood in front of the shed. Macho Man was searching for something. The key to the padlock?

"It was right here," he said to Andover. "I left it on that pot right there."

"Find it," said the familiar patrician voice. It had lost its diplomacy and charm.

The search became more frantic.

"It is not here. It must have fallen," said Macho Man.

Lawrence ran back to the *yali*.

It was our one chance, and it would last not more than a minute.

"Is your boat ready?" I hissed to Leila. "You must get help."

She hesitated, then said "yes, yes," jumped into the boat and began rowing.

I slithered to where Faye was hidden.

"Are you all right?" I whispered.

"I will be," she answered. "But you must get away, Elizabeth. It's not worth our both being caught. And he stands to lose more from killing me than you. So go."

"What do you mean? What stakes are on you that aren't on me?"

Faye stared at the house. "Oh, for god's sake, just go," she said to me, irritably. "You surely must have guessed by now that I'm undercover.

My co-horts are looking for me, I'm sure. They'll eventually figure that Andover is not who he appears to be. It's Andover's fear of my connections that has kept me alive. You, now, you're a straight journalist…"

Her voice broke off as Lawrence, the two men who had captured me, and a stocky, leather-coated man came out of the house and headed toward the potting shed. It would be only moments now before they discovered we were not there. Our chances, frankly, didn't look good.

148

*"How despicably have I acted!" she
cried. "I, who have prided myself
on my discernment! I, who have
valued myself on my abilities!"*

Jane Austen, *Pride and Prejudice*

Outside the shed, voices now blended with footsteps. Under the circumstances, not reassuring. All the more frightening because they were familiar.

While Lawrence supervised opening the shed, one of his henchmen and the stocky guy in the leather coat started searching the garden. Now that he got closer, I recognized the man who had come out of Lawrence's house as Howard Black, the *börek* klutz from the party earlier tonight.

Faye and I lay motionless behind the bushes, waiting for flashlight beams to catch us.

All of a sudden, Leila's disembodied voice came from one of the big chestnut trees that hugged the garden wall. "You won't get away with it, Andover. Son of a Donkey Andover. I am armed."

There was a nice element of surprise in the tactic; the four men in the garden froze for a moment. Then Lawrence's hand reached into his pocket, and the autumn night was shattered by a volley of shots—and screams from at least two people.

I pushed Faye down and lay over her, trying to cover both of us with the enveloping black shawl. The shots were the prelude to all hell breaking loose. Sustained pounding on the front wooden gate gave way to splintering. Were they using a ram to break through the solid wood?

"Police. You are covered. Give up now," came the barked order. In English. With a start, I recognized that voice. So he had been working!

Rescue was at hand, and I raised my head.

Leila had fallen out of the tree —had she been shot? Unseen by the police who were busy rounding up dangerous culprits, she crawled toward Lawrence.

Lawrence, too, had taken at least one bullet. He was lying on the ground, while police handcuffed his three accomplices. He looked badly hurt, but his eyes were open. He was not watching the police; he was watching Leila. As she crawled closer, he reached out. For a weapon?

I shouted, "He's going to shoot!"

Maybe he *was* going to shoot. I'm sure that was his intent. But at that moment, İrfan Algar came running out of the house, straight to Lawrence, calling with desperate sobs, "Lawrence, Lawrence." Lawrence glanced toward Algar for a moment.

Leila aimed directly at Lawrence's forehead, and now she pulled the trigger.

"That," she said quietly, "was for Erol." Then she slumped to the ground.

The night was full of İrfan Algar's heartbroken cries, as he cradled Lawrence's shattered head in his arms. Even the police left them alone for a minute.

A sister's need for revenge had had its inevitable resolution. It would be a long time before İrfan reached resolution of his loss.

1ᖷ9

Many will show you the way once your cart has overturned.

Turkish proverb

The evening breeze blew brisk and chill. While it was tempting to sit outside and listen to the gentle lapping of water against the restaurant sides, we decided to step inside, out of the wind. A ferry approached, lights aglow, looking warm inside.

"But how did you know to go to Lawrence's house?" I asked the group in general.

Faye, Mehmet *Bey*, and Jean frowned over their glasses of *rakı* at the restaurant in Bebek. We were celebrating a heartfelt Independence Day. Perihan Kıraz looked musingly at the rich red of her wine.

On my right sat a less-grumpy-than-usual Haldun, leg propped up in a cast. Ayla *hanım* sat beside him, positively glowing. Sultana the cat sat protectively on Haldun's lap.

"Let's give credit where credit is due," I said, answering my own question in the interests of summing up. "Haldun made the connection and telephoned me just in time."

As usual, Haldun was all modesty. "We should have known a long time ago," he said gruffly, looking around the little circle of journalists, lawmen, and archeologists. "All roads led to Andover, but since rumor had always had it that he was the covert leader of C.I.A. operations here, there were logical excuses."

I looked to Jean. "Was he the C.I.A. chief?" I asked.

There was a long pause. Secret agents really don't like to talk.

"No comment," he finally said.

We all took that to mean yes.

"So he was playing more than one double game? Subverting the law instead of upholding it?" Like Haldun, I found it hard to imagine that none of us had thought seriously of him as a suspect in Peter's death. "When did your branch realize that side of it?"

"I said, Elizabeth, I can't talk about it. Suffice it to say that the Andovers of the world are some of the biggest threats to security, just because they are so plausible. Their own governments keep believing them way past normal limits. At a certain point, people like Andover forget about demands of duty; all they think about is self, self, self. Franklin and some of the rest of us were getting inconveniently in his way."

"Are you saying the shots that night when we were going out to dinner came from Lawrence's men?" I involuntarily rubbed my still-sore knees.

"No, that was something else," said Jean, always one for mysteries. "That was just a little drug ring I had been a nuisance to."

I combined *roka* leaves with white cheese on my plate while continuing my questions: "When did Lawrence get involved with the antiquities trade?"

"We've pieced that together mostly with Kutlu's help."

Mehmet *Bey* nodded at Haldun. "It became clear from Franklin's notes and Kutlu's observations that Andover's basic obsession was with antiquities, which satisfied both his love of beauty and his pocketbook. Franklin was about to blow the whistle on that, which would have deprived Andover of his house, his possessions, and his dignity in public. To say nothing of providing him with prison accommodations and menu. An unacceptable scenario for such a proud man."

"So who actually killed Peter?" I asked. I had to know.

Mehmet *Bey* and Jean Le Reau looked at each other and spoke together.

"Leila Metin."

Leila? Horrible.

"But you said," I looked at Haldun, "that Peter and Leila were good friends." The same rumor about Faye and Peter prevented me from saying "lovers."

"That was one of the ways Andover worked," said Mehmet *Bey*. "He liked to use people who knew each other. It increased his hold over all of them."

150

We all sipped from our glasses and watched as a great bulky oil tanker made its ponderous way up the Bosphorus to the sadly-polluted Black Sea and across to Russia.

"I still don't understand what Andover was doing with antiques, ex-actly," complained Faye. She sat quite still, pale and thin, slowly recu-perating from her ordeal. "You must remember I've been out of the pic-ture for several crucial days. I was just starting to think ceramics when I happened to follow Metin."

"Well," interjected Perihan, who had been listening up to this point. "You are aware, I'm sure, of the enormous profits being quietly made in the international underworld through the sale of precious antiquities."

Faye nodded. That was common knowledge. She had told me pri-vately that her undercover specialty was terrorism.

"Go on," she said, taking a large bite out of her *pide* bread with roasted eggplant salad.

"Andover's great obsession was ceramics and pottery. He especially fell in love with 16th century Iznik work, and had begun to collect it."

Here I had to break in. "I saw an original Iznik vase—and tile—in his house, but couldn't believe they were genuine. Of course, Lawrence was a competent man of complex talents, so he decided to do things on a larger scale."

"Let me get a word in edgewise," interrupted Haldun. "I've had enough of talking to nurses and doctors, goddamit. Andover wanted the originals just for himself, at first. Then he realized how much money he could get for selling them, and he looked around for someone who could supervise expert copying of the original pottery. He was able to find just the right person, about five years ago."

"Leila," I said, my interruption earning a scowl from the storyteller.

"Yes, Leila. An expert in design and in ceramics. An expert in a crucial position at Topkapı, where original tiles were often lying around waiting for a room to be restored. And, last but not least, an expert with a fatal flaw in the form of her high-risk brother."

"But what was the relationship between Leila and Ahmet Aslan?" I asked finally.

"A potter in Ahmet Aslan's factory was surreptitiously providing copies, after Leila gave him the design and the color scheme," said Haldun. "Aslan himself didn't know. He doesn't seem to have been as alert as he should have been about his own workers."

Jean Le Reau stirred. "We were interested in Aslan's factory because somebody there was putting small amounts of heroin between tiles being exported. It turns out that was just a red herring cleverly put in our path by Andover."

Haldun waved his arm imperiously. He enjoyed being the center of attention, and I had to admit he had earned the position this time.

"Aslan was a logical one to plant all this stuff on, being a Kurd in turbulent times like these. It's easy enough to create suspicion of all kinds regarding a rich, urban Kurd."

I shifted uncomfortably and glared at Jean. He raised his eyebrows and shrugged.

"We all suspect those we want to suspect," he muttered.

The air smelled of sautéed olive oil, onions, arugula, and *rakı*, as well as Turkish tobacco.

"Speaking of red herrings, what was the terrorism connection?" I glanced at Faye. Would she answer?

She did. "You can't call terrorism a 'red herring' because it's very real and it's a problem," she said. "The bombing of Professor Fener's house, though, was not your garden variety of terrorism. It was murder, ordered by Andover because Fener had shown too much interest in some of the Topkapı tiles. He was very knowledgeable about which pieces had emerged from the Iznik dig. Leila apparently told Andover about Fener's questions and later made the connection between her information and what had happened. It was her tragedy that Andover chose her own brother to do the deed, since he had been trained in bomb-making by the Silver Wolves."

"So that's why you were following Erol," I said. "You knew he had set the bomb. Did you know who had hired him?"

Faye sighed. "I didn't suspect Andover until I saw him actually give the order for Erol Metin to be killed," she said. "By then, I was too close, and of course they had been following both Erol and me."

"You were held because you saw the Metin murder?" Held, and perhaps forced to make a phone call? "Was it you who telephoned the Pera and asked them to let someone in to get papers from my room?"

Faye swallowed hard. "I had a gun to my head, and several unpleasant hours to reminisce about at that point," she said. "I thought if I said it would be someone from your office that you would cotton to the fraud immediately. Nobody could ever suspect Bayram of that kind of thing. . ."

"She did, as you say, cotton to it pretty fast," murmured Mehmet *Bey*. "She asked pertinent questions about that phone call."

Well, I had indeed suspected Bayram for a few minutes, but this was not a moment for self-recrimination.

"Getting back to the ceramics," I said. "When Haldun gave me a hint they might be a critical part of the puzzle, I went to Topkapı to check it out. Yesterday, was it? Seems like ages ago. Sure enough, right there in the second room of the tradesman's entrance to the *harem*, the room with all those green and yellow Iznik colors, there was a stack of tiles. We don't have the one I snatched from the pile because Mehmet *Bey* here tells me my good friend Sevim's house was burgled after she escorted me to Lawrence's *yali*." I paused. "At least she wasn't home at the time. But I guess the way things worked out, it's rather a moot point."

I turned to Mehmet *Bey*. "Do you know which of Lawrence's cronies did that burglary, by the way? Was it the young man with the mustache?"

"His name is Bozkurt, and he is a bad element—largely due to Andover's influence. Andover was attracted by his physical perfection and quickly became his mentor and friend." Mehmet *Bey* poured himself another finger of the warmth-inducing *rakı*. "Bozkurt would do virtually anything Andover told him to, including murder, as in the case of Erol Metin. It is indeed a good thing the family of the ferry official was not at home when he broke in. We found the tile and your clothes in Andover's house. He must have been quick about doing the job."

Ayla *Hanım* poured a little, just a little, more *rakı* for her husband. I had my mouth full of crusty *sigara börek* and was happy to sit there with new-found friends. Given what we had all gone through together, they felt like old friends.

"What was the role of the American, Howard Black?" I asked suddenly, again to the table at large.

This time, to my surprise, Jean opened his mouth. "Black was Andover's international contact on selling antiquities," he said. "We had some guys following him, because there was also a drug element in the business, but they hadn't cracked the Andover connection."

"Was that because you thought Lawrence was part of your team?" That came out nastier than I intended, but I couldn't help it. Rub it in, don't rub it out. Not one of my more admirable characteristics.

Jean looked at me intently. "Maybe."

"By the way, what are Leila's chances?" asked Faye. Her voice was weak, and she looked unusually vulnerable. I was very, very grateful to the fierce, cold woman who had saved our lives.

"She is still in intensive care," said Mehmet *Bey*. "The doctors say she will probably pull through. It depends on whether she really wants to, they say." He spoke directly to Faye.

"I will go see her," said Faye decisively. "She and I have a few things in common. Maybe I can talk her into wanting to live."

I remembered the suggestion that Faye and Peter, like Leila and Peter, had had, shall we say, connections. Triangles can be tricky businesses, with no one able to say what the final angle will be.

"If Leila lives, will she go to jail?" I asked Mehmet *Bey*.

"We will probably have to charge her with manslaughter and complicity in the copying of antiquities," he said slowly. "But in light of her sacrifice to save both you ladies, we will not be pressing very hard." He got a smile from Faye at that. "I wouldn't be surprised if she got off lightly."

Did Mehmet Durmaz have a wife at home? Or was he perhaps in a mood to help comfort Faye after her harrowing time?

151

No matter where you go, Kismet [Destiny] will follow.

Turkish proverb

Twilight fell over the Bosphorus, and the big tankers making their tortuous way up the straits turned on their lights. We had already ordered swordfish *kebab*s, laced with green peppers, onions, tomatoes, and garlic, when Ahmet Aslan came into the restaurant. I waved to him, and he came toward our table.

"Join us," I invited, despite a frown from the man on my left.

Aslan nodded and sat at the opposite end of the table from Jean and me. His fathomless dark eyes sparkled at me, in particular, until they rested on Faye, when they sparkled at her. Admiring and enticing women was just one of Ahmet's attributes. He's so handsome he can't help it.

"Happy Independence Day," I said to the table as a whole. "A bit late, but we are all independent again."

The call to prayer began at the nearby mosque, muted by the closed veranda windows.

"Excuse me just a minute." I walked out on the veranda. The melancholy sound echoed across the water. I needed a moment. .

The wind was brisk, to say the least, out on the veranda. It wasn't yet freezing, though, and there was not a wisp of the Bosphorus fog.

The *muezzin's* voice rang confidently, repeating the familiar, comforting Arabic words: "Allah is great. There is no god but Allah, and Mohammad is his prophet."

That tribute is for you, Peter. You lived a good life and loved the Middle East. Man's arrogance and greed brought you down. I find satisfaction only in the fact that your end came here, in your beloved city, doing what you liked best.

It was nearly time for me to return to Washington—the *Trib* had already named a new Istanbul correspondent, who would be arriving in a few days. I'd stay to help with the transition and then leave this set of adventures behind. A step sounded on the veranda behind me. Jean shivered as he came toward me.

"Sad to be going?" he asked quietly.

I turned to face him, smiling into his secretive blue eyes. "Not really," I said. "But it's been a nice interlude."

"Ah." My friend, who would ever only be a friend. "I wish it could last."

"If it lasted, it wouldn't be an interlude."

I walked back into the restaurant.

Epilogue

*...between times, and when the
moon gets up and night comes, he is
the Cat that walks by himself, and
all places are alike to him. Then
he goes out to the Wet Wild Woods
or up the Wet Wild Trees or on the
Wet Wild Roofs, waving his wild
tail and walking by his wild lone.*

Rudyard Kipling,"The Cat that Walked By Himself"

Sultana had enjoyed the trips to the hospital, either in Ayla *Hanım's* basket or on her own four paws. It was even better having Haldun at home in the Üsküdar house, where she could sit on his lap or on the comforter folded on the chair near him.

At night, she still explored outside. Part of her patrol was the house where the garbage had smelled strange. But someone had cleaned up the garbage.

The white cat crouched around the corner when anyone came out of the house, which wasn't often. The person was usually a young man. The young man who had petted her hadn't been around lately. In the ritual way of cats, Sultana wondered what had happened to him. For a while, she would remember Haldun's friend, the woman who had petted her.

Then she would curl up in her usual place. Sultana did not worry about any of these strange human events.

Acknowledgements

It has taken me so long to get to the point of publication from that first "gleam in the eye" of writing a mystery, I have used most of my family and friends as supports along the way. I have also benefited from years of friendship with hospitable people in Turkey and Yemen, where I have been so fortunate as to have lived and visited, time and again. There is no way to mention all the wonderful people who, often unknowingly, have contributed to this work.

There are, however, a few who need special mention:

My husband, Jim, has read every version of every chapter and without him I wouldn't have made the leap from reporter to novelist. Jim, I love you and will always be grateful.

My daughter, Anne Welles Auer, has graciously applied her artistic talents to the book covers, giving the series its unique look.

Carla Coupe of Wildside Press is an amazing editor/publisher who guided me along the path, always patient, precise and encouraging.

Liz Trupin-Pulli of JET Literary, my agent, has added her years of editorial talent to making these books as linguistically precise as possible.

Other heartfelt acknowledgements appear below to friends and writing companions who have read, critiqued, and encouraged my work—and to friends in Turkey and Yemen who, through countless dinners, trips, late-night drinks and all manner of friendship over a twenty-year period have helped me enjoy and understand their complex cultures:

Anwar Ahmed (Hadhramaut, Yemen)
Hassan Bahashwan (Hadhramaut, Yemen)
Hamit Balkır (Istanbul, Turkey)
Nancy Beardsley
Cordelia Benedict (Ankara, Turkey)
Rasha Benjamin (Cairo, Egypt)
Ginie Çapan
Oğuz Çapan (Turkey)
Linda Cashdan
Katherine Dibble
Güngör and Güngör Dilmen (Istanbul, Turkey)
Ginny Eisemon (India)

Jeff Gall
Dave and Edna Green
Betty Hanson
Matt Hanson
Kathryn Johnson
Paula Harrell (Jordan)
Anne Hillerman
Sandy and Miriam Lieberman (India, Indonesia)
Jancis Long
Kristina Hanson Lowell
Janelle Masden (Jakarta, Indonesia)
Shahira Mehrez (Cairo, Egypt)
Noor Meurling (Jakarta, Indonesia)
Aziz Nesin (deceased, alas) (Turkey)
Fran Porter (India)
Marjorie Ransom (Yemen)
Kamal Rubaiah (Sana'a, Yemen)
Caroline Todd (Charles Todd)
Linda Scheffer (Turkey)
Cengiz Tekin (Istanbul, Turkey)
Elizabeth Thompson
Phoebe Tobin (Istanbul, Turkey)
And the Rector Lane Irregulars:
>   Donna Andrews, Carla Coupe, Ellen Crosby, Val Patterson,
>   Noreen Wald (special mentor), Laura Weatherly, Sandi Wilson

If it takes a village to raise a child, it appears to take several villages for me to get to the finish line! Warmest thanks and love to all those mentioned and to those not mentioned who are not forgotten. You know who you are and I love you! Onward to more adventures!

About the Author

PEGGY HANSON enjoys an international life and loves to share it with her readers. The Deadline series starring journalist Elizabeth Darcy is her first venture into fiction. The books reflect years of living in Turkey, Yemen, India, and Indonesia, as Peace Corps volunteer, international radio broadcaster with Voice of America, and teacher of English as a second language. Like many reporters, she always chafed at having to stick to facts. Elizabeth Darcy has no such constrictions and can go places that might be off-limits and deal with adventures as they come her way.

Peggy lives near Washington D.C. with her husband and an elderly Indonesian cat.